"A promising debut! Delights with charming characters, lots of heart, and a clever whodunit."
—Christy Fifield, national bestselling author
of *Murder Ties the Knot*

"*Snow Way Out* . . . is everything I love in a cozy mystery . . . [This series is] off to a magnificent start. Christine Husom's unique story line using characters who own a snow globe shop and joint coffee shop is one that is different than most I have read and it works . . . *Snow Way Out* . . . is an absolutely delightful story to cozy up on the couch to."
—Fresh Fiction

"This was a wonderful debut to a promising new series . . . I look forward to spending more time with this great cast of characters."
—Melissa's Mochas, Mysteries & Meows

"This is a pleasantly appealing and delightfully charming addition to the cozy mystery genre, and I can't wait for my next visit to Brooks Landing."
—Dru's Book Musings

Berkley Prime Crime titles by Christine Husom

SNOW WAY OUT
THE ICED PRINCESS
FROSTY THE DEAD MAN

FROSTY THE DEAD MAN

CHRISTINE HUSOM

BERKLEY PRIME CRIME
New York

BERKLEY PRIME CRIME
Published by Berkley
An imprint of Penguin Random House LLC
375 Hudson Street, New York, New York 10014

ISBN: 9780425270820

First Edition: December 2016

Printed in the United States of America
1   3   5   7   9   10   8   6   4   2

Cover art © Julia Green
Cover design by Lesley Worrell
Book design by Laura K. Corless

This tale is dedicated to my grandchildren.
They are special gifts and have shown me
there is another dimension to love
that I could never have imagined existed.

ACKNOWLEDGMENTS

I've been very fortunate to have a dream team to work with at Berkley publishing group: Senior editor Michelle Vega, her assistant Bethany Blair, publicists Danielle Dill and Roxanne Jones, and production editor Yvette Grant. Edie Peterson and Elizabeth Husom for their proofreading skills. My agent, John Talbot, for his vision, and my family for their unfailing love and support. My sincerest gratitude and thanks!

"It's craziness, pure and simple—"

The loud male voice from the back of my friend's coffee shop caught my attention as I stepped through the archway from Curio Finds into Brew Ha-Ha.

"—I can't believe you'd want that factory moving in west of town. That's prime cropland." I followed the direction of the voices to the table where Mr. Marvin Easterly was shaking a large pointer finger in front of Mayor Lewis Frost's chest.

"Now, now, Marvin. You need to appreciate that Wonder Kids Clothes would be a real boon to our town. It'll spread the tax base and take some burden off the residents."

"That's what you say. And it might help you city folks,

but it robs those ninety acres from the township's tax rolls."

Mayor Frost didn't miss a beat. "Not to mention that it will bring in thirty new jobs to start with. That's thirty area people who will able to work close to home."

"Hmmpf. Jobs, snobs. I've lived next to that farm all my life. What I can imagine are all the cars coming and going to get those thirty people to and from their jobs. Not to mention the semitrucks making deliveries and picking up the finished products. Nothing but a lot of noise disturbing the peace as far as I'm concerned. There're places that are better suited for that plant and you know it. I'm not the only one in the township opposed to it, and you know that, too."

Frost and Easterly were the only customers in either of our shops; a little break during the pre-Christmas season. My coffee shop owner friend, Pinky Nelson, had left to run a quick errand, and I'd stepped into my own shop—one that specialized in unique items and snow globes from around the world—to grab my cell phone moments before the argument ensued.

I hung in the background near the archway, between the front counter and the back sitting area, wondering what direction their disagreement might take. A number of early morning customers had talked about the Brooks Landing City Council meeting the night before. According to them, it had gotten so heated that Assistant Chief Clinton Lonsbury and Officer Mark Weston were on standby in case they were needed. And it was a good thing, too, because they'd had to escort several people out of the meeting before it got completely out of control.

I patted the cell phone in my pocket. If the argument got any worse, I'd call on my police officer friend Mark for some help with this second go-round.

Marvin Easterly got in one last jab. "There are people wondering if you've got some special interest in that clothing factory, what with the way you've been talking it up. And I'm one of them, to tell you the truth. If you've been working some deal under the table, then it's time to come clean about it."

The bell on Brew Ha-Ha's door dinged. City council member Harley Creighton burst in and didn't even notice me plastered against the wall as he marched by. He stopped at the mayor's table. "Am I interrupting?" Steam rose from the top of his head and out of Harley's ears, nose, and mouth. It took me a second to realize it was from the cold December air he'd brought in with him.

Mr. Easterly stood up. "I was just leaving. And mark my words, Mayor, you have not heard the last of this." He huffed and puffed all the way to the door.

Creighton pulled out a chair with force. Its legs scraped the floor, producing an irritating sound that grated on my nerves.

"What a fiasco our meeting turned into last night, Frosty. A doggone free for all, and it went downhill from there. You lost command of the meeting." Creighton barely took a breath before he went on. "It's bad enough you're in favor of that microbrewery setting up shop here, encouraging folks into another bad habit. But suggesting that we use tax incentives to bring in this clothing manu-facturing business is irresponsible in my book. You've been pushing your own agenda too many times these last months and I'm sick of it. I quit." He slammed his fist on the table, got up, rushed past me, and went out the door.

The mayor's problems were getting worse by the minute. I'd heard complaints from a variety of people about local politics since I'd returned to my hometown of Brooks Landing. I'd served for years as the legislative affairs director for Senator Ramona Zimmer in Washington, DC. And because of that, people considered me a bit of an expert in the world of politics. I'd done more behind-the-scenes research for sound policymaking and hadn't worked as much with legislators in the public domain, however.

The sentiment from a number of the city residents was that Lewis Frost had let his position as mayor go to his head more and more the last months, evidenced by things he'd said and done. Some people were surprised he'd been reelected in the last election for another two-year term. Word was that if he ran again he'd have trouble holding onto his seat. But that would be up to the voters when the time came.

I knew Frosty more as a faithful customer of Brew Ha-Ha and less as the mayor of Brooks Landing. I often read the minutes of the city council meetings in the local newspaper but didn't recall anything special that indicated he was abusing his power in any way. I was interested in the goings-on, but managing Curio Finds for my parents and helping Pinky in her coffee shop captured most of my time and attention.

Elected officials were under public scrutiny, and that wasn't always easy. I could attest to that. The senator I'd worked for had lost her reelection run after a much-publicized scandal involving her husband, Peter, and me. I was innocent, but Senator Zimmer fired me anyway, blindly believing her cheating husband instead of accepting the truth. After the incident, I'd lost a great deal of respect for both of them so it was just as well my working relationship with the senator had come to a screeching halt, devastating as that was for me.

I thought about Harley Creighton's emotional words. Was he serious about giving up his seat on the city council? I was curious why he was so opposed to a microbrewery setting up shop in town. In addition to an off-sale municipal liquor store, Brooks Landing had a number of other establishments that served alcohol. Microbreweries were growing in popularity and sprouting up in other communities in the county as well. Folks loved supporting independent ventures, whether it was a winery or a microbrewery or a children's clothing factory.

I understood why Mr. Easterly wanted to keep the westerly area around him rural but, on the other hand, I'd heard the farmer who was offered a tidy sum for his property was psyched up about it. There were always at least two sides to every story.

Mayor Frost noticed me hovering nearby and shook his head. "Camryn! What a fine mess we're in." *We?* "Did you hear Creighton say he's up and quitting the council, and here it is three weeks before Christmas. Who are we going to get to step into his seat at this time of year?"

"I wouldn't know, Mayor. It'll take time to arrange a special election," I said.

"No, fortunately we won't have to do that. We'll appoint someone to fill the last year of his term. If we can't talk Creighton into staying on, that is. The good thing about the appointment process is all the time and money it saves. Elections aren't cheap." Frosty frowned like he was considering his options. "Harley Creighton and I have butted heads more times than I can count the last few years. And now that I think about it, I'm not so sure I'd be sorry to see him step down."

The bell on the shop door dinged, announcing a new arrival. It was Rosalie Gorman, another city council member. The fire in her green eyes matched her flaming red hair. Had someone sent out an announcement that Brew Ha-Ha was the place to discuss city business that morning?

Rosalie came straight toward me looking far from pleased and it caused me to subconsciously brace myself. "The city clerk told me the mayor was here," she said.

I nodded and lifted my hand, indicating the table where he sat. It was the city clerk who'd been alerting people where Frosty was, no doubt with his permission and blessing. It was to the mayor's credit that he made himself available to everyone who wanted to talk to him.

Rosalie's cold look pierced right through me. "If you'll excuse us, there is something I need to discuss with Mayor Frost. In private."

Her dismissal made me want to come back with, *Then you shouldn't be meeting in a public place*. But I zipped my mouth shut, had a final glance at Frosty's doomed-looking expression, and slipped away. If Rosalie wanted a cup of coffee she would no doubt summon me back. I didn't want to cross her, if at all possible. She'd been in Curio Finds a number of times and I'd always given her a wide berth.

I moved behind Brew Ha-Ha's service counter as Pinky came through the door bringing in a bag of groceries. A blast of arctic air clung to her long, willowy body. "Holy moly, Cami, it's downright frigid out there."

"It's downright frigid back there, too. And the chill is not coming from our man Frosty," I said quietly and pointed toward the table area with my thumb.

She lifted her shoulders and eyebrows as if to say *What?*

"Rosalie Gorman is talking to Mayor Frost." We kept our voices low.

Pinky shivered. "Brrr, so you're saying it's about as cold back *there* as it is out *there*?" She moved her head left toward the seating area then right toward the outside wall.

"Pretty much. Rosalie is mighty upset about something."

"Maybe I'll creep in closer so I can hear what they're saying." Pinky lifted and lowered her eyebrows.

"Not a good idea, Pink."

She shrugged. "Three different people stopped me at the grocery store to give me their two cents' worth about the city council meeting last night. I'm not sure why they did that, either. Just about everyone in town should know by now how much I hate politics."

"Not all policy decisions are political."

She set her groceries on the back counter, blew some air out of her lungs, and threw up her hands. "Well, you could have fooled me. There is way too much bickering over every little thing, if you ask me."

I held up the palms of my hands. "People have differences of opinion. And what constitutes a big issue or a not-so-big issue depends on where you're sitting. That's why we have a city council and a mayor as our local officials. It's up to them to sort everything out and decide what needs to be done. But they can never please all the people all the time."

"And that's why I make a variety of coffees and other drink concoctions, and bake different kinds of muffins and scones. So there *is* something to please everyone."

"You people pleaser you." I reached over and gave Pinky a friendly pat on the back.

She smiled. "Yep. What time did you tell Emmy to come in?"

"Ten."

"You know Emmy's gotten pretty good making all the different drinks we serve. She's not the fastest person on the planet but she makes up for it by being such a great worker."

"Very true." We'd hired Emmy Andersohn to help us over the Christmas season. She was in her early seventies and very reliable. We'd also hired Molly Dalton, but she'd tragically died at the end of her first day on the job. We were still reeling from the loss nearly a month later. Emmy had agreed to continue working for us despite the trauma she went through after getting arrested and jailed as the prime suspect in Molly's murder. Thankfully, she was cleared a short time later.

"Pinky, won't it be a relief to get into the January business slump? Getting here early and staying late is wearing us out," I said.

"Your parents offered to lend a hand if we need them." Pinky stepped away from the counter, removed her coat and hat, and laid them on a stool until the coast was clear and she could put them in her back room.

"And they are helping by doing most of the ordering. Dad even connected with a new supplier of snow globes in Holland after they sent us a catalog. They have some unique ones so Dad placed an order, and it should be here today. At least I hope so. The snow globes have been flying off the shelves and out the door."

"Well yeah. Christmas. Snow globes. Gifts. They all go together."

Movement outside caught my eye and I pointed at the flakes falling. "As does snow."

"Great, more shoveling," she said.

The meeting between Mayor Frost and Councilwoman Gorman got boisterous. Rosalie's voice went up several decibels and then there was a loud sound, like something had fallen. Pinky's eyebrows shot up, then her face scrunched together. I felt mine do about the same thing as we took off for the back area.

The mayor was bent over picking up the chair that Rosalie had apparently knocked over. Accidentally or deliberately, we didn't know. Her face was the color of beets. "You just better watch yourself from now on," she said and pushed past Pinky and me without so much as a "pardon me."

Mayor Frost noticed us gawking at him. "Rosalie gets overly excited about things at times. You get used to it," he said.

My dad was expressive and more outwardly emotional than my mom, but he didn't knock over chairs. "Is there anything we can help you with?" I said, and Pinky stuck her foot against my ankle, apparently leery of what I might be getting her into.

The mayor picked up his overcoat, brushed some crumbs off the front of it, and then slipped it on. "Oh, no, no. But thanks for the offer anyway. I've learned to roll with the punches. And not to get too upset when people misinterpret things or gossip about me for this or that reason."

Gossip: one of Pinky's favorite pastimes. The very word piqued her interest and she removed the foot she had planted on my ankle as she took a step forward. "Really? So, Frosty, what kind of stories are they telling about you?" she said, a little too brightly.

Mayor Frost waved his hand back and forth. "Nothing for you girls to worry your pretty little heads about. Well, it's time for me to get back to business. Oh, and I apologize if we disturbed anyone here. When Mr. Easterly asked to meet with me, I thought it'd be good to talk over a cup of coffee. But . . . well let's just say it didn't go quite the way I thought it might."

Pinky had missed the action, but said, "No problem at all. It's a slower time of the day for Brew Ha-Ha, between the morning rush and coffee hour. And most people haven't caught on that Curio Finds is open an hour earlier for the month of December. Have they, Cami?"

I shrugged. "Not so much on weekdays anyway."

"Well, enjoy the rest of the day, girls." The mayor gave us a nod and then left.

Pinky and I picked up the mugs and plates from the mayor's table, carried them to her serving counter, and set them in the soapy water-filled sink. I glanced up at the Betty Boop clock on the wall above it: 9:45 a.m. The place would be filling up with customers any time now. "Pinky, you were here all the years I was gone. I know there are complainers who don't like the job the mayor's been doing. But most of the people must like him since he's been reelected over and over."

"Frosty was always popular, but he's lost a few fans lately. Some folks think he's losing it."

That might have been the gossip he was referring to a minute ago. "I didn't meet the mayor until I moved back home, but he's always seemed 'with it' to me. I've talked to him a number of times when he's stopped in for his morning coffee."

"I sure haven't noticed that he's forgetful or confused either, but we don't exactly have in-depth conversations," Pinky said.

"When did he move to Brooks Landing, Pink? He wasn't around when we were growing up."

"I'm not exactly sure, around twenty years ago. He was CFO of some manufacturing company in Minneapolis and commuted for a while. After he retired, he got more involved in the community. And then he was elected mayor however many years ago that was, six or so, I guess." Pinky shrugged and filled a stainless steel cream container.

"With the way Frosty was talking this morning, maybe he should consider a second retirement and not run again in the next election." I thought about his visitors. "You know Marvin Easterly, the one who farms west of town? He was the guy with the mayor before you went on your errands."

"Sure."

"Things heated up between them pretty fast after you left. Mr. Easterly had finished what he had to say and was about to leave then Harley Creighton tracked down the mayor here. First Creighton read Frosty the riot act, then he said he was quitting, giving up his seat on the council. A minute later, Rosalie Gorman stormed in and told me to leave so she could talk to Frosty in private."

Pinky shook her head. "Stormin' Gorman, that's what a lot of folks call her."

I laughed. "Gee, I wonder why."

"So Harley Creighton said he was quitting? I bet he'll change his mind after he thinks about it some more." Pinky picked up her coat and hat and headed to her back room.

"We'll find out soon enough, I guess," I said.

Pinky got back as the bell on the shop door dinged. It was Emmy with the first of the coffee-break crowd following behind her. Good timing. Emmy first went to the storeroom in my shop to deposit her coat and things, and then returned to the coffee shop ready to serve drinks and ring up orders. After a shaky start, she had come a long way in a month. Thankfully.

I noticed a small group of customers in my shop and

went through the archway to greet them. "Nice and cozy in here," one said.

"I smell coffee," another said, then threw back her head. Her nostrils opened wide as she took a deeper whiff.

"Gift ideas first, then we can indulge ourselves with a good cup of coffee," the third said. The others agreed to the plan.

"Is there anything I can help you find?" I said.

The three of them looked my way and one said, "Thanks, we're browsing for now, but we'll let you know." They started on their paths through the aisles admiring some of the unique music boxes, candleholders, trinkets, and snow globes. My parents had items for almost everyone on a person's shopping list. Tooled copper, blown glass, kiln-dried pottery, carved wood treasures. You name it.

A young woman I hadn't noticed was there stepped out from behind a shelf and cleared her throat. She looked like she was in her late teens, early twenties at the most. She gently waved her hand at nothing in particular. "Are these all the snow globes you have in stock?" Her manner of speaking was unlike most young peoples'. It was slower and her word pronunciation was distinct and clear.

I moved over to her side. "Yes, this is it. Everything we have is on display, but we're expecting a shipment sometime today and another later in the week, I believe."

"What time do you expect your delivery will arrive?" she said.

"Usually they come right around noon, although it could be later. The delivery guys have been especially busy this month with extra orders." She nodded, and then cocked her head slightly to one side and stared at a spot high up on the wall, like her mind had gone to a faraway place. "Is there something special you're looking for?" I asked.

She switched her attention back to me. "No, but I thank you. I asked you only to see if there was more to choose from. Of course, you have many choices now, but I thought I would ask just the same."

One of the things I'd learned working in retail sales was people oftentimes didn't know what they were looking for specifically but they knew it once they saw it.

The young woman attempted a smile, but made it only about halfway. "Good-bye," she said and slipped out the door. I took a step closer to the large shop window and watched her walk away. She was waiflike, and something about her reminded me of some of the young homeless people I'd seen on the streets of Chicago and Washington, DC.

But Brooks Landing, Minnesota, was not the place to be homeless in December when the average high temperature was around ten degrees below freezing. And if the wind was howling, it often felt like the town was situated on top of a glacier. I wondered if the girl was really interested in a larger selection of snow globes or if she was in search of a refuge from the falling snow flakes. Perhaps asking about another delivery gave her a legitimate reason to return later.

I shook my head, and switched my focus back to the other customers. They were busy picking up a variety of snow globes, shaking each one of them, and watching to see how the snow settled on the different scenes. "Oh, look, this is a music box, too. How cool is that? You can listen to *White Christmas* while the people ice skate in the falling snow," one said. And then all three of them sighed like they couldn't imagine anything better.

2

The women selected a number of items so Emmy came into Curio Finds and helped me gift wrap their purchases. Then Emmy followed the trio into Brew Ha-Ha, and lent Pinky a hand with serving them beverages and treats. I boxed up two special orders I'd received from a pair of Brooks Landing snow birds who spent their winters in Arizona. They were loyal customers and had asked me to send them photos of our new stock via e-mail. From those, they selected the items they wanted to buy for gifts.

When I heard a loud, familiar voice next door I set the boxes aside to find out what Sandy Gibbons, longtime reporter for the local newspaper, was all excited about. "Oh, there you are," Sandy said when she spotted me. Emmy nodded as she passed by me then disappeared

CHRISTINE HUSOM

through the archway into Curio Finds. The young shoppers seemed a bit put off by Sandy's enthusiasm and moved from the counter to the back seating area with their mugs. When Sandy singled me out, I was tempted to follow them.

"Hi, Sandy." I'd known her for most of my life. She had always seemed like she was about sixty years old, from the time I was a little kid to now. When I returned to Brooks Landing, I was surprised she looked about the same, right down to the dyed brown hair she had professionally styled each week. She must have passed the seventy-year milestone by now.

"So. The word is Harley Creighton told Mayor Frost that he was stepping down from his council seat after they had a big showdown right here in Brew Ha-Ha." She pointed her finger and moved it up and down toward the floor like she was marking a permanent spot.

"Who told you that?" I asked, knowing there were only three possibilities. I looked at Pinky and she shook her head. That left two possibilities.

"I rarely reveal my sources," she said with a smile. "You were here and I understand you heard the whole thing."

"I couldn't say," I said with a smile of my own.

"Oh, come on, Camryn. A witness statement would give my story more credibility."

"Sandy, you named the two men who supposedly had the conversation. One of them gave you the scoop, so talk to the other one."

She crossed her arms and let out a big breath. "He won't take my calls."

"If what you heard is true, then it won't be long before everyone in town knows about it."

"That's the trouble. I want to know now so I can include it in my article for tomorrow's edition. It'd be a great ending twist, sort of the final straw of what happened the day after all the controversy at last night's meeting. And that reminds me, I've been trying to track down Assistant Chief Lonsbury and Officer Weston, but neither one of them are answering their cell phones."

Pinky leaned in toward Sandy. "I'm sure they'll call you back when they can. And really, I don't know why all those people can't just find a way to get along and not get so riled up. I heard it was all over a microbrewery and a clothing factory. I mean, isn't it a good thing to get more businesses in town? It'd sure help me out here. More people in town would mean there'd be more coffee drinkers, right?"

"Especially if they stayed at the microbrewery too late the night before," Sandy said.

Pinky laughed. "Good one, Sandy."

Sandy zeroed in on me. "Well, Camryn, if you're not going to give me a confirmation, I'll just have to go see if I can find someone who will. And don't give a thought about me running around in the snow while I'm looking." She turned and picked up the large bag that held her writing supplies from a counter stool.

"Be careful out there, Sandy," I said with sincerity as she headed out the door. "Doesn't she remind you of the Energizer bunny from that battery commercial? She just keeps on going."

"You are right on there. I don't think she'll ever throw in the towel and retire," Pinky said.

"I don't think the paper will let her. She gets her stories, by gosh and by golly," I said.

"I think she's even snoopier than I am."

I'd have to think about that one. "I hear Emmy talking to a customer so I better get back to my shop."

Emmy was waiting on an elderly couple that was still spunky enough to get out for some shopping in the snowy conditions. Emmy was pointing out different snow globes with winter and Christmas themes. Since she had everything under control, I greeted them then went back to my counter to finish packaging the gifts for mailing.

A brown UPS delivery truck stopped outside our shop. The spry young driver jumped out, opened the side door, and pulled out a box. It was just after eleven a.m., earlier than usual. "Hey," he said as he hurried in, set the box on the checkout counter, punched in something on his device, and then handed it over to me to sign.

"You're ahead of schedule. Nice." I scratched out what served as my signature and gave it back to him.

"I got an extra early start today. And it's a full load so I better keep moving. Thanks," he said and took off.

I called out, "Thank you," to his back.

Emmy showed the couple a snow globe they both loved, and they joined me at the counter where she rang up their purchase. I found a gift box and asked if they wanted it wrapped. "No, thank you. It's a gift we're giving each other. A little tradition we started almost sixty years ago," the gentleman said as he put his arm around the woman's waist.

I found a card and stuck it in the bag along with the globe. "Here's a certificate for twenty percent off your next purchase."

"That's lovely, thank you. Merry Christmas," the woman said.

"And the same to you." I handed the bag to the man and watched as the two made their way out the door and safely to their car.

"What a sweet couple. I try not to get sad when I see two people who are able to grow old together," Emmy said as her eyes grew moist.

I touched her hand. "I'm sure this time of year is sad for a lot of people who have lost loved ones. And you went through a lot when your husband died." In fact, she'd been falsely accused of poisoning him and had spent months in jail before she was acquitted.

"That was bad all right. But I've had a few years to deal with it and have come to accept it, somewhat. But Irene Ryland, losing her daughter Molly like that. That's who my heart goes out to most of all this year," Emmy said.

"Me, too. I'm glad you and Irene have become friends. And the offer still stands if you want to spend Christmas with the Vanellis. Again, the friendly warning that my family gets pretty loud at our gatherings."

Emmy swiped her tears away and smiled. "I appreciate that. My friend Lester has asked us—both of us—if we want to get together with him. So we'll see. We haven't really talked about it; Irene and me, I mean. She may have other plans."

"No pressure, just know that you are welcome."

She nodded and pointed at the box the UPS man had delivered. "Would you like me to help you unpack that?"

I looked at the label. "It's from a new supplier in the Netherlands my parents are trying out. They sent us a catalog month and my parents put in an order. I guess they carry mostly new snow globes, but they run across old ones, too. And, that's our specialty, as you know. The older and more unique, the better."

I opened the drawer under the counter and found a box cutter. Then I sliced through the packing tape and spread the flaps open. Under the packing peanuts, there were four plain brown square boxes. Emmy watched over my shoulder.

"Here you go. Let's see what treasures are inside these." I lifted the first box out. Emmy took it, set it on the counter, then pulled out a snow globe with an ornate bottom and a scene of a gingerbread house in the woods. Two characters that appeared to be Hansel and Gretel stood side by side, holding hands near the front door.

I picked it up, gave it a shake, and we watched the snow settle around the pair. "I love it," I said.

"Oh, my, this will sell in no time," Emmy said.

We removed the other three from their boxes, and the next two were as delightful as the first. The fourth one felt heavier, and I noticed the base was more solid. When I looked at the globe, I was struck by its unusual scene. There was a cabin with pine trees behind it. A man stood by its front door and was holding a long-barreled gun, pointing upward, not in the shooting position. Three bears appeared to be walking toward him, closing in on him. I studied the man's face and he looked calm, like he wasn't afraid of the bears at all. I tried to figure out what the scene was depicting. It was more sinister than the others. Would any of our shoppers be interested in it? It must have looked better in the catalog than in person.

I picked up the order sheet with the wholesale and retail prices listed and handed it to Emmy. "This says it's the first of three shipments." I picked up the phone and dialed. "I'm going to give my parents a jingle."

"Hello Cami," my dad answered.

"Good morning, Dad. I wanted to let you know we got our first snow globe order from the Dutch company."

"Glad to hear it. How do they look?"

"They're high quality. One's a little different, but the others are very nice."

"Different, you say? Well, I asked for their top sellers, and any old, unique ones they came across."

One certainly fit the description of being unique. "We got four in this order with more coming."

"Only four? We ordered twelve, but I suppose this close to Christmas, they're scrambling to keep up with demands."

"I wouldn't doubt that. Thanks, Dad, I'll catch you later."

"All right, my dear."

We hung up and I pointed at the new snow globes.

"Emmy, go ahead and mark these. I'm going to run to the post office and get these packages we wrapped up mailed to our customers in Arizona."

Emmy picked up the pricing gun. "I'm happy to do that."

I grabbed my coat, gathered up the packages, and walked the two blocks to the post office. It had quit snowing, making the journey less slippery. I'd hoped to avoid the lunch-hour crowd, but when I saw the long line, I glanced up at the wall clock. It was 11:47, later than I'd thought. I made small talk with others in line and twelve minutes later, it was finally my turn.

The two workers behind the counter had a growing stack of boxes behind them and they looked harried. As wonderful as the season was, it created extra work for a lot of people. I greeted my helper as pleasantly as possible, and almost got a smile out of him. Maybe on another day. Like a lazy afternoon in the middle of summer.

When I got back to Curio Finds, I noticed Emmy looked about as stressed out as the postal workers had. "Oh, Camryn, I'm glad you're here." She was alone in the shop so I knew her tension wasn't because she was swamped with customers.

"What's up?" I said.

"First Mayor Frost came by to talk to you, not a minute after you left. It seemed kind of urgent. He went to get some lunch and said he'd stop back after that. Oh, and by the way, he looked at the new snow globes sitting on the counter here and asked me to put one of them on the back shelf for him. He'll get it when he comes back."

"Okay." I wondered if Sandy had tracked down the mayor and had led him to believe I'd given her more information than I had. "Did he seem upset?"

"Not exactly upset, but he wasn't his usual easygoing self, either."

"Mmm."

"And there was a young woman who came in a minute later to see if we'd gotten our snow globe delivery yet."

"I bet it's the same one who was in here earlier. Was she small, on the petite side, with eyes almost too big for her face?"

Emmy nodded. "That sounds like the one; a little slip of a thing."

I got out of my coat and draped it on my arm. "Did you show them to her?"

"I did, and she looked at each one very carefully and asked if that was all we'd gotten. I told her there was one more but the mayor had spoken for it and I'd put it away for him. She asked if she could see it, in case he decided not to buy it so I showed it to her. I hope that's okay."

"I don't see the harm in that."

"When she saw it, she said that was her favorite one of all. I told her I could give her a call if the mayor decided not to take it. But she said she'd stop back later instead."

"We can always order another one for her. We should be able to get it in time for Christmas. Which one was it?"

"The one with the man by the cabin and the bears."

"They both wanted that one? It shows you how much I know—I thought we'd be lucky to sell it."

Emmy gave a little shrug. "To each his own. Camryn, do you mind if I take my lunch break now?"

"Not at all, and enjoy." She usually brought a packed

lunch from home and Pinky said it was just dandy for her to eat it at one of the coffee shop tables.

As I was finding a temporary home for the last snow globe from the order, my attention was drawn to a man looking in the shop window. He was a giant of a man, and seemed especially so with the big fur collar on his long wool overcoat and a furry hat with both forehead and ear flaps. The sheriff in the movie *Fargo* wore one like it. A trapper hat.

He nodded when he saw me, then made his way into the shop and pulled off the sunglasses that had fogged up as soon as he was in the warm room. "I see you have snow globes," he said with a slight accent I couldn't pinpoint. European, but just barely, like he had been born in Germany or Latvia or Poland but had spent most of his life in the United States.

"Yes, we do. Do you have anything special in mind?"

"Perhaps a winter scene with bears."

"Bears?"

"Yes."

Was there a new fad I hadn't heard about that had made bears suddenly popular? "I'd be happy to order one for you. Coincidentally, we got one in a shipment this morning, but it's been spoken for."

"By spoken for, you mean it is still here?"

I nodded. "A gentleman asked us to set it aside and will be in later to pick it up."

"Perhaps I could see it, and if I like it, you could order another one for me."

"Sure, let me get it." I went to the storeroom shelf

where we kept special orders and I shook my head as I picked up the snow globe and had a second look at it.

When I carried it out the man's eyebrows raised ever so slightly, like he'd seen it before. He nodded. "Yes, that would be just the thing for my brother. Perhaps you'll consider selling it to me for more than the asking price." *To each his own is right.*

I shook my head. "Sorry, that wouldn't be fair. But I'll put you on the list if the others don't want it after all."

"The list?"

"There are two ahead of you. The gentleman I mentioned and a young woman."

He frowned. "Ah, well, that's it then. Perhaps I will stop in again another day. There is no need to put me on a list. If I decide to place an order, I will let you know."

"Sure, that's just fine."

Mayor Frost came rushing into the shop like he was being chased. And with all the controversy swirling around him, maybe he was. I was still holding his promised snow globe as the man and I ended our conversation. "Camryn, you must have seen me coming," he said when he saw it.

"Hi, Mayor."

He withdrew his wallet from a back pocket, pulled out a credit card, and handed it to me. "Why don't I pay for that now, and then I have something important to talk to you about."

The other customer slipped into Brew Ha-Ha. "Thanks for stopping by, sir," I called out to him. He raised his hand in a wave without turning around.

"Who was that?" Frost asked.

"I don't know."

"I don't recall seeing him around town before," he said.

"No, me, either. But there are people from all over who come to Brooks Landing to shop."

"That's true, and what a good thing that is for our business community and overall development. It's nice that buyers from the outside are helping to build our local economy."

I rang up the mayor's sale, put the snow globe in its box, and when he said he didn't need it wrapped I put it in a bag, and handed it to him. "So what do you want to talk to me about?'

He looked around like he was checking to see if we were still alone. He moved close to me and lowered his voice. If he was there to question me about Sandy Gibbons asking me for a statement, I was not guilty. And if he doubted that, there was always Pinky to call in as my witness. "I want you to submit your name to be considered for appointment to the city council."

"What?" My ears must have been plugged because what I heard couldn't have been what he said.

His bright blue eyes shone. "Throw your name in the hat for the council seat that'll be opening up. You have as much political experience as anyone in town."

"I worked for a senator researching legislative issues and policies."

"Perfect! That's what we need, someone who does her homework." He clapped his hands together.

"Aren't you jumping the gun here, Mayor Frost?

Doesn't Harley Creighton have to officially resign, like write a letter or go before the council? Make some kind of public announcement?"

The mayor waved his hand back and forth. "He does, but that's just a formality. Creighton may have even called Sandy Gibbons to tell her." So Creighton was his own snitch?

Pinky came into my shop and caught what must have been a doozy of a look on my face. And I knew my color was a deeper tone than usual, given how hot I felt. "Cami, are you all right?" She looked from me to Frost. "What's going on?"

"I just gave her something to consider. To strongly consider. Stop by the office when you get a break, and we'll hash it over some more."

I shrugged. "I'll see if that works out. It depends on our customers."

"I understand. Well, if not today, tomorrow then." He lifted his shopping bag in a good-bye salute and left.

Pinky swooped in with her long legs and arms as only she could do. "What was that all about?"

"You will never guess, so I won't make you. Mayor Frost wants me to file, or apply for, the city council seat that Harley Creighton is supposedly vacating."

She pulled her chin in and drew her eyebrows together. "Is he crazy? You've got a job, and you haven't even been back in Brooks Landing for a whole year yet."

"I know. But as far as having another job, I think the others on the council do, too, except the mayor, of course."

"You're not seriously considering it, are you?" She crossed her arms over her waist.

"Not seriously. I've only had like five minutes to try to process the mayor's question, much less think about what would be involved in the job. He said my background would be an asset."

"Well sure it would, to the folks in town here. You work hard and you take everything you do to heart."

"Isn't that what elected officials are supposed to do, serve the people?"

Pinky raised her eyebrows. "I think some of them forget that part."

The shop door opened and the young "slip of a woman" came in. Three visits in as many hours. "Hi, again," I said.

"You remember me."

I smiled in affirmation. "How can I help you?"

"Well, there was another woman here who told me she had put a snow globe aside for someone. But if he did not want it, I could buy it."

The very popular snow globe where three bears were about to attack a man. "Sorry, but the man actually did buy it. I'd be happy to see if I can get another one like it for you."

She gave her head a quick shake back and forth. "No. Thank you." And then she took off.

Pinky inclined her head toward me. "That was different. She's different."

"I know. She reminds me of some of the homeless kids I used to see in the cities I've lived in. Not dressed quite warmly enough, with backpacks strapped on their backs."

"Maybe we should go after her."

"And then what? She must have money if she was planning to buy a snow globe. And a rather pricey one at that."

"Not that I'm suspicious or anything, but maybe you should take a close look at your shelves, make sure nothing is missing. That girl could be saying she's interested in a snow globe you have put away on a shelf in the back room, and then take the opportunity to steal something else when you're gone."

"You do have a suspicious mind, Pinky. And you're right; I know it's happened before. We've had items stolen when there have been a lot of customers in the store. And we don't notice until after everyone's gone that something's missing. Fortunately, it's a pretty rare occurrence."

"Yeah, I know your parents were bummed a couple of times when a one-of-a-kind trinket or one of their rare snow globes disappeared. And that reminds me, I've been meaning to ask you this. I know they're doing ordering for the shop from home, helping you out that way, but have they said whether they're coming back to work here, at some point?"

"They haven't made a commitment one way or the other and I haven't pushed them for an answer, either. Eight months, even four months ago, I would have said, 'Sure, as soon as Mom is strong enough.' But they've gotten used to being free to do other things, like going to my nieces' and nephews' games and concerts. And babysitting the grandchildren when they're needed. If we hadn't hired Emmy, I think they would have been here to help out when they could. But since she's here, they don't have to."

Pinky gave me a mild shove. "If you get on the city council, they may have to come back big time."

B usiness over the next hours was fairly steady with a few busy spurts thrown in the mix. At 4:15, things had died down enough so I felt comfortable asking Emmy if she'd be okay on her own in Curio Finds for a while. I wanted to talk to Mayor Frost about what he had in mind. If—and it was a big if—I did get appointed to finish out Creighton's term, I figured a year would be doable. Maybe.

"Call me if you get swamped. I'll keep my cell phone in my pants pocket so I'll feel it buzz," I told Emmy.

"No need to worry, Camryn. But I will call you if I need to," she said.

"Thank you." I grabbed my coat and headed into Brew Ha-Ha. "Pinky, I'll be back in a bit. Are you about ready to head for home?"

She looked up from her counter where she was washing cups. "Maybe in a half hour or so. You're going to see Frosty, aren't you?"

"Yes, and I won't be long." At least that's what I thought. But things turned out much differently.

3

The cold air bit my cheekbones and nose as I made my way down the sidewalk to the city administration building where the mayor and council members, along with the city administration staff, had their offices. The council chamber where the meetings were held sat perpendicular to the offices on the east side. The mayor's and councilors' offices were on the north.

It was a sturdy, one-story brick structure that had been constructed about twenty years before. The police station was housed in the same building and the two departments shared a common front entry then split into separate units. The city offices were on the left, the police on the right. I went through the city hall entry and saw two workers shutting off lights behind the service counter.

It was warm inside, especially in contrast to the

outside temperature. I slipped off my coat, slung it across my arm, and made my way back to where the inner offices were located. I'd visited the city administrator a time or two, so I knew my way around. It was just after 4:30, the official closing time. The city clerk, Lila, normally worked at a front desk, and along with her other duties also served as the receptionist. But she wasn't there. As I was considering whether or not to call out and announce my presence, Lila strolled in from a back area, donning a hooded, lined, fleece coat. She visibly jumped when she saw me.

"Oh, Camryn, I wasn't expecting anyone this time of day. I was just leaving."

"Sorry, I didn't mean to startle you. The mayor asked me to stop by."

Lila got close to me before she spoke. Her brown eyes widened and her voice lowered, like she was about to share a secret. "Mayor Frost should have a revolving door installed back there. People have been coming and going from his office all afternoon. I kind of lost track, but I don't think anyone's in there with him now. Should I go check for you?"

"That's okay, I'll do that. Thanks, Lila, and enjoy your night."

"You, too. I'm locking up, but you'll be able to get out after your meeting. The doors have push bars and don't lock from the inside. And even if they did, Mayor Frost has keys, of course. The hallway and entry lights stay on all night, too." The sun was about to set and it would be dark in minutes.

"Sounds good, and thanks again."

"Sure thing," she said as she grabbed her purse and walked toward the door I'd just come through.

The near silence in the deserted office space was disquieting. *It'll be comforting to talk to a live person,* I thought as I walked down the corridor that led to the individual offices. I stopped at the one with the nameplate Mayor Lewis Frost on it. He'd always talked about his open door policy, but it was closed shut at the moment.

I knocked and waited. No answer. I knocked again, a little louder, but still no answer. He might have left when Lila was away from her post, before I'd gotten there. "Mayor Frost?" I called out and gave the door a final knock. I was about to leave when I noticed the light from his office was shining out from under the bottom of the door. Maybe he had earphones in and was listening to music or the news and couldn't hear me. I'd seen him wearing a pair when he was taking walks.

After I'd convinced myself Frosty was working at his desk, connected to earphones and oblivious to the outside world, I turned the knob and pushed the door open. He'd asked me to stop by to talk, after all. But he wasn't at his desk, or anywhere else in sight. His chair was pushed aside, like he'd gotten up and left in a hurry. He'd even left the lights on. I was about to turn tail and leave when I saw what looked like the base of the snow globe the mayor had purchased mere hours before. It was lying on the floor near the desk, but the globe wasn't next to it. What had happened?

The snow globe had to have hit something hard enough to break it, and the office floor was covered with a soft carpet. I glanced up at the shelves behind the desk.

It could have fallen from there and struck the bottom ledge. I hoped Mayor Frost wouldn't think I was snooping, but I crept over to see where the rest of it was. And when I found out the answer, there was no turning back. There were broken pieces of glass and wet snow flakes lying next to Mayor Frost, who was sprawled out on the floor behind his desk.

I screamed, then an uncontrolled reflex made my hand fly to my mouth to stifle more squeals that were desperately trying to escape. But none of the noise I was making roused the mayor. He was lying on his back with one arm across his belly and the other stretched out at his side on the floor. His fingers were pointing at the snow globe glass and snowy-water mess on the floor, the same place his eyes appeared to be staring.

I studied his chest and it was still, not rising and falling like it should have been. I looked for the pulse on his neck and couldn't see it from where I was standing so I squatted down and held my breath as I reached across his shoulders. I placed my two fingers on his neck in search of it. But no matter how I positioned and repositioned my fingers, I didn't find a pulse.

I was alone with a dead man. It wasn't the first time I'd been in that predicament, but that did not make it one iota easier. My denial, my initial disbelief, shifted into belief. *I'm alone with a very dead Frosty.* I stumbled to my feet and almost toppled back on top of the mayor. I grabbed the edge of the desk for support and that's when I felt something wet. I looked at my hand. There was a red substance on my palm, and it had a peculiar, familiar odor. Salty, earthy. Blood. *Blood. Blood!* I braved another look at Frosty, and that's when I noticed a small brownish spot on the carpet by his face. His injury must have been on the side of his head that was turned toward the floor.

I moved as fast as my running-challenged body would carry me with my blood-stained palm straight out in front of me, as far from my face and the rest of my body as possible. The only thing I could think was I needed to find a police officer. And the obvious and best place was at the police station. An office so close, and yet so far away. I called out, "Help, help, help . . ." as I ran through the empty, and now terrifying building, then pushed out through the door and pulled open the door to the police station. Margaret, a woman who'd grown to dislike me more with each passing month, was sitting with her usual stern face behind her desk. She'd been glued to her chair every time I'd been there before. But not this time. When she saw me coming toward her with my bloody hand extended, first she jumped up, and then she collapsed across her desk.

I prayed she hadn't had a heart attack and died. Assistant Chief Clint Lonsbury would have trouble restraining himself if I'd brought death to his police station. "Margaret, Margaret, please wake up, tell me you're all right. Help, is anybody back there? Clint, Mark, Jake?" Clint and Mark, especially, were the two I knew best. I'd met Jake a couple of months before.

Clint appeared around the corner then his hand fell on the gun strapped at his side. "What in tarnation is going on out here?" He saw Margaret slumped across her desk and me holding out my arm with my bloody hand, which was getting increasingly heavier and was starting to drop. I grabbed it with the other hand and tried to keep it from falling to my side, but I was getting weaker and weaker by the second. I'd never passed out in my life, and I hoped against hope this wouldn't be the first time. I needed to concentrate on something besides the drying blood on my hand.

"I think I scared Margaret. I hope she's okay. But the mayor's not—he's on the floor in his office. He's dead. I found him there like that and came to get help." The words spilled out of me.

Clint shot me the most incredulous look—his face squeezed together like he was struggling to believe or even understand what I was saying. "Stay right where you are," he said then rushed over to Margaret, who was beginning to stir. She wasn't dead, thank God. She turned her head to the side and opened her eyes.

Clint put his hands on her shoulders. "Margaret? Can you hear me?"

She blinked a few times. "Assistant Chief Clint?" She pushed herself up, sending the papers on her desk flying in fourteen or so different directions.

"Easy now," Clint said as he helped her back into her chair. "I'll call for an ambulance."

Margaret looked around, like she was getting her bearings back. "No ambulance." And then she spotted me and pointed. "It was that woman. She scared the living daylights out of me."

Clint threw another look in my direction. Maybe he heard my teeth chattering as my jaw bounced up and down uncontrollably. And he must have noticed I'd started trembling because he said in his most authoritative voice, "Camryn, you need to sit down before you fall down. We don't need another casualty around here." He had a way with words that often made my dander go up. But the positive effect they had that time enabled me to back up to the row of chairs and sink down onto one of them. I rested my arm on my leg, palm up, and avoided looking at the hand that was covered with evidence of a possible crime.

Clint made two quick phone calls. "Mark, get down to the PD. Now." Then, "Audrey, your mom needs a ride home." That's all I heard before he said, "Margaret and Camryn, I need both of you to stay put, right where you are without moving, and I'll be back as soon as I can." He pulled out a set of keys and took off at a fast clip out the police station door and then keyed into the city office door.

Margaret stared at me and I kept my eyes on the door, hoping Mark would hurry up and come rescue me from this nightmare, and from Margaret's unforgiving look. Every second felt like an hour. Mark finally rushed in, and all I wanted was a big hug from him, but that wasn't going to happen. His eyes moved from my face, down my body, then locked on my open palm.

"Cami, what's going on? Where's Clint?"

I used my right hand to point at the door the same moment Clint came through it.

"Frosty's dead all right," he said.

Mark's head jerked back and Margaret let out a high-pitched cry that made my skin crawl.

Clint pulled out his phone. "Buffalo County? We need your major crimes unit at city hall. Mayor Lewis Frost died in his office. It's definitely not natural, and it doesn't appear to be accidental. Thanks."

Mark stepped in closer to Clint. "Mayor Frost, murdered?"

Clint lifted his shoulders. "That's the way it looks."

Margaret squealed again, and Clint looked at his watch. "Your daughter will be here any time now, and we'll be locking up shop a little early today. Make sure Audrey stays with you tonight, so you're not alone. Agreed, Margaret?"

She nodded.

"And we need to keep the mayor's death between us until we've done some investigating." Clint looked directly at Margaret. "You'll want to talk to your daughter about it, but *no one* else. She can't tell anyone yet."

Margaret nodded again. Her daughter came in wearing a worried expression. I turned my hand palm down, so she wouldn't see the blood. "Mom?"

"Just a little fainting spell. I'll be fine."

"A *little* fainting spell? We should go to urgent care."

"No. Let's go home, and if I need to see a doctor, we can go later."

They gathered Margaret's things and were out the door in a minute.

Clint hovered over me. "Where'd that blood on your hand come from?"

"The mayor's desk."

"And how did it get on your hand?"

"I grabbed onto the desk to catch myself when I almost fell on Mayor Frost, and I didn't know there was blood on the edge of the desk—I didn't see it—until it was all over my hand."

Clint drew in a deep breath. "What were you doing in the mayor's office in the first place?"

"I was supposed to meet with him, but he didn't answer his door. I thought maybe he hadn't heard me knocking so I opened the door. I didn't see him behind his desk, but I noticed the snow globe he'd just bought was lying on the floor, broken. And when I went over to check it out, there he was, on the floor behind the desk. I wondered if the snow globe had fallen off a shelf and knocked him out. I checked for a pulse, but I couldn't find one, and when I grabbed the desk to stand up, that's when I found out about the blood."

"Camryn Brooks—" Clint started.

Mark interrupted. "Mayor Frost."

Clint nodded. "Right. Camryn, you're staying with us until we get this sorted out. And the county will need to swab your hand."

"Hang in there, pal," Mark said, as he linked his hand through my right arm and we followed Clint down the long hallways to Mayor Frost's open office door. Clint stopped and turned to me. "Okay, start from the beginning and tell me exactly what happened from the time you got here to the time you arrived at the PD. And why you were meeting Mayor Frost in the first place." He and Mark both took out memo pads and pens, ready for writing action.

I relayed every detail that pertained to the mayor beginning with the morning visits he'd had at Brew

Ha-Ha from farmer Marvin Easterly, Councilman Harley Creighton, and Councilwoman Rosalie Gorman. And that Mayor Frost had stopped by Curio Finds twice that afternoon looking for me, and that he'd found me on his second visit.

When I got to the part about the mayor wanting me to consider a seat on the city council, both Clint and Mark gave me looks that suggested I shouldn't take even one baby step down that path. I told them about talking to Lila on my way in to see Frosty, and that she'd told me a number of people had visited him that afternoon.

"She'll be the next one we talk to," Clint said. "Go on."

I detailed the rest of the story, then Clint and Mark stepped into the office. "Wait out here, but don't touch anything," Clint told me.

I looked inside and noticed my coat was lying on the floor where I'd apparently dropped it when I first saw Frosty. "Um, that's my coat. And that's the base of the snow globe." I pointed to it. As if they couldn't see the items in front of them but could see me gesturing behind their backs.

The phone inside my pocket buzzed. "It's probably Pinky wondering where I am, or maybe it's Emmy because she needs help at the shop," I said.

"Go ahead and see who it is," Clint said.

Fortunately, the phone was in my right pocket so I pulled it out with my uncontaminated hand. "It is Pinky."

Clint nodded. "You better answer so she doesn't keep calling you. Or worse yet, come looking for you. Tell her you've been detained."

Tell her I've been detained? That'll go over big with

her. I cleared my throat and pushed the talk button with my thumb. "Hi, Pinky." My voice sounded as shaky as the rest of me felt.

"Cami, is everything all right? I thought you'd be back by now."

"I'll be a while yet. Have Emmy take over so you can go home. I'll tell you all about it later. I've gotta go."

"Cami, tell me what's going on. You sound really strange."

"I do? Sorry, gotta go, and I'll call you as soon as I can." I hung up before she could utter another word.

"After that conversation she probably will come looking for you," Mark said.

"She won't be able to get into the building since the doors are locked," Clint said, as his phone rang. It was about a ten-second conversation. "We'll be right out," he said then disconnected. "Speaking of locked doors, the county crime guys are here."

"I'll go let 'em in." Mark took off past me.

When I looked back into the office something glittery in the carpet caught my eye. It was a dazzling diamond-like gem, and I had a perfect view of it from where I stood. My phone was in my hand and I snapped a picture of it then took a step into the room, forgetting my orders. "Where do you think you're going?" Clint said.

"Look." I pointed with my phone then stopped in my tracks. I'd learned the lesson of obedience from past mistakes.

Clint came closer and bent over to examine the gem. He fished a pair of protective gloves from his pocket, pulled them on, and then picked up the small object and held it in his hand. As he lifted it toward the light hundreds of sparkles every color of the rainbow danced.

I was drawn to its astounding beauty. "It's huge. Where would it have come from? There isn't a piece of jewelry with it that I can see."

"We'll take care of the investigation, Camryn." Clint liked keeping unofficial me in one place, and official him in another. I moved back to my appointed place on the other side of the door.

Mark and two Buffalo County deputies from the major crimes unit came down the hallway with duty bags filled with the equipment they needed to process the scene. I stepped aside to give them passage and they both eyed me before heading into the mayor's office. I'd watched county deputies work on two other occasions, and had picked up a little bit of how they operated.

The deputies were dressed in tan polo shirts embroidered with the sheriff's star, their department, and names, E. Holden and G. Thompson. They were wearing black cargo pants with pockets in front, back, and on the side. Clint addressed them as Emily and Greg, and I guessed they were both younger than me.

"We found this in the carpet." Clint opened his gloved hand to reveal the gem, and Mark, Emily, and Greg all took a second to admire it. Emily was the team's photographer and took pictures of the diamond. Then Mark produced a small evidence bag, and Clint dropped it into it. "I wonder who lost this, and when," Mark said.

"No one's reported it missing, not yet anyway. We'll find out when the room was last vacuumed and pull together a list of the mayor's visitors since then," Clint said.

Deputy Greg moved his foot around on the carpet. "It's got enough of a shag so I can see if the diamond was laying upside down, it'd stay hidden until it was moved."

The deputies changed their focus to Mayor Frost.

"Did you call the ME?" Deputy Emily asked Clint.

"No. I'll do that now." He pulled out his phone and took care of it.

"What about his family?" Deputy Greg said.

Mark shook his head. "His wife passed away some years ago. He only has the one son that I know of. Jason. He's a teacher out east. Vermont, I think." He pointed at a group photo of a man, woman, and three kids that appeared to be in their teen years. "Jason's married with a family of his own."

"We'll get the info from Mayor Frost's personnel file," Clint said.

Deputy Emily snapped pictures of everything in the room—including the coat I'd unwittingly dropped—while I repeated my story to Deputy Greg who stood on the other side of the door frame from me. Then he swabbed the blood on my hand. When he finished, Greg told me I could go wash the rest of it off, and then I was free to go. "Unless you need her for anything else, Assistant Chief Lonsbury?"

Clint shook his head. "Not for now. And like I told you before, Camryn, we need to keep a lid on this until we can notify the mayor's family and prepare a statement for the public. At least a preliminary one. Understand?"

I nodded. "But Pinky—"

Clint interrupted, "Will need to wait for another hour or two."

"Umm, is it okay if I take my coat?" I asked of who-ever might care.

The deputies and police officers looked at each other, then Clint nodded. "Sure, go ahead. Mark, pick it up for her, and see that she gets out the door okay after she cleans up."

Clint didn't trust my ability to wash up and leave on my own? Well, on second thought, maybe a little help was a good idea. Mark scooped up my coat and held onto it as he directed me to the restroom. The sink had a faucet that had to be manually turned on. And it stayed on until it was turned off, thankfully. It saved me trying to find the sensor for a two-second blast of water that I'd have to repeat over and over and over and over. I washed and scrubbed my hands until my skin was garnet-red and getting raw.

How had I ever gotten mixed up in Mayor Lewis Frost's death? Not to mention that it was smack dab in the middle of all the disagreements surrounding him and his city council. And Christmas was just around the cor-ner besides. If the people in town and outlying area weren't in enough of a tizzy already, they would be as soon as this latest dire news was announced.

4

Mark was shifting his weight from side to side when I stepped back into the hallway, obviously impatient. He'd likely been wondering what was taking me so long and got his answer when he took a quick look at my hands. He helped me into my coat and nodded at a door at the end of the hallway. "Did you park out back, or in the side lot? I didn't see your car out front."

I shook my head. "I didn't drive here. I walked."

"You want a ride back?"

"Thanks, but the walk will feel good, maybe help me burn off some of my stress."

"If you're sure. It's gotten nippy out there." A Minnesota way of saying it was well below freezing.

"Yep, I'm sure." I waved my hand at the back exit. "I'll go out this way."

"Let me get the door so you don't touch the push bar."

He used a single gloved finger, depressed the bar, and opened the door. Police officers had to think of everything.

"Thanks, Mark."

"I'll catch you later. Cami, are you going to be all right?" He said it in a way that soothed me.

"Yep."

The cold late afternoon air felt clean and refreshing. I breathed it in, but not enough so it burned my nostrils or lungs. I pulled the hood of the coat onto my head and hooked the button to keep it securely in place. Then I found my woolen mittens in the pockets and put them on.

As the door closed shut behind me, I turned around and stared at it. If someone needed a quick escape, with little risk of being seen, that would probably be the best door to exit. I stood for a minute taking in the surroundings, wondering if the killer had in fact come out this way.

Frosty's death scene had embedded itself in my mind, every detail of it in full color. When I had first seen him lying on the floor, I'd been too shocked to fully process what I was looking at. I hadn't even noticed the blood on the carpet by his head. Despite that, my brain had somehow managed to capture a snapshot and had plunked it into my memory bank.

I started my journey back to Curio Finds reliving those first moments. The base of the snow globe was the first thing that had caught my attention. Was the mayor fighting with someone who had gotten so mad that he'd picked up the snow globe and knocked him over the head with it? That would have been a hard blow to break the globe from its base. And the blood on the mayor's desk meant he must have hit his head on the way down. Or, had the killer cut himself on the broken glass and it was his blood on the desk?

My hand twitched inside my mitten thinking about the blood I'd carried on my hand for those long minutes. Eewy eewy, eew. And the way the mayor seemed to be staring and pointing at the broken snow globe and its contents was eerie. Poor Frosty. He probably died from a snow globe blow to the head. What a way to go.

My thoughts bounced from wondering where in the world had the diamond lying in the carpet come from to what had caused the mayor's death. If his death had to do with the decisions he'd been making, there were a number of people who could have been responsible. Harley Creighton had accused the mayor of pushing his own agenda for a time. What had Harley meant, specifically?

The mayor's office would be filled with documents on all the matters that came before the city council, and from individual constituents. Not to mention all the e-mail correspondence he'd had. Some of it would be confidential, no doubt. It was possible Frosty had surprised a burgling information thief who'd grabbed the first thing he got his hands on and hit him with it, intending to knock the mayor out, not kill him.

I was back at the shops before I was ready to face the music with Pinky. I slipped into Curio Finds, but it was empty. "Emmy?" I called out.

Both she and Pinky came in from Brew Ha-Ha. "Cami, I can't stand it anymore. What is going on?" Pinky said.

"I will tell you everything, as I always do, just as soon as I can." I pulled off my mittens and unbuttoned then shrugged off my coat and laid it on the stool behind the counter.

"What in the world did the mayor have to say in that drawn out meeting?" Pinky persisted.

"I can't get into anything right now. Really, Pinky, I can't. And hey, you've put in a very long day here. Emmy and I will finish up, and you and I will talk a little later tonight."

She planted her hands on her hips and frowned. "Cami Brooks, you're trying to get rid of me."

Yes, I was, before I melted down in front of her. "You've had to stay late enough because of me."

She bent her head down so her eyes were level with mine and stared. "You'll tell me ASAP?"

"Yes, I will." I nodded and our foreheads bumped.

Pinky stared for another few seconds, no doubt trying to wear me down, and then she finally broke her eye hold, much to my relief. "Okay. I told Erin I'd stop by so I'll get going." Erin made up the third point of our nearly lifelong friendship triangle. And she, too, would be blown away by Frosty's death. His murder. Pinky gave a little wave and headed into Brew Ha-Ha to collect her things.

The look on Emmy's face told me she was curious as all get-out, but much too polite to say anything. I put an arm on her back. "And, you, too, Emmy. I'll tell you as soon as I can."

She smiled. "I know you will, dearie."

"It's less than thirty minutes until closing time, so feel

free to go home. It's pretty dead in here." I cringed at what I'd said before I even finished the sentence.

"That'd be fine. I'm looking forward to sitting in my chair and putting my feet up. I'm more tired than usual for some reason," Emmy said, and then sighed.

"That sounds like a fine idea." If she only knew.

Emmy got into her warm outerwear and made her way to the door. "See you tomorrow, Camryn."

"Good night, Emmy, and thank you."

It wasn't five minutes later that Pinky called. "Cami, I drove by city hall and there are a bunch of police and county sheriff cars there. And the medical examiner's van is there, too." Pinky'd barely had time to warm up her car since she'd left.

"Pinky, you know I'm sworn to secrecy."

"Somebody *died* when you were there. That's why you looked so spooked."

Actually, he was dead before I got there. "I can neither confirm nor deny that."

"Listen to you. You sound just like a politician already."

She was right. "What else can I say?"

"I can't go to Erin's now, not with everything that's happening with you. I'll let her know I'm on my way back there."

"Pinky, really, there's no reason to come back here. It'll probably be a while until we hear anything."

"Somebody *died* at city hall. They can't keep that a secret for long. Sandy Gibbons will be like a bloodhound following a scent in no time."

And if no one told her I was the one who found Frosty's body, I'd be off the track and not at the end of her trail. For the time being at least.

I had trouble focusing on anything besides the image of Frosty, as dead as dead can be, lying on the floor pointing at that snow globe. It was as though he wanted the police to know what had killed him. That wasn't the difficult part to figure out. The key factor the police needed to know was who had used the snow globe to knock Frosty over the head.

The sound of a car bumping into the curb outside got my attention. Then a second car pulled to a stop behind it. Pinky and Erin. There were my dearest friends, and had been since childhood. But when I needed to keep a secret, they were the last people on earth I wanted to be around. And this wasn't any old run-of-the-mill secret. Pinky came in first, effectively hiding small fry Erin, who came in behind her. Pinky stepped to the side the same moment Erin threw her hands up in the air, making it look like she had just jumped out of a cake.

Pinky closed the gap between us with her long strides before I had a chance to take a single step back. "Cami, this is serious. What's going on? Mark's police car is sitting in front of city hall, along with the county crime van and the medical examiner's van. And Mark won't answer his phone."

Erin pinned me in on the other side and her dark eyebrows drew together. "You'd tell us if something bad had happened to Mark, right? Like if he'd died? He couldn't have been the one to die." Erin and Mark had been an item in high school, but things had never been the same between them after they'd gone off to separate colleges. They'd both eventually returned to Brooks Landing where Erin started her career as an elementary school teacher and Mark was hired as a Brooks Landing police officer. It was evident Mark's feelings were stronger than Erin's in the romantic department, but there was no question that she loved him dearly. We all did. But not in *that* way.

"I saw Mark at the city hall when I was there, and he was fine. If someone died at city hall, I can promise you that it wasn't Mark."

"Cami Brooks . . . oh, never mind." Pinky dramatically whipped off her coat and cap and walked to the back seating area in her shop. Erin and I followed her. Erin slipped off her down-filled jacket then she and Pinky hung their coats on the backs of chairs. We sat down for a very uncomfortable, stretched-out moment of silence.

"Would you guys like something to drink? I'm buying," I said and attempted a smile.

Erin reached over and took my hands in hers. "Cami, your hands are shaking."

I looked down at them and she was right. "I guess I'm a little chilly."

"Your hands don't shake like that from being cold. That's from being nervous, from adrenaline," she said.

"How about I try calling Mark again, see if he answers," Pinky said.

I pulled free of Erin's hold and turned to Pinky. "Let's give him some time. He'll get back to you as soon as he can."

Erin looked around. "Did you hear that?"

CHRISTINE HUSOM

"What?" Pinky and I said together as we tried to hone in on the sound.

"It's probably the old pipes in the ancient hot water heating system. You can hear them when it's quiet in here," I said after listening for a few seconds.

"It's kind of spooky in here after dark when no one else is around," Erin said.

"Stop trying to scare us, Erin. It's hard enough not to feel creeped out knowing Molly's ghost might be haunting the place," Pinky said.

Here we go again. "I only saw her ghost in my dreams, and not in our shops, Pinky," I said.

Pinky let go of a big breath. "But in those dreams, she was always in our shops."

Erin looked at her watch then changed the subject. "It's a little after six. Maybe we should go somewhere else to wait for whatever bad news it is we're waiting for."

"In any case, we can finish locking up." I got up and headed into my shop to take care of that when Mark came through the door and startled the heck out of me. "Mark!"

"Cami, you're looking a little peaked. With good reason, of course."

Pinky and Erin heard Mark's voice and came bounding out from the back. "Cami won't tell us a thing, except that you aren't dead," Pinky spit out.

Mark's eyebrows shot up toward the ceiling. "Now why would you think a thing like that?"

"Because we saw all the emergency vehicles at city hall, not to mention the medical examiner's van. That's a dead giveaway." She frowned when she realized what she'd said.

Mark's lips tugged upward. "Well said. Okay. Cami was ordered by our assistant police chief not to tell anyone what happened until we'd made notification and we were ready to release an official statement."

Pinky and Erin moved in close on either side of me and each locked an arm on my waist. "What is it?" Erin said.

"Mayor Frost died in his office."

"You're saying Frosty just up and died?" Pinky leaned toward him.

"A heart attack?" Erin said.

"More like a head attack. A blow-to-the-head attack."

Erin and Pinky stepped in closer to Mark, taking me with them. "Somebody killed our mayor?" Erin said.

"With a snow globe blow to the head. And Cami was the unfortunate one to find him." Mark shook his head back and forth like he didn't believe it himself.

When Pinky and Erin turned in to face me they almost bumped into each other. "Cami, you poor thing," Erin said.

"The way you keep ending up in the wrong place at the wrong time is just plain as unlucky as can be," Pinky said.

I knew Pinky was referring to Washington, DC, where I was falsely accused of an indiscretion, and to what happened after I'd returned home to Brooks Landing. The first months were uneventful, but then the floodgates opened and I had happened upon the bodies of three victims in as many months. I nodded and felt tears pop out of my eyes and run down my cheeks.

"Now, now, let's get you something calming to drink," Erin said.

"You know we don't have any alcohol here," Pinky said.

"I was thinking along the chamomile-tea-with-honey lines," Erin corrected her.

"Oh, right. That we've got."

"Clint's helping the county guys wrap things up, collecting evidence, then he'll want to talk to you some more. Do an official interview, Cami," Mark said.

I didn't know if I could a face an official interview. The unofficial one was about as much as I could muster tonight. The three of them shuffled me over to Pinky's serving counter. "We've got to lock up," I said.

"Erin and I will do that. You sit, and Pinky will get your tea," Mark said.

I watched the three of them work with my mind only half registering what they were doing. Who had killed Mayor Lewis Frost with a snow globe he'd bought only hours before? There was something about the globe and its scene that felt wrong to me. But never would I have imagined it'd be used as a weapon to hurt anyone.

I looked down at the counter and spotted a penny I could have sworn had not been there a second ago. Pinky thought I had extrasensory perception, which I did not. And I surely hoped it stayed that way. I did, however, have a propensity to spot pennies that I believed my mother was sending from heaven, sometimes to comfort me, sometimes to alert me. A young woman had described finding pennies as an alert, a heads-up. So I wasn't the only one who believed it was possible.

When the shop doors were locked, the signs in the

windows were turned to Closed, and the only light left on was the one above Pinky's counter, the four of us gathered as we had hundreds of times over the years to talk about things. Fortunately, 99 percent of the time the topics were far more mundane than the one we had on the table tonight.

My friends made me go over the details of the day, starting with Frosty's first contentious meeting, then the next, and the next. And his two subsequent visits to Curio Finds where he finally tracked me down. On the second visit, he'd purchased the fateful snow globe, and then he asked me to consider the open seat on the city council. Mark jotted down in his memo book the extra things I hadn't mentioned at city hall.

"A thing of beauty was not a joy forever for Frosty," Erin said.

"Or even for a whole day," Pinky added.

"I wouldn't go so far as to say that particular snow globe was a thing of beauty or a joy to look at. At all," I said.

"What do you mean?" Mark said.

"It was strange. There were three bears that were closing in on a man who was standing outside a cabin. He was holding a gun, and he had what looked to me like a resigned, maybe even peaceful, look on his face. Like he knew the bears were going to get him and he didn't care."

"That sounds pretty bizarre," Erin said.

"I'll say. It seems strange Frosty picked that one out of the scores you have on the shelves over there," Pinky added.

"I know. And it had just come in and didn't even make it to a display shelf. Frosty saw it sitting on the counter, and spoke for it when we'd barely put the price tag on it."

"Well, Mayor Frost did have three bears come after him today, according to what you said, Cami. And those are the ones we know about. Maybe he liked the fact the guy had a weapon he could use if he needed to. Not that Frosty would ever use that kind of weapon, but maybe he had some tactics up his sleeve he was planning to use to calm everybody down," Mark said.

"And now he can't." Pinky sniffled. "I always liked him. He got coffee here almost every morning."

"Did you get a hold of his son to let him know, Mark?" I said.

Mark raised his eyebrows and nodded. "Not the phone call you ever want to make. He was pretty shell-shocked, especially when Clint told him his father may have been the victim of a homicide. Jason said he'll get here as soon as he can tomorrow."

"Poor guy. Why is it that things like this always seem worse during the holidays?" Erin said.

"Because they are," Pinky said.

"I thought Clint would have finished up by now. I better go see if there's anything he needs." Mark stood up.

"Mark, there are so many people that Frosty was having problems with. It's going to take forever to talk to everyone," I said.

"We'll figure it out," he said as his phone rang. He wrestled it out of its holder, glanced at the face, and pushed a button. "Yes, boss. . . . I'm still at Brew Ha-Ha with Cami and Pinky and Erin. . . . Right." He hung up and pointed at me. "Clint will be right over to talk to you."

It was one of those moments in life when the ability to disappear into thin air seemed like the most desirable gift on earth to possess.

5

Clint phoned Mark a short time later, letting him know he was standing outside Brew Ha-Ha. Pinky swooped her way over to the door, unlocked it, and pushed it open for our assistant police chief. The arctic air reached our seats in seconds. Clint walked toward our group with purpose in each step with his eyes trained on me in particular.

A range of emotions darted through me: sympathy that he had the murder of the city's most prominent elected official to solve, dread that he was about to give me the third degree, and finally admiration of his "eye candy" good looks. I kicked myself for letting the last thing enter my mind, unbidden or not. As irritating as he was at times, he was very pleasing to look at.

Clint's phone rang. "I may have to take this." After a

quick glance he shook his head. "I'll talk to our illustri-ous reporter later. She's already gotten the press release. Mark, I see you left your car on the next block over so people wouldn't immediately track you down here. I did the same thing."

Mark nodded. "It'll make folks wonder what's going on over there. Clint, do you have the list of the people you want me to talk to?"

Clint nodded, and the two of them walked over to the archway between the shops where Clint tore out a sheet from his memo book and handed it to Mark.

"I'll get right on this," he said.

They moved back to the counter then Clint said, "Camryn, I'd like to go over some things with you, either in your office or at one of Pinky's tables."

I picked up my mug. "Pinky's." Then I started off in that direction.

"We'll wait for you," Pinky offered.

"You know what, thanks, but I'm going to head home after this, so why don't we all catch up tomorrow?" I said.

"If you're sure," Erin said.

"I'll see that she gets home safe and sound," Clint said.

The hopeful looks on both Pinky's and Erin's faces told me they were reading more into his words than he'd intended.

Mark lifted a hand. "I'll be in touch with what I find out, boss."

The girls grabbed their coats and Mark herded them out the door as they called out their good-byes. The lock clicked shut then Clint turned to me. "Let's sit down. I want you to take me through every encounter you had with Mayor Frost again, what you overheard. And if there is anything else you've remembered."

"Okay." I gave him the details once more, but there wasn't much regarding the mayor to add to the account. I added a little side commentary about the odd snow globe, however. "It's not one I'd want sitting in my house, yet there were two more people who were interested in buying it if Frosty didn't."

Clint shook his head. "When we cleaned up the pieces, it didn't look overly special to me."

"What made it different, what gave it a sort of ominous feeling was that the man was standing on his porch with his gun in one hand and his other arm up, like he accepted that the bears were going to get him." I took the last sip of my tea.

"It seems to me you're reading way more into it than there is."

"I don't know. I've seen more snow globes than I can count, and none have been that strange."

Clint shrugged. "Different strokes for different folks."

A yawn that felt like it started at the tips of my toes pushed out my diaphragm and forced my mouth open before I could stifle it. The unsettling and heartrending events of the day were hitting me full force. "Clint, if you don't have any more questions I'd like to go home."

He studied me a moment. "No, no more questions for now. I'll follow you home; make sure you get there all right and safely inside."

Clint was over the top when it came to safety. "You don't have to do that."

The look on my face must have prompted him to reconsider. "I'll watch from my vehicle."

"All right."

"If you'll give me your keys I'll go start your car, warm it up."

Oh, well that was an offer I was not about to refuse. I flipped the lights back on in my shop then retrieved my keys from my purse in the storeroom. Clint was close behind me. I turned and handed them over. "Thank you. Just turn the lock to get out." I pointed at the door.

"I'll let it run a while then drive around to the front." He disappeared outside of Curio Finds in seconds. I slipped into my coat then picked up the purse I'd dropped on the checkout counter and was about to go into Brew Ha-Ha to turn off the light when my shop door opened. I wondered if Clint had forgotten something. Instead, it was the young woman who'd been interested in the three bears and lone man snow globe that Frosty had bought.

"Hello, I saw your shop was open, but it looks as though you are closing for the night," she said.

There was something about her that tugged at my heartstrings. "Yes. We aren't actually open this late. I was just taking care of some things. Can I help you find something, as long as you're here?"

She shook her head. "Thank you, no. I was just walking by. I will come back another time."

"It's awfully cold to be out walking. How about a cup of something hot to warm you up?"

"I do not want you to bother."

"No bother. I can have a cup of hot chocolate ready in about ninety seconds."

"All right. How much does it cost?"

"Nothing tonight, it's on the house. We have leftovers from today that we'll have to throw away otherwise. I'd feel better if it warms someone's tummy instead."

Her face brightened. "Thank you, that would be very nice. One of those take-with-you cups would be good." She had a quaint way of phrasing things, and a dialect that I tried to place. But she was guarded and I sensed it was too soon to ask questions she might consider personal.

"Okay, one hot chocolate to-go coming right up." I slipped off my coat, dropped my purse on a chair, and walked behind Pinky's counter. She had hot chocolate in a decanter in the small refrigerator. I took it out, poured some in a disposable cup and set the microwave on seventy seconds. It was just the right amount of time to warm it to a drinkable temperature without it boiling over.

The young woman smiled when I put the lid on and set it in front of her. "Thank you. It smells very tasty."

I smiled back. "Do you live close by?"

"Yes, madam."

"If you need a ride, I'd be happy to give you one. A friend of mine . . ."—okay, it was a bit of a stretch referring to Clint as my friend—". . . is actually warming up my car now." Speaking of the devil, he pulled up in my Subaru and parked by the curb in front of the shops. The streetlight caught the shiny metal of his badge on the front of his blue stocking cap as he got out of the car. I pointed at the shop window. "And here he is now."

The young woman took a look at Clint then grabbed

her cup. "I must get home. Thank you, madam." Two "madam"s. I was starting to feel old, and supposed I was in her eyes. My thirty-seven years to her eighteen or so. She dashed toward Pinky's door and found it locked when she pulled on it. She turned to me with what I read as a panicked look on her face. Did being locked in frighten her?

"It's okay, you can get out that door. Just turn the lock," I said, lifting my hand and demonstrating.

Clint had come in the Curio Finds door and was in the archway between the shops as the young woman darted out Brew Ha-Ha's door. "Who was that?" he said.

"I was about to ask her name when it seemed she suddenly had to get home." Maybe it wasn't only getting halted by a locked door that had upset her. It occurred to me she may have been making a fast exit to avoid running into Clint. Was she a runaway, after all?

"What was she doing here so late?"

"She said she was walking by and saw the lights on and thought we were still open."

"That kid shouldn't be running around town alone after dark in the bitter cold," Clint said.

"I agree. She told me she lives near here. Maybe in one of the apartments above a business." Downtown buildings constructed in Brooks Landing in the 1920s commonly had a store or professional service on the street level, and an apartment upstairs for the owners. That practice had ceased long before I was born, but most of the buildings still stood and many had apartments on the second floor that were rented out to tenants. Our buildings, Curio Finds and Brew Ha-Ha, didn't have second stories.

Although on that frigid night, as I was growing wearier and wearier after the long day—mostly from the horror of finding Frosty dead like that—the thought of crawling up a single flight of stairs to a place called home seemed like an answer to my prayers. In fact, even a cot with a sleeping bag in the storeroom would have suited my needs tonight if Pinky hadn't kept bringing up the subject of Molly's ghost haunting the place. Although 95 percent of me didn't believe it was true, there was still enough of a niggling doubt to keep me on edge.

Clint bent his face closer to mine. "Are you okay? I lost you for a minute."

That snapped me out of my reverie. "Oh. I'm not exactly okay, but I'll feel better when I get home."

Clint picked up my coat and helped me into it. As I reached for my purse, he picked that up as well, and handed it to me. "Let's make it happen."

I nodded and watched Clint as he shut off the lights and then locked Pinky's door. We walked through my shop, and I flipped off the lights and locked up. When we stepped out onto the sidewalk Clint slid his hand under my arm and held it firmly as he guided me to my car. He opened the door and I slid in, adjusting my coat under me. "Thank you. I know you still have work to do, so you really don't need to follow me home," I said as I pulled the seat belt across my middle.

He bent over, leaned his head in close to me, and spoke quietly. "It's not far and I told your friends I would.

I don't believe there is a threat to the public, but until we find the killer, we should use extra caution. And you especially, since you're the one who found Mayor Frost. Wait here and I'll bring my car around." He shut the door then jogged down the sidewalk and around the corner, out of sight.

A few cars drove by, but the street was mainly deserted that frosty winter night. *Frosty.* Oh, my, when I thought of how his upsetting day of battling with angry people had ended, my tired mind went into overdrive trying to figure out who could have done that to him. I didn't know any of the three people I'd heard arguing with him well enough to even hazard a guess. Lila said there had been a number of visitors in to see the mayor. But who was the last one, the one before I got there? The killer. There must have been a struggle and at least two crashes, judging from my observations of his office. So why hadn't Lila heard anything? And then to make things more curious, there was that large gem lying on the carpet.

Clint pulled up in his police car behind me and I took that as permission to head on home. I lived about a mile away, and the police escort was not necessary. But I had to admit it was comforting to have one on that dark night. *Until we find the killer, we should use extra caution. And you especially, since you're the one who found Mayor Frost.* Clint's words from a few minutes before hadn't registered in my brain until then. Surely he didn't think I was in any special danger, did he? Whether he did it on purpose or not, Clint, too, often acted like I should have my own personal bodyguard.

I barely remembered the short drive home, and that

was not a good thing. And admitting it to Clint would be even worse. I lived in a homey 1960s brick Tudor-style house that had belonged to my birth mother's dearest friend on earth. When Sandra McClarity joined Berta Brooks in heaven the past year, I liked to think the two of them had picked up where they'd left off over thirty years before.

I rented the largely-furnished house from her children, and loved living in a place that had always held a special place in my heart. The home sat in an older part of town where the blocks were plotted so alleys divided neighbors' back yards. Most had garages that were accessed from the alleys, and others had upgraded by adding garages that attached to their houses. It would be a nice feature to have in the cold days of winter or in inclement weather. I pulled into the alley and pushed the button to open the automatic garage door. That was the perk I'd added when I moved in so I didn't have to wrestle with the heavy overhead door. I kept an extra opener in my purse and always fished it out before I got out of the car.

Clint's car was idling in the alley as I stepped out of the garage and pushed the button to close the door. He rolled down his window. "Your house is locked, right?"

"Right."

"Okay. Be sure to lock up again as soon as you get inside."

It was one of his favorite warnings for me. "Yes, sir." My teeth were starting to chatter, and that time it was the freezing air causing it. I dropped the opener back in my purse and pulled my keys from my pocket. When I reached the back door my fingers were stiff from the cold, even with my leather driving gloves on. I either needed to buy a warmer pair or wear my wool mittens instead of the gloves. I fumbled to get the key in the lock and finally got the door open.

Clint called out from his car. "Let us know if you need anything."

I waved, stepped into the warmth then shut and locked the door behind me. I flipped on the kitchen lights and leaned back against the wall, hoping the friendly vibes the house gave off would surround me and help me feel better. My cell phone rang and my body jerked in response. I dug it out of my pocket and saw it was Pinky calling.

"Cami, Erin and I are wondering if you want some company tonight."

"No, thanks. I just got home and I need to call my parents before they hear about Mayor Frost from someone else."

"Good idea. But after word gets around the rest of your family, you'll be on the phone all night."

"Let's hope not. I'm really beat and need to quiet my mind. I can't seem to stop thoughts about the mayor from spinning around up there."

"Me either. Erin says the same thing. And we didn't even see what you did. I just want to remember how he looked when he came in for his morning coffee. That's the image I'm going to hold onto—his smiling face. And it's better than the expression he'd get when someone got after him for this or that. I couldn't make myself listen to that chatter half the time." Pinky disliked conflict and avoided confrontations whenever possible.

"I understand, Pink."

"Erin wants to talk to you."

There was a pause then Erin came on the line. "Cami, call if you need us to come over. You'll do that, right? I'm going to help Pinky bake for a while. But we can take a break."

That brought a smile to my face. Erin was not exactly domestically inclined when it came to cooking or baking. That meant Pinky was behind schedule and either she'd begged Erin for assistance, or Erin had volunteered, as she so often did. Even with her full-time teaching position, she had filled in at our shops here and there since Black Friday, when the Christmas shopping season had started off with a bang.

When I took off my coat I got a quick reminder that my thermostat was turned down to 60 degrees Fahrenheit, like we did at the shops. It conserved energy and saved money, and there was no reason to keep the temperature up when I was gone. I turned the thermostat to 68 degrees then flipped a living room lamp on, plopped down on the couch, and pulled a throw blanket over me.

The little bird popped out of the clock and its single cuckoo let me know it was 7:30. I still had my phone in my hand and punched in my parents' home number. My dad answered with less enthusiasm than usual.

"Hi, Dad. Is everything okay? How's Mom?"

"Hello, Cami. Everything's fine here. We're just tuckered out for no good reason other than it's cold out and gets dark so early."

"A lot of people are affected by the short daylight

hours. Look on the bright side, in a few weeks we'll start gaining light again, little by little."

"It's always good to get on the other side of the winter solstice, that's for darn sure."

"Dad, have you and Mom heard the news about Mayor Frost?"

"No, what happened?"

"He died today."

Dad made a sound like "haah," then said, "He died? I thought he was the picture of health, for an older guy that is." My parents were about the same age as Frosty.

"Actually, it seems that someone was responsible for his death. And when I went to meet him in his office I was the one that found him."

"I can hardly believe he's gone. Wait a minute, Cami, are you saying he was killed, and *you* found him?" His voice climbed up a few notes.

"Unfortunately, yes."

"Hold on, Mom wants to talk to you."

"Your father held the phone so I could listen, too. My poor dear. Tell us what happened."

I gave a summary of the day's events. Then I went into deeper detail about finding the mayor and how I'd checked for a pulse before I ran for help. I left out the part about getting the blood on my hand and scaring Margaret so badly that she conked out from fright.

Dad came back on the line. "We just can't figure out what he would've done that got him killed. It's no secret as mayor, Frost gets into disagreements with people over this and that, but that goes with the job. It doesn't seem like the kinds of things that would get a guy killed."

"Cami, go back to the part about Mayor Frost asking you to consider a seat on the city council." It was Mom back on the phone.

When I repeated that piece, I heard her clicking her tongue, an indication she didn't know if that was such a good idea. "I know you're very sharp when it comes to legislation, and you have all that experience working for Senator Zimmer, but is this something you'd really want to do? I mean, with running Curio Finds, you might have people tracking you down at work with any number of issues."

"That's a possibility."

"And it'll be so different from the kind of job you had in Washington, doing research behind the scenes. That's where you always liked to be," she added.

I'd been a shy kid who would rather have endured a week without ice cream if it meant I didn't have to get in front of the class for any kind of speech. "You're right, Mom. At the state and national level, I wouldn't have been comfortable being in the public eye. Not that I'm hiding any skeletons in my closet. But it's different at the local level. Sandy Gibbons's newspaper articles covering the highlights of the Brooks Landing's city council meetings has not yet gained national appeal."

Mom chuckled at the thought. "That's true. You'll give it very careful consideration, won't you, Cami?"

"I will."

"We'll be happy to come stay with you if you need us," she said.

"Thanks, but I'll be fine."

After we disconnected, I sat and stared for a while,

trying to free my mind of the image of Frosty lying there lifeless in his office. It was something I knew would always be there. Not front and center like it was now, but never too far back in the recesses of my brain. Who had killed him and why? I'd witnessed him having heated discussions with three people that morning. I hadn't heard Rosalie Gorman's specific beef, but she'd warned him about watching himself before she stormed off.

I thought of Lila, the clerk at city hall. Did the killer walk by her on his, or her, way to Mayor Frost's office? Or was Lila away from her post when the killer snuck in, as she had been when I arrived? It may have been mere minutes between the killer's arrival and my own. A series of prickly sensations skipped their way up my spine as I realized that if I'd arrived before the killer had made a hasty escape I may not have gotten out of there alive.

6

My dreams were vivid during the night and Mayor Lewis Frost was the main character in each one I remembered. He was going about normal activities like walking down the street with his earphones in, listening to something on his device, as he often did. Then he was sitting at a table drinking coffee with some people I couldn't identify, and then he was presiding over a city council meeting. All the while he was seemingly unconcerned about the activities of those around him, like he didn't have a care in the world or feel threatened in any way.

In the last dream he was standing in Curio Finds holding the snow globe with the three bears and lone man he'd purchased. That's when I woke up. My heart was beating loudly in my chest and a sinking feeling of guilt settled in the pit of my stomach. Frosty was attacked with that same snow globe, the one I'd sold him.

I sat up in bed then pulled a fleece robe around me. My furry pink bunny slippers—a gift from my pink-loving friend—were sitting on the floor next to the bed. No matter that they weren't my usual style. I slid my feet into them, appreciating both Pinky's thoughtfulness and their comforting warmth. It was almost like having the soft little creatures attached to my feet. They were the only things I'd ever worn that had little faces, complete with floppy ears, a mouth, a nose, whiskers, and eyes that looked alive in a certain light. Like now. I closed my eyes and chided myself for being silly. Even if they had been real, they were bunny eyes. Sweet little bunny rabbits, not big bad bears.

My stomach rumbled, reminding me I'd skipped supper the night before. I shuffled my tired self into the kitchen, opened the refrigerator, and smiled when I spotted the leftover honey and balsamic vinegar-glazed chicken breast on the shelf. I'd made two servings a few evenings before to have a second meal on hand. I popped the container in the microwave then sat down at the kitchen table a couple of minutes later with the chicken and a tall glass of milk. I'd get my fill of carbs with one of Pinky's muffins or scones midmorning, but my body was telling me I needed protein to start the day right.

As I chewed and swallowed bite after bite, I thought of Mayor Lewis Frost and how he'd died. But by whose hand? I finished eating and pushed the plate aside. A notebook and pen were lying on the table. I slid them in front of me and wrote Lewis Frost at the top of the page. Mayor of Brooks Landing. *Poor Frosty*. He'd been well-liked by the majority of people. But, there was a handful who didn't like him or his politics. That was true of virtually everyone who served in public office. I'd heard harsh words from two people who didn't agree with his stance on certain issues. Plus whatever Rosalie Gorman had to say was not something she wanted overheard. Not a good sign.

I wrote down Lila's name first. Not as a suspect, but as a person who likely had some valuable information. She'd know what the protocol was for getting in to see the mayor, for one thing. Open door policy or not, she was the first line of defense. It seemed to me the mayor would want to be informed if someone was there to see him, even if they had an appointment. But Lila had let me find my own way back to the mayor's office without so much as a call to let him know I was there. Lila. I pushed the pen into the paper next to her name, thinking about her. She'd freely shared that the mayor had a number of visitors that day, and I hoped she'd be as open with me on my next visit.

Marvin Easterly. He was livid when he loudly voiced his opinion to the mayor, arguing that the neighboring farm land should remain rural. He did not want a factory encroaching on the peace and quiet he and his neighbors had been accustomed to forever. Marvin didn't strike me as a violent man, by any means. But that was no guarantee he hadn't lost his cool, grabbed the snow globe, and hit Frosty with it before he could stop himself.

Rosalie Gorman. She'd been angry when she left her meeting with Frosty at Brew Ha-Ha. Stormin' Gorman. The only thing I knew about her personal or family life was that she was divorced. I realized the times she'd come into Curio Finds, my guard had gone up and I hadn't been overly friendly to her. Her personality was on the brash side and off-putting to me. Professionally, Rosalie was ambitious and had built a successful real estate business. She'd also been elected to serve the city by a majority of the people.

But according to her city council reputation, Rosalie was difficult to work with, at times. She pushed and pushed and pushed when there was something she really wanted. I'd known many people like her, more than I could count, during my years in Washington, DC. I'd heard she'd gotten nasty with a few people on different occasions, both inside and outside of council chambers. If I decided to apply for the vacant council seat and got appointed, I'd need to find an effective way to work with her. When I was younger and greener, people like her tended to frighten me because I didn't know what they were capable of. Now I was more wary than anything else.

Harley Creighton. He had very strong opinions and had "butted heads" with the mayor time and time again during his stint on the council, according to Frosty. Word was he had aspirations of running for mayor someday, after he had gained some experience in city government. And he would run against the sitting mayor, if he had to. But from what I had overheard him saying yesterday morning, which the mayor later confirmed, Harley Creighton was giving up his seat. Would he change his mind now that the man who caused him so much grief was gone for good?

Had Marvin visited Mayor Frost at his office, he would have gone in the main entrance. The public entrance. Rosalie and Harley, on the other hand, would have had access through the back entry, either with a key or an identification card they swiped. Lila told me the mayor had keys, but that may have included a key card.

My cell phone rang in the bedroom and I managed to get to it before the fourth ring when the voicemail picked up. I snatched it off the nightstand, pushed the Talk button, and sat down on the bed. "Good morning."

"Good morning? Holy moly, Cami, have you seen the news?" Pinky was pumped.

"By seen, do you mean on television?"

"Yes, a bunch of my customers were talking about how all the major Twin Cities' channels had a blurb about Mayor Frost's suspicious death on their early morning news broadcasts. Since we don't have a TV here, I turned the radio on to our local station and just caught it there."

My heart pitter-pattered. "What are they saying about the mayor's death, exactly?"

"Okay, what they said on the radio was, 'Lewis Frost, mayor of Brooks Landing was found dead in his office yesterday afternoon. He died under suspicious circumstances, and it is under investigation.'" Pinky recited it like she was a newscaster herself.

"So they didn't get into any details, and I'm selfishly glad they didn't name the person who found him. Not that they usually do, but they often say, 'was discovered by a coworker or family member,' something like that."

"No, they didn't say 'local business manager,' thank

goodness. And I kept my big trap shut this morning with everyone talking about it here, too."

"I appreciate that. When she finds out, Sandy Gibbons will be hounding me before you know it."

"That's for sure. Cami, when I heard it on the news like that, it seemed even more real than it did last night." Pinky's voice quieted.

"I know what you mean. Tragic news takes time to really sink in."

"When he didn't stop by for his usual cup of coffee this morning, it made me so sad knowing he'll never walk into Brew Ha-Ha again."

"It's very sad. We'll all miss him."

"There are customers coming in, so I gotta go." Pinky hung up before I had a chance to tell her I'd be there as soon as I got ready.

Erin phoned me halfway through my morning routine. "Cami, how are you holding up?"

"Pretty good, I guess. More than a little shocked."

"I can't begin to imagine. I wanted to check in with you before my students arrive, see if you need anything."

"I don't think so, but thank you."

"All right, well I'll stop in at your shops after school, see if you and Pinky need help."

"Good, I'll see you then. 'Bye, Erin."

"Toodles."

The bell on Brew Ha-Ha's door dinged when I stepped into the shop. Pinky glanced up from her task of whipping up frothy Cocoa Coffee Delights. It was her drink special of the day I noticed when I glanced up at her sign. There were a number of customers at the counter so I headed to my back storeroom, dropped off my coat and things, then returned to lend a helping hand. We kept busy for another ten minutes until everyone had a beverage of some kind, and most of them had a muffin or scone besides.

A woman around my age wearing a stylish fur hat and a long wool coat walked up from the back seating area and stopped. "When does Curio Finds open?" she said.

I'd extended the hours for the season, opening at nine instead of ten. The clock read 8:34. "I can open now, if you'll give me a minute to turn on the lights."

She narrowed her eyes on me then smiled. "I'd like that. I arrived early, thinking you'd be open at eight. I have an interest in snow globes." *Have an interest in?* The way she said it sounded official, professional.

As far as the specialty shops in the area, most opened at ten. Eight o'clock was considered early in Brooks Landing, unless you had a hardware store or lumberyard or restaurant or coffee shop. Other retailers opened at nine. Antique, shabby chic, and shops like ours that sold collectibles opened at ten. I don't know when those norms were established, but I figured they were based on customer traffic and the hours the majority of people shopped.

The woman followed me into Curio Finds, keeping a respectable distance. I flipped on all the lights and unlocked the entry door. But I kept the sign turned to the Closed side until later. I slid in behind my checkout counter and turned the key in the cash register, ready to ring up the day's sales.

"Anything in particular you're looking for?" I said.

"No. But thank you." She looked like she was on a mission as she examined one snow globe after another. I knew from past dealings that some collectors took their searches and their finds very seriously.

"Are you a collector, a dealer?"

"You could say I'm a collector."

Her answers were curt enough to cut me off from further probing. She picked up a snow globe we'd gotten in the infamous order yesterday. The order that included the scary bear scene, the one that had been used in Frosty's murder. She held up one that was far less ominous and featured a woman standing with her arms in the air, like she was welcoming the falling snow. A cabin, much like the one in the scary bear snow globe, stood behind her. The mood in that scene was the polar opposite of the bear scene. It would have been my choice, hands down, between the two. But the unnerving one had sold immediately and the soothing one was still on the shelf.

The woman studied it for a time then asked, "Where did this come from, a supplier in Minnesota?"

"No, as a matter of fact, it's from overseas. From a new company—new for us, that is. We got our first shipment yesterday, as a matter of fact. Their name is . . . let me look at the invoice." The sheet I needed was conveniently lying on the counter in a pile of recently received orders. "It's Van Norden Distributing out of Amsterdam."

She nodded. "You said your first order from them arrived yesterday, so that means you're expecting more?"

"We are, but I'm not sure when."

"Okay, thank you." She set the snow globe back on the shelf and made her way out the door. Her manner and behavior made me curious, and drew me to the window to see where she was headed. She slipped around the corner and disappeared from sight.

I flagged Pinky down when she passed by the archway. "Who was that woman?" I said.

"No clue," she said with a wave of her dish towel. She joined me in Curio Finds.

"Has she ever been in your shop before?" I said.

"Not that I know of, but it's possible. When it gets crazy busy, sometimes it gets to be one big blur of who is gracing me—and my business—with their presence."

"That's true enough. Pinky, think about it: did anything about her, that woman, I mean, strike you as odd?"

"Like what?"

"For one thing she was here very early, hanging around, waiting for me to open."

She shrugged. "Some people are early birds. They like to get up and on with their day, so it doesn't seem all that odd to me."

"Maybe not, but she guessed we opened at eight, and the shop hours are posted in my front window and . . ." I pointed to the sign on the wall next to the archway, ". . . right there."

"Not everybody notices signs."

"That's true, but I was standing right next to it when she asked me."

"I repeat, not everybody notices signs."

"But she seems like the kind that would. In fact, I

could have sworn she glanced at it when I was answering her. And then when she checked out my shop, she looked at the stock of snow globes we had. After she found one she seemed very interested in, she asked where it came from, asked if we were getting more, and then left."

"Cami, why are you making such a big deal about this? Maybe that sixth sense of yours is out of whack because of the way you found Frosty yesterday and now you're going to start wondering if everyone is up to something or other."

I lifted my shoulders in a quick shrug then nodded. Pinky was probably right. Not that I had a sixth sense per se, but my regular five senses did seem like they were on heightened alert. And likely would be until Frosty's killer was found and put behind bars. I looked at Pinky's Betty Boop clock. Lila would be at her city hall post soon.

Pinky's phone rang and she went behind her counter to answer it. "Brew Ha-Ha, how can I help you? . . . Hi, Emmy. . . . Sorry to hear that, but we'll be fine here. You take care of yourself. . . . Thanks and 'bye." She hung up and told me what I'd surmised; Emmy was under the weather and couldn't come to work.

"I hope she'll be okay. Oh, and that reminds me, Erin said she'd come by after school. It looks like we'll need her help after all."

Pinky nodded. "Things work out somehow."

"Hey, Pink, do you have any groceries to pick up or need a break before the midmorning rush?"

"No, I'll be good until later."

"Then if it's all right with you, I'd like to go talk to someone about something."

She put her hands on her hips and lowered her chin. "Really, Cami, like you can't say who it is?"

"I'll tell you when I get back. That way, if someone asks for me you can say I had an errand to run, and if there is a particular person or two that wants details, you won't have any."

"Ah, you mean like Assistant Chief Clint or Officer Mark or Sandy Gibbons."

"Or anyone. Thanks, I'll be back in a jiffy."

I definitely chose the wrong time to visit Lila. When I rounded the corner to her desk, who but Sandy Gibbons herself was there interviewing her. Pinky had jinxed me by saying her name out loud mere minutes before. Both women turned their attention to me before I could slip away unnoticed. But I tried to make a quick getaway anyway.

"Camryn Brooks, you come back here." Sandy slid her chair back then planted her hands on Lila's desk and pushed herself up. "Lila here tells me you were the one who discovered Mayor Frost's body in his office yesterday."

Lila's face colored. She bent her head down and her eyes found something on her desk she was visibly more comfortable focusing on than me.

"I'll come back later," I said and tried again to run away.

But Sandy was on my heels. She grabbed my arm and turned me around. "Please, Camryn, I just have a few questions." She was no spring chicken, but she had impressive strength. And I was convinced it was just as well to get her inevitable questions answered, and the sooner the better.

"Sandy, you probably know better than I do what I can or can't say. And the less I say for the newspaper, the less trouble I'll be in with the police for saying something I shouldn't have."

Sandy ignored my concern and lifted her hand, revealing the pen and notepad she was holding. She shifted the pen to her right hand, prepared to write. "So, tell me, why were you in the mayor's office in the first place?"

Golly, that was a whole other can of worms. "I had something I wanted to talk to him about. Something personal." But it was something that could become public before long, depending on my decision.

"Personal? Ha. Well, I'll respect that, for now. Lila left work as you headed on back there. Everyone else was gone for the day. Then what?"

"I knocked on Mayor Frost's door—"

"So his door was closed."

"Yes, but he was expecting me so I knocked again then went in. And I found him lying on the floor, not breathing."

"What else did you see? Evidence of a struggle, a fatal injury, what?"

"Sandy, the police are doing the investigating, so you'll have to ask them."

"Well, they're calling it a homicide investigation so I know you must have seen something to back that up."

"I told the police everything, but that's all I can tell you."

"Camryn. Okay. So what did you do after you found him?"

"I ran to the police station and called for help. And they did. Help. That's all I have to say."

"That's all?"

"That's all."

Sandy let out a loud breath and stuck her pen and notepad in her pocket. "I'll see if the police have any more information to share then." She looked at Lila. "Thank you," she said then headed down the hallway, no doubt marking the police station as her next destination.

"Sorry, Camryn, I didn't mean to speak out of turn, telling Sandy that," Lila said and stood up.

"You didn't speak out of turn. I am the one who found him. I know how persuasive Sandy can be. I've been through this before. It's just that if word gets out who found Mayor Frost, all kinds of people will ask me for the details. It's human nature."

"I suppose that's true. I have to confess that I want to know more. I mean, not the really bad parts, but I want to know what happened to our mayor." Tears filled her lower lids and she sniffed. "He was almost like a grandfather to me. Maybe not quite old enough for that, but Frosty was the kind of guy I'd want for my grandpa."

Lila was sincerely distressed. Not that I suspected

she'd had anything to do with his death in the first place. I reached over and put my hand on her shoulder for a moment. "How long have you worked here?"

She sniffled. "Just over eleven years."

"So you've gotten to know a lot of people, seen a lot of changes around here in all those years, huh?"

She nodded.

"When I worked for Senator Zimmer in Washington, even though I didn't work in constituent services, I know there were always people who were upset with decisions she made. Most e-mailed or phoned, but there were some that stopped by to talk to her in person. And once in a while their conversations got close to being rowdy."

Lila thought for a second then smiled. "I know what you mean. Mayor Frost had the best temperament for handling people like that."

"When I stopped by yesterday, you said that he'd had a number of visitors. I happen to know a few people who had words with him earlier in the day, at Brew Ha-Ha."

Lila raised her eyebrows. "Really, like who?"

"A farmer from Chatsworth Township, two of the council members. Do you remember who Mayor Frost's visitors were yesterday, before I got here?"

"I suppose it doesn't hurt to tell you, now that he's gone. Marvin Easterly, the farmer from Chatsworth Township you're probably talking about, came by and was in the mayor's office a while. Then I heard Harley Creighton talking to him in the hallway and it was loud enough for me to hear all the way back to my desk. He was saying something about quitting, and that really surprised me because I thought he loved his job, at least that's what I've heard him say more than once.

"Come to think of it, all the councilors were in and out yesterday afternoon." She shuddered then very quietly added, "And Rosalie Gorman was another one who seemed upset, maybe even more than anyone else. I heard her say, 'Lewis,' like she was mad at Mayor Frost, and then she went into his office and slammed the door behind her."

"So she was in the mayor's office alone with him?"

Lila nodded and moved like a shiver had raced through her. "And she didn't come out for a long time."

The thought made me want to shudder, too. I wouldn't want to be trapped in a room with her for two minutes. "Anyone else visit him?"

"Let's see, the pastor from his church, and a plumber who dropped off a bill for some work he'd done for the mayor. One or two others I didn't know. But that was earlier in the afternoon."

"So who was the last one or two before me?"

"Just the councilors. That I know of, but I'm not always at my desk, like if I'm making copies or delivering papers, things like that."

"I understand. Okay, last night Officer Mark Weston let me out the back way. Is that door kept open during business hours?"

She pointed with her thumb in the direction of the door I was referring to. "Oh, you mean the one back there?" When I nodded she said, "No, that's for employees only. You need an access card to get in."

I'd figured as much. "One last question, Lila: Who

was the last person that walked by your desk before I got here?"

"The last person that walked by my desk? Either direction? Gosh, I don't know. Other people that work in the office here, I guess."

"No member of the public, any of the councilors?"

"No visitors that I noticed. And the councilors would probably go out the back way, since that's where their parking lot is."

As would the person who needed a quick flight. And that person would not want to be seen by anyone in the city hall offices. Last night I'd surmised the killer had snuck out the back way, and now I was convinced of it. And who would be more familiar with the back way out than one of the employees?

7

If someone had posed the question, Margaret would probably name me as the one townsperson she'd least like darkening her door again. But I owed her an apology. Especially since—and she could never find this out because it wasn't nice—the look on her face and the way she fainted when I'd come rushing in looking for help had struck me as hysterically funny during the middle of the night. I'd been dreaming about Frosty and when I woke up I needed to think of something else, and then Margaret and the look of utter disbelief and fright came to mind and tickled my funny bone. I was exhausted and overwrought and slap happy and couldn't stop it, and it helped ease some of my tension. Margaret's dislike for me would deepen even more if she found out I'd had a laughing jag at her expense. It was something that was best kept secret, even from my closest friends.

Margaret was at her post and looked like she'd recovered well enough from the incident. She didn't smile when she saw me, as per normal. But she didn't scream or faint either, so I counted that as a step in the right direction. "Hi, Margaret."

"Camryn."

"I wanted to tell you how sorry I am about yesterday, scaring you like that. I didn't think about how I must have looked with the blood on my hand and everything. I wasn't able to think about anything except getting help for Mayor Frost."

Margaret nodded. "I understand, and I don't blame you for what happened. I mean. about me having that fainting spell. My daughter talked to the doctor and he thinks the blood just rushed to my head when I stood up so fast like that."

"Well you look good now." I stuck my hands in my coat pockets, ready to leave, when I felt something in the left one I'd forgotten about. It was a stack of twenty-five dollar gift certificates enclosed in envelopes from Curio Finds. I'd tried to drop them off at the local food shelf a couple of days before, but they were closed. The volunteers there knew individuals who were in particular need, and would slip them into their bags of groceries so they would have a nice surprise when they got home and unpacked their bags. It was fun for us, and a small way to give others some happiness at Christmas.

I pulled one out of the stack and handed it to Margaret. "What's this?" she said.

"A little peace offering."

Margaret opened the envelope and withdrew the card. "Oh, my, how nice. But really, that's not necessary." She replaced the card and tried to give it back to me.

I shook my head. "It's yours."

"I don't know what to say. Thank you." And then she smiled. At me. For the first time. And for the first time I got to see how attractive she was when she did.

"You're welcome." I waved and made my way out the door. Then it was my turn to smile. I think the wall around Margaret may have developed a little crack.

I drove my Subaru back to Curio Finds, parked in the lot behind the buildings, and took the shortcut through the walkway between my shop and the one to the north of it. About halfway to the sidewalk, I spotted a young woman passing by, the same one who'd been in the shop yesterday and had returned later that evening. I called out, "Hey, wait up." But either she didn't hear me or didn't think I was talking to her. I picked up my pace, but wasn't fast enough to catch up to her. She'd disappeared, probably into one of the neighboring businesses.

Before I opened the door, the window displays in our shop caught my attention and I paused a few seconds to admire them. Curio Finds was dressed for the holidays. My parents had helped me set up three decorated and lighted Christmas trees—small, medium, and larger— along with a variety of different sizes of wrapped gift boxes to set snow globes on. The garland and lights gave a festive added touch. Frosty had told me how cheery it

looked when he walked by, and I smiled thinking it had
given him little moments of joy.

I stepped into the shop and was greeted by the welcoming aroma of a spiced beverage and the scowling face
of Rosalie Gorman who came through the archway from
Brew Ha-Ha as I was slipping off my coat. One of the
people on my list I had deep concerns about. She could
be nasty, but just how nasty? I needed to talk to her.
Eventually.

"Got a minute, Camryn?"

My instinct was to say no, but without any customers
in the shop to use as an excuse, I nodded. I walked to the
checkout counter and draped my coat over the stool
behind it. Pinky stuck her head into my shop, gave a
quick glance at Rosalie's back then at me, shook her head,
and disappeared back into her own domain.

Rosalie came toward me with deliberate steps and left
little space between us when she stopped. It reminded
me of the three bears in the snow globe scene, approaching the man in perceived attack mode. It was somewhat
of a relief there was only one of her to contend with. "You
were the one who found Lewis . . . ah . . . Mayor Frost
yesterday," she said.

Word was getting around. "Yes, I did. Sad to say."

"What time did you get to his office?"

"Right around four thirty."

"And you saw Lila, she was still there?" Rosalie
persisted.

What was she getting at and how much information
should I give her? I had questions for her, and she was
the one interrogating me. Maybe if I answered hers, she'd

answer mine, too. Although she might be trying to throw me off since I knew she and Frosty had had a disagreement that ended with her spitting out a biting warning to him. Out of common courtesy—not to mention the fact that I'd been firmly dismissed by her—I hadn't eavesdropped on their conversation.

But I later wished I had. It would have been easier than trying to wheedle it out of her now. What would she own up to, and what would she leave out? Frosty was the only other person who knew what had transpired between the two of them, and he'd taken that information to his death.

I nodded as the answer to her question. Yes, Lila was still there.

Rosalie pressed on, "Anyone else that you saw or heard?" Ah, maybe she'd been there after all and had narrowly escaped before I saw her. She could have been nearby and taken off when she heard me knocking on his door and calling out to the mayor.

My chin lifted slightly and my eyes narrowed. "You mean like you?"

Her mouth dropped open and her face colored to a shade of rosy purple. "You think you saw me?"

"Rosalie, I didn't say that."

"You implied it, and I'm not going to stand here and listen to any more from you." She turned and made a huffing sound as she headed out the door.

Pinky stepped through the archway. "What was that all about?"

"It seems she was on a fact-finding mission, and the reason behind it makes me more than a little suspicious."

CHRISTINE HUSOM

Pinky's long legs carried her to my side in two strides. "Cami Brooks. Seriously. Tell me you're not getting yourself mixed up in Frosty's murder. I know you're already mixed up in some of it, but I'm talking about the whodunnit part. You aren't, are you?"

"Not exactly."

Her graceful arms looped a wide circle on either side of me then her hands settled on my shoulders. She bent over so we were eye to eye. "You saying 'not exactly' is exactly what's got me worried. Cami, we've been best friends practically our whole lives. I know you can't help yourself when it comes to trying to make things right after they've gone wrong. But you've had some close calls with some scary people lately and I don't want you to get hurt. Neither does Erin or Mark or anyone else who loves you."

I reached up and put my hands on hers. "Thank you." And then I was saved from further explanation or excuses when the ding of the bell on her shop door announced that a new group of customers had arrived.

Both shops were busy until early afternoon when we got our first real break. I was standing behind my checkout counter when Pinky came in and plopped down on a nearby stool. She stretched her legs straight out in front of her and pushed back the headband that had crept lower on her forehead. It could only hold up her wild curls for so long before it slipped.

"Holy moly, Cami. Now we know how much help Emmy is when she's here."

"We sure do. Pinky, we should think about keeping her on after the holidays. Both of us have been tied down to our shops for too many months."

"There's more to it than that, if I'm reading you right."

"I won't deny that I'm thinking about the council seat, but that's not the main reason. When I took over for my parents, they planned to come back when Mom got better. But now I think they'll just help with ordering and keep going to rummage sales and auctions looking for cool things. That's the part they really love anyway. And maybe give us a little time off here and there, but I doubt they'll ever be back to their old schedule."

"I've been thinking the same thing. And let's face it, if I was seventy-something, I'd be ready to do other fun things, too. Who can blame them?"

"Not me, that's for sure. I know how hard they've worked all their lives."

Pinky frowned slightly. "Cami, about this city council thing, it seems like it got to be a dangerous job for our mayor all of the sudden."

"I'm not worried. If I got appointed to fill out Harley Creighton's term, it'd only be for a year. No one has any gripes against me that I know of. If I don't like it, I won't run in the next election."

Pinky waved her hands above her head then dropped them on the back of her neck. "That's what you say now, about nobody having any gripes against you, I mean, but just wait."

Clint and Mark came trooping into Curio Finds looking as tired as all get-out. Pinky sat up straighter and I stood up taller. "You guys look like you could use a good strong drink," she said.

Mark shook his head. "Yeah, but we're still on duty."

Pinky chuckled. "You being in uniform gave that part

away. No, I meant one of my special caffeinated concoctions and a fresh buttery muffin to go with it."

Being tempted with a buttery muffin made my mouth water. The four of us headed into Brew Ha-Ha and we all had drinks and muffins in front of us in no time. Pinky and I stayed behind the counter, and the men settled on seats.

"Any progress, Assistant Chief Lonsbury?" I said.

Clint had to get in one very noisy slurp of his coffee before he looked at me with raised eyebrows over the top of his cup. "Nothing conclusive, but it's early days yet."

"We collected a boatload of fingerprints," Mark said.

"Including the set you left on the mayor's desk in full living color," Clint added.

My response was to turn the color of the bloody fingerprints I'd unwittingly left behind.

Pinky nudged me and some of my coffee sloshed out of the mug I was holding. "I'd have done the same thing," she said in my defense, but must have given it a second thought because she added, "Well, maybe not. I might not have been brave enough to get close enough to check the poor man's pulse."

Clint shrugged a shoulder then sucked in another loud sip of coffee. You'd think he did it on purpose because he knew how much it unnerved me. "I'm not blaming her, Pinky." He looked at me and added, "And I agree, it was a brave thing to do." And then my blush deepened. Whether it was his unexpected compliment or his striking good looks, I couldn't say.

It was an optimal time to use the restroom. "Excuse me." I slipped away and cautiously opened the door to our shop's bathroom, flipped on the light, and peered inside. It had been my habit since I'd found our employee, and former classmate, inside the room, poisoned to death.

Pinky didn't necessarily mean to scare us, but she'd convinced herself that Molly was haunting the place. Unexplained things had happened, and we had yet to get to the bottom of them. Although my head didn't believe her, my heart had its doubts.

I noticed nothing unusual or alarming in the little— and by "little" I mean teeny tiny—bathroom. I stepped inside and locked the door. Then the lights went out and little shivers danced up my spine and down my arms. I couldn't get out of there fast enough. That was the most evident thing that happened on occasion. The lights would go off and on without explanation. And the electrician hadn't figured out the reason.

I rejoined my friends just before both shops got popular with the shoppers once again. I'd hoped to get more information from Mark and Clint, but that would have to wait until another time.

I t was nearing three o'clock when Pinky carried a mug of hot chocolate into Curio Finds and set it on the counter. A number of snow globes and other gift items had sold, leaving gaps on the shelves, so I was reorganizing. "Here's a mistake I know you'll enjoy. I misunderstood a customer and added mint to it," she said.

"Thanks."

My shop door opened and I turned to see a young woman. Her stocking cap had ear flaps and was pulled down so it covered most of her forehead and cheeks, but I recognized her in an instant. She'd been in the shop several times and I'd called out to her from the alley walkway that morning. "Hello again, and welcome to Curio Finds."

"Hello, thank you. I am just looking. Is that all right?" She noticeably shivered.

"Of course, take as long as you like." She appeared too thin, even with her winter coat on. "How about a hot drink to help warm you up? Pinky, my coffee shop neighbor, just brought me a hot chocolate with mint. But I'm too full to drink it right now, and I hate to see it go to waste." That wasn't completely truthful, but if she thought she was doing me a favor, she'd be more likely to accept it. I picked up the mug and handed it to her.

"If you are sure?"

"Yes, please."

"All right. Thank you." She stretched both hands around the mug and pressed them flat against it, no doubt warming them. Then she brought the mug to her lips, inhaled deeply, and took a sip with a smile of appreciation on her face. She could give Clint lessons on how to drink hot beverages quietly without the threat of alerting the whole neighborhood. "Who would think of putting mint in hot chocolate?"

Where had this girl been? "Someone who's made a lot of people happy ever since. I don't believe we've even exchanged names. I'm Camryn Brooks, the manager here."

Her eyes had a wary look when she nodded and said, "I am Nicoline."

I smiled. "Pretty. And unusual."

"It is Dutch. I am named for my grandmother."

That was it, the hint of a foreign accent. "Is that where you're from?"

Her eyebrows shot up. "Why do you think that?"

She didn't want to answer the question, so I decided to let it go. For now. "It's not that I do, I was just making conversation."

Nicoline nodded, took another sip of her drink then pushed her stocking cap back enough so a good-sized bruise was revealed on the edge of her cheekbone near her ear. I stepped within reach and laid my hand gently on her shoulder. "Gosh, that looks like it hurts. What happened?"

"Oh." She pulled her cap back down to cover up the injury again. "I was clumsy, and . . . fell . . . and my face struck . . . the frame on the door."

I didn't believe her haltingly delivered explanation for a minute, especially since falling against a door frame would have produced a different shaped bruise than the one she bore—it was on the round side, like it'd been delivered by a person's fist, or maybe a fast-pitched base-ball. But I didn't want to push too hard, not two minutes after we'd exchanged names. If I scared her away, there would be no chance of pulling out the truth and hopefully helping her.

"So sorry that happened to you."

She nodded again then looked out the window and flinched like she might have right before she was hurt. I glanced up, but all I caught was a tall person walking by who soon disappeared from sight.

"I need to get going," she said. Something negative, perhaps harmful, was going on in the young woman's life. I was sure of it.

"Are you on break from school?" I said.

She finished the drink and set the mug back on the checkout counter. "School? No. I am not as young as I look. Or so I have been told."

"That's something you'll appreciate the older you get."

That didn't bring the smile to her face that I'd hoped it would. "I thank you. Good day." She turned and headed for the door.

"Please stop in again. Any time at all."

She gave a little nod and out the door she went.

Pinky poked her head through the archway. "Someone's here to see you." And then she mouthed, "Harley Creighton."

Oh, great, the city council member who'd told Mayor Frost he was quitting in no uncertain terms. I switched my thoughts from Nicoline to Frosty and all the people he'd been having trouble with, including the man who was waiting for me in Brew Ha-Ha. I lifted my hands and shrugged my shoulders, my expression asking, *Any idea what he wants with me?*

Pinky frowned and moved her eyes back and forth. Apparently it was her silent way of saying no without being too obvious. She looked so silly I almost laughed.

I rounded the corner from my shop into hers and went to the back table area where Pinky was pointing. Harley must have felt more comfortable there than in Curio Finds. But he'd saved me from tracking him down so I wasn't about to fret about details.

"Afternoon, Camryn." He sounded far more chipper than when he'd been talking to Frosty the day before. Way too cheerful, in my opinion. Especially under the circumstances.

"Mr. Creighton—"

"Harley." He eyed me like he was about to ask me out on a date. What was his marital status anyway? No one had ever mentioned it, and I'd never thought about it one way or the other.

I nodded and my body stiffened, wondering why he was there.

"Do you have a minute to sit down?" he said.

"Okay." I pulled out a chair on the opposite side of the table to keep some distance between us. Creighton had a bit of a creep factor going, as far as I was concerned. It was possible his beady brown eyes and his unnatural-looking blond comb-over played into that.

Harley leaned across the table to close that distance. "The word out there is that you're interested in the vacant seat on the council."

That was the last thing I'd expected him to say. If anything, I thought maybe he'd come to offer some sort of an apology or excuse for his behavior the day before. "Um . . . you mean yours?"

He head jerked back a bit. "No. I admit I may have made some noise about that yesterday. But it wouldn't be right for me to leave now. It would cause too much disruption and wouldn't be fair, not after what happened to Mayor Frost and all."

"So you're planning to stay on until they find a replacement?"

"Let's just say I'm planning to stay on and leave it at that."

With Frosty out of the picture, the man he'd so often battled with, life on the council would be easier for Harley. "Oh, okay." I tried to come up with something pithy to say, but that wasn't what came out.

Harley pressed on. "So you agree that's the best thing for me to do?"

I didn't know enough to either agree or disagree. I'd read the council meeting minutes in the newspaper fairly often, but they didn't spell out every detail of the discussions about each matter before it went to a vote. There were disputes and disagreements among the council members over various issues, as one would expect. I'd have to poke around, ask some people I trusted for their opinions about the kind of job Harley was doing before I could render an informed opinion of my own. I shrugged. "The people who voted for you would expect that. But if you're not happy in your role—"

"There have been some moments here and there that were tense, but I've enjoyed serving overall."

That's not the way it had sounded to me yesterday. "So you heard I was interested in a seat on the council. That's not completely accurate, but I've been thinking about it since Mayor Frost asked me to consider it. But now . . . after what happened to him. . . I don't know what I'll do."

He extended his arm across the table, and I sat up straighter in my chair so he couldn't touch me, if that was his intention. "I hope you'll go for it. We'll need to appoint a new mayor to fill in until the next election. It'll be one of the sitting council members. And from what people tell me about your experience working for Senator Zimmer in Washington, I think you'd be a great fit."

Did he now? "Like I said, things have changed since yesterday. I'm not ready to make a final decision yet."

"I get that. I think everybody in town is shocked about Frosty dying in his office like that."

Including you, Harley? And Frosty didn't just die. Somebody had killed him. Whether it was intentional or not had yet to be determined. When I gave it a little thought I realized it might prove useful to keep an open dialogue with one of the prime suspects. "You are right about that, Harley."

8

I was behind the serving counter in Brew Ha-Ha washing some mugs when Erin Vinkerman, our third "all for one and one for all" musketeer came in with a sweet smile on her face. I knew it was to cheer me, and in fact, it did. By a lot. "How was school?" I said.

"The kids have been little angels. Something about Christmas being right around the corner brings out the best in them every year. We're going to make snow globes tomorrow as gifts for their families, and they are all excited. So thanks to you and Pinky for having that snow globe–making class here in October and giving me the idea."

That infamous class where it turned out that half the people there had a connection to the most unpopular man in Brooks Landing, and ended up having unpleasant words with each other after the class had ended. But that

CHRISTINE HUSOM

was nothing compared to the dead body I came across in the city park on my walk home that night. I shook my head at the memory.

Erin frowned slightly. "I know you're thinking about all the drama that happened with some of the people at the class." Erin was one of those people. "But I'd rather remember how much fun the class itself was instead."

"It's good to put a positive spin on it." I had trouble forgetting, however. "Erin, you're a natural when it comes to arts and crafts. Are you planning to make the snow ahead of time, or will you demonstrate how it's done to your fourth graders?"

"No, I actually found a recipe online where you use Styrofoam instead of that method May taught us, you remember, precipitating benzoic acid. Those might look more like real snowflakes, but with having to heat the water and all that, it'll be easier with Styrofoam. You just use a grater to get little white flakes."

"That's clever. Who comes up with stuff like that?"

Erin nodded her agreement and said, "Where's Pinky?"

"Taking an inventory of her coffee beans, seeing what she needs to order. She's been going through a lot of them lately." Pinky ordered beans not only from companies in the United States, but also from around the world.

"She sent me a text about Emmy being sick, so I'm here to work."

"Thank you."

"You're hanging in there?" Erin said.

I nodded. "Doing pretty well, all things considered. But I'll rest much easier when they find Mayor Frost's killer." We chatted about him for a while then I filled her

· 108 ·

in on my visits with Harley Creighton and Rosalie Gorman. "I'm having trouble figuring them out. Both of them. Another mystery to me is how the council members manage to work together with those strong personalities."

"I know what you mean. So what is up with Harley Creighton? First he says he's out then he tells you he's in. It really makes you wonder. And then he actually asks you to take a run at the open seat. Are you still thinking about it?"

I sucked in a quick breath. "I told Harley I wasn't ready to make a decision, but that's only partly true. I've gone back and forth a thousand times, and what keeps bubbling to the surface is the obligation I feel to Frosty."

"Seriously, Cami? Why is that?"

"Okay, Erin, this is probably going to sound a little strange, but as it turns out, Frosty asked me to consider an open position that was actually created by his death."

Erin frowned slightly. "I think I'm following you—which is scary by the way—but I'll have to let it sink in some more."

"It's something you'll understand more with your heart than with your mind, Erin."

"I'll try. But even if you feel you owe that to the mayor, think of all you've got on your plate already. Running this shop has been more than full time for you."

"You're right about that, especially this month. But if Emmy stays on, and my parents keep up with the ordering, we'll make it work."

Erin gave me one of her *Don't say I didn't warn you* looks then said, "I'll go see if I can help Pinky and get her home at a decent time."

That reminded me. "So how did your muffin and scone-baking session go last night?"

Erin shook her head. "Pinky's got it down to a science with her fancy commercial mixer and baking equipment. She doesn't even have to measure ingredients. I did what she told me to do, and she assured me I was a big help. Ha, I'll take her word for it." She smiled and headed to the back room.

I went back to Curio Finds for some alone time before the next potential rush of customers. I sat down behind the checkout counter and picked up the Marilyn Monroe snow globe Erin and Pinky had made for me after the original one got broken. I gave it a shake and watched the snow-flakes touch Marilyn's bare arms and legs before they dropped to the ground around her feet. The funny thing about snow globes was the scenes were often not set where snow would actually fall. But it didn't seem to matter. It was still delightful to watch snow fall on just about any scene imaginable.

My thoughts turned to Marvin Easterly and his op-position to the children's clothing factory going up in his neighborhood. I understood why he felt the way he did, but I also recognized it would be a big boost to Brooks Landing's economy. Mr. Easterly had talked with the mayor yesterday morning at Brew Ha-Ha, and then later paid him a visit at his office. Was it to apologize for his behavior, or to try to convince him to change his mind? If that was the case, and the mayor had stood his ground, could their disagreement have escalated into a physical altercation, one that led to murder? I needed to talk to Marvin Easterly.

I set the Marilyn Monroe snow globe down and went to Pinky's back room where she and Erin were finishing up with the inventory. Pinky stood straight from her bent over position and stretched her back. "What's up?"

"Checking to see how long you'll be here, what time you're planning to leave," I said.

"You need to go on another errand, a.k.a. fact-finding mission?"

Erin raised her eyebrows. "Is that some sort of new code you two have?"

I cut to the chase. "I thought I'd take a quick drive out to Marvin Easterly's farm; see what it's like out there."

They both scrunched their faces at the same time, a good indication that neither one of them saw any value in that at all. Pinky turned to Erin. "Trust me, it does no good to try to talk her out of these mission trips she's bent on taking lately."

Pinky's idea of a mission trip was very different from mine. "It shouldn't take long, but if you're leaving soon, I'll go tomorrow."

"Nah, go ahead. I need to get my coffee bean orders in today and that'll take a while."

"Thanks." I hurried to get my things. The sun set right around 4:30 p.m. and I hoped to get to Mr. Easterly's before dark.

I'd looked up Easterly's address earlier in the day, and followed County Road 53 west from the downtown area of Brooks Landing. It ran along the north side of Green Lake to its western shore then continued to the edge of town into Chatsworth Township. I focused on the beauty of the land and scenery around me. Chatsworth Township was picturesque with its rolling hills and many lakes. Aside from more concentrated housing around some of those lakes, and a few businesses—including a large apple orchard with a century-old barn that drew in huge crowds from September through November, a horse riding stable, a downhill ski area, and a bar and grill that was a destination for bikers—the majority of the acres were used for farming operations, and were either planted in crops, or utilized as grazing pastureland for livestock. Every part of the township could be delightfully captured as a winter wonderland snow globe scene.

Marvin Easterly's farm was less than a mile from the Brooks Landing city limits. I stopped my car in front of the property that was at the heart of the dispute. The western edge was perhaps a quarter of a mile from Easterly's house. The land itself was flatter than the surrounding areas and would require a minimal amount of earth moving, compared to nearby land. I hadn't known the previous property owners, and only knew of the current ones. They dabbled in raising animals, mainly for their children's 4-H projects, and had a large organic vegetable garden. They rented out the majority of their acres to another farmer: namely, Marvin Easterly.

So it wasn't only the rural view he was concerned about. Easterly also faced the loss of income he got from ninety acres of corn one year and soybeans the next. My car windows were starting to fog up, so I slid the lever on my dashboard from heat to defrost, then drove up Easterly's driveway. As I pulled up between his house and barn, the man himself came out of the barn toting a large milk can in each hand like they were light weights. The only sign that he was exerting in the least came from the clouds of stream swirling around him from his expended breaths.

I wasn't certain how many gallons each can contained, but judging from the old milk cans my parents had picked up at auctions, I guessed they were either the six- or seven-gallon size. And since one gallon of milk weighed close to nine pounds, that meant he was lugging between fifty- and sixty-something pounds in each hand. He'd be a very worthy arm wrestling opponent.

I parked the car, but left it running as I popped out. His eyebrows lifted in surprise when he saw it was me. "Hello! I see you're doing your chores," I said.

"Just finishing up with the afternoon milking. Can I help you with something?"

"I hope so. If you have a few minutes, I'd like to talk to you about the clothing factory the city council is considering. And also about Mayor Frost." I stopped myself from saying, *and his untimely death.*

"Hmm. Well, let's get in out of the cold. You look like you're about to turn into an ice sculpture."

My eyelashes were freezing together, now that he mentioned it. I followed Easterly to his house. The weight of his body combined with the heavy milk cans he carried produced a loud crunching sound on the snow with his every step and dispelled the quiet of the late afternoon. I didn't feel personally threatened by Easterly, but I fingered the canister of Mace in my pocket to be sure it was there. I'd started carrying it when I lived in

Washington, DC, and it gave me a sense of security, even in my small hometown. "I'll get the door," I said and stepped around him. I pulled open the old screen door of the side entrance. It led to an enclosed, unheated porch.

"Thanks," he said as he stepped inside and set the milk cans on the wooden floor. "My neighbors like fresh milk so I set aside some each week for them."

"That's a lot of milk."

He kicked off his barn boots and set them on a side rug. "Enough for four families."

That meant Easterly was on good terms with at least four families in the area. He pushed open the entry door that led to his kitchen. I started to remove my own boots, but he waved his hand. "Leave them on. The floor is linoleum and easy enough to wipe up."

I stomped off the snow I'd picked up on the driveway and followed him inside. He didn't call out and it made me wonder if anyone else was there. Hanging on the opposite wall, prominently displayed, was an aerial photo of a well-kept farm. I pointed to it. "Is that your place?"

He pulled off his jacket, cap, and gloves. "Yup. Taken about twelve years ago."

"Nice. I can see why you love it here and want it to stay rural around you."

"Make yourself at home, take a load off." He pulled out a chair and sat down.

The room was clean, but lacked a decorator's touch. A small wood table with salt and pepper shakers and butter dish sitting in the middle of it and four wood chairs surrounding it took up half of the floor space. The old wood cupboards had been painted white, and the countertops were a gray Formica with some swirls of other colors mixed in and dated back to the fifties, was my guess.

I unbuttoned my coat and sat down across from him. "You said you've lived here all your life?"

"Every one of my fifty-four years. Yup. Born and raised here. This farm has been in the family for nigh unto a hundred years." No wonder he was so steadfast in his resistance. A factory as a next-door neighbor would be a big change.

"What about the rest of your family, are they nearby?"

"I'm all that's left. My brother died young, and I haven't found the right woman who would have me yet. Sorta been married to this farming operation, you could say." Like Pinky and I were to our shops.

Couldn't find the woman who would have him. And no family. Did that make him feel like he'd have nothing to lose if he got caught for committing a heinous crime? I touched the Mace in my pocket again, in case my questions brought out the same anger he'd shown toward Frosty.

"You and the mayor were having a pretty heated discussion in Brew Ha-Ha yesterday," I said.

"I kind of lost it, and I owe you coffee shop folks an apology for that."

"Thank you."

He nodded. "I haven't always liked how Mayor Frost has done business. The way this whole factory idea came out of the blue is suspicious, if nothing else. He didn't even talk to the township officials. The first any of us heard about it was when one of the township supervisors called me up after he saw it posted on the city council meeting agenda. And come to find out, Frost had talked to my neighbor about selling a couple of months ago."

"The mayor talked to them?" I hadn't heard that part before.

"That's right. I found that out after the meeting Tuesday night. That's why I was so irked. That's not the way a mayor should do business."

I knew more about the duties of elected officials at the national level, and not as much at the local level.

"Those factory folks should have gone to the whole council with their proposal, and then taken it from there. There's something fishy about the way Frost went about it, but I haven't gotten to the bottom of it yet."

Easterly might think my next question was out of turn, but I asked it anyway. "I understand you went to see the mayor at his office yesterday afternoon."

"I needed to apologize for acting like a damn fool in the coffee shop. I wasn't sorry for everything thing I said, but I was sorry I yelled at him like that."

"And he was okay with that?" I wanted to add, *and still alive when you left?*

"As far as I know. He was acting a little peculiar, distracted-like. All he said was, 'Thanks for stopping by. We'll talk about it some more later on.' It seemed like he was expecting someone else any minute."

I nodded. Was that someone Rosalie Gorman, the

one who'd reportedly pushed her way into the mayor's office and slammed the door shut behind her? Stormin' Gorman.

"Did he talk to you about it later?" I said.

"Nope, he never got the chance."

9

I drove back to the shops mulling over Marvin Easterly's words. I was confident what he'd told me was true, but also questioned if he had told me the whole story. Considering how passionately opposed he was to the factory going up next to his property, and the words he had thrown at Mayor Frost, would he have let himself be dismissed so easily?

Had it been me, I would've been too curious to leave without learning who the mayor was expecting. It may have been Gorman, but there were other possibilities. Easterly suspected Frost had been involved in some underhanded activities. If I were him I'd have hung around a while to see who showed up. Just in case it was a party he suspected was in cahoots with Frost. It'd have given him some proof to support his beliefs.

Easterly might very well have done just that. Then after the person left, he may have gone back into the mayor's office and confronted him. A disagreement could have escalated into a physical fight. One that ended in the worst way possible, before Frosty "got the chance" to talk to him again. I'd witnessed how strong Easterly was when I saw him toting heavy milk cans with ease.

It hadn't been a completely satisfying discussion with Marvin Easterly, but it was heads above the ones I'd had with Rosalie Gorman and Harley Creighton. They'd both taken an offensive approach when they visited me, putting me on the defense, instead of the other way around.

When I got back into town I noticed there were several parking spots on the street in front of our shops, a sign that shopping was slowing down for the day. I opted to park in one of them, leaving the prime ones open for our customers.

Erin was talking to a couple at the front serving counter of Brew Ha-Ha and sipping on a drink from a mug. I nodded and smiled as I walked by. Pinky was sitting at a back table typing away on her laptop. "Still at it?" I said.

"Yeah, I'd rather get my ordering done here. It's too boring to do it all by myself at home. How was your *errand?*" She winked at me when she asked.

"Fine, with details to follow." I couldn't say much with customers in the shop. I slipped off my coat and headed into my shop to hang it up. Curio Find's door opened and a man came in. I threw my coat on the stool behind the counter.

"Hello, can I help you with anything?"

He studied me with eyes the shade of cornflower blue. And the more he stared, the more I thought I should know him, but couldn't place him. A former classmate, maybe? He looked like he was close to my age, of average height, and with pleasing facial features. "Camryn Brooks?"

It hit me who he resembled right after I said, "Yes."

He nodded and said, "I'm Jason Frost."

I closed the gap between us and extended my arm. "Oh, Jason, I'm so sorry for your loss, for everything you're going through."

He pulled his gloves off and shook my hand. "Thanks. It's been a big shock."

"Would you like to go sit down, have a cup of something hot?" I waved in the direction of Brew-Ha-Ha. "We can make you just about any kind of coffee, tea blend, or chocolate you can think of."

He pursed his lips, looking like he was going to say no then lifted a shoulder and nodded. "Well I guess a hot chocolate does sound good right about now. And you have a few minutes to talk?"

He must have been here about his father because he'd never visited Curio Finds before. "Sure."

Erin lifted her eyebrows when Jason and I came through the archway, no doubt curious who he was. "Erin, would you be so kind to make a hot chocolate for Jason here. We'll be at a table."

"Sure thing. You want one, too, Cami?"

I nodded. "Thanks."

Pinky had closed her laptop and was gathering her things together in the back area. "Pinky, this is Jason Frost."

She dropped her papers back onto the table then swooped in and gave him a hug before he knew what was happening. "I loved your dad. I can't tell you how sorry I am." She was a couple of inches taller than Jason and when she bent over her headband slipped down over her eyes. And in the seconds it took for her to right herself, her face went through a variety of contortions. She often unintentionally provided some comic relief in tense moments.

Even the corners of Jason's lips lifted. "Thanks."

"Jason, have a seat. Would you like me to take your coat?" Pinky said.

"That's all right." He took it off, hung it on the back of a chair, then sat down. "I'm here to talk to Camryn."

Pinky's head bobbed up and down. "Okay."

Erin delivered steaming mugs, topped with generous mounds of real whipped cream and sprinkles of cinnamon.

"Thank you. Erin, this is Jason Frost."

Jason visibly tensed, probably expecting another embrace. Instead, Erin laid a gentle hand on his shoulder for just a moment. "So sorry about your dad. I know how hard it must be." And she did, too. Her father's death had been very difficult for her. He had rescued her from an orphanage in Vietnam, and provided her and her mother with a good life. She'd always been especially close to him.

"Thank you. All of you. It's so unreal. My poor cousin is pretty distraught, too. And my aunt doesn't seem to know how to take it," Jason said.

"Is that your dad's sister?" I guessed.

Jason sniffed and nodded. "They've had some differences, and I don't think they were completely resolved." He gave his head a little shake. "Sorry. I don't know why I mentioned that. I'm not exactly thinking straight."

"Of course you aren't," Pinky said. "You're here to talk to Cami, so we'll get out of your hair." If it hadn't been such a long day for her already, I knew she would have hung around.

Erin helped Pinky get her things together and they headed to the front of the shop.

It took Jason a moment before he said, "You found my dad, and maybe you can't answer this question, but did he look like he suffered?"

Dear Lord, what a question. "Jason, I've been thinking about that a lot actually, wondering the same thing. I can tell you my experience as a kid when I got knocked out playing ball one time. I don't remember feeling any pain at all, until I woke up that is. So if I had to guess, I don't think he did."

"So he didn't have a pained expression on his face?"

"No, he didn't." I'd have described the look on Frosty's face as surprised more than anything else. But there was no reason to share that with Jason.

"Thanks. Knowing that helps a little. My dad was a people lover, not the kind of man you'd think would get killed."

"I know. The police are investigating, looking at all the evidence, and they'll figure out who did it."

Jason nodded. "The police said Dad had just bought a snow globe from you, maybe as a Christmas present, but then it was used to . . ."

"I feel awful about that, too. The scene in the globe was a man standing in front of a cabin with three bears approaching him."

Jason's eyes grew misty. "My favorite bedtime story when I was little was 'The Three Bears.' If he bought it as a gift, it was probably for me."

Frosty didn't want it wrapped, but it may have been a gift. It was best not to get into the sinister aspect of the scene so I smiled a little. "Or he may have gotten it for himself because he was thinking of you."

He pulled out a hankie and wiped his eyes. "The police said they found a diamond on the floor in his office. No one's come forward to say they lost it. So the police are wondering if it came from a piece of jewelry Dad was planning to give as a Christmas gift. They think it might have fallen out of its setting and are looking into robbery as a possible motive."

I nodded. I hadn't heard that, but I'd wondered the same thing.

"You know about that?" he said.

I would probably get in trouble with Clint, but I pulled out my phone and found the photo I'd taken of the gem. I handed it to Jason. "If it's a diamond, it's the largest one I've ever seen."

Jason looked at it and nodded. "The police showed me a photo of it, too, a closer shot. My grandmother had a pendant in the shape of a heart with a large diamond about the same size as that in the center. And there were a number of smaller diamonds around the edge. She willed it to my dad, but I can't imagine why he would have had it at his office."

"Could he have been planning to give it to someone for Christmas? Or maybe he was having it cleaned?" I said.

Jason looked down like he was considering the possibilities. "If he was planning to give it to someone outside the family, he would have told me about it. My aunt had expected to inherit it, but my grandmother left it to my dad instead. As I said, my aunt and my dad had some differences, and that was one of the things she was most upset about. She even offered to buy it from him. I suppose it's possible he decided to give it to her after all. Or to her daughter, my cousin Anne."

"Your dad must have kept that pendant under lock and key, right?"

"I'd sure think so, but I don't know where he kept it. This might be hard to believe, but we've never talked about it, not since my aunt made a stink about it after my grandma died, and that's over six years ago now."

"That's not hard to believe." Disputes in families over heirlooms caused problems many people didn't like to think about, much less talk about.

We were quiet for a time then Jason said, "After my mother died, my dad became a bit of a ladies' man, mainly because so many women were after him."

"Really?" That came out quickly and didn't sound very kind. "Sorry, I didn't mean it that way."

Jason smiled. "I didn't take it that way."

"You're right, your dad was a people person, and with so many single women out there, I can see why he was so popular."

"From the little he said about it, I figured he was often juggling a couple of women at a time. Once he let it slip that there was one woman in particular he'd taken out who was overly possessive. She got jealous when other women even looked at him."

Frosty, a Casanova? And a jealous woman who didn't like it when other women even looked at him? Maybe something happened that pushed her over the edge. I tried to sound casual when I said, "Oh, who was that?"

"I don't know. Dad didn't tell me and wouldn't say any more about it. It was one of those things he tried to make light of after he'd said it. I think out of respect for Mom, and what she'd meant to both of us."

"I can understand that."

Jason stood up and grabbed his coat. "I should get going."

"Are you staying right here in town?"

He nodded. "My aunt invited me to her house, but she lives in Minnetonka and I'd rather be at Dad's. My cousin is coming over later so we can spend some time together. Dad was like a father to her, and it seems like she's taking this harder than anyone, maybe even me."

"It's good you have family around, and there are a lot of us who would be happy to help you in any way we can."

"I appreciate that. My wife, Lea, wanted to come with me, but we decided it'd be better for her to stay home with our kids until things are more settled here. And after I make Dad's final . . . arrangements."

After Jason left, I puttered around Curio Finds thinking over the things he had told me. I was surprised he'd shared so much personal information. Hmm. There was a family treasure—his grandmother's pendant—that his father had inherited and his aunt coveted. The single diamond lying on Frosty's office floor was, without question, very suspicious. Did the pendant, or another valuable piece of jewelry, have anything to do with what happened to Frosty? And what about the mysterious, possessive woman in his life? Had she found out something about another girlfriend that set her off, and she picked a fight that ended in his death?

I thought of all the times I'd seen Mayor Frost, and couldn't remember him being out with a woman, even once. Not that we socialized together. But when he walked, he was alone, and when he stopped in at Brew Ha-Ha for his morning coffee on his way to work, he was alone. I wandered into the coffee shop as Erin was ringing up some to-go coffee purchases. After the trio of customers left, I said, "What do you know about Mayor Frost's love life?"

She pursed her lips then raised her eyebrows. "Ah, nothing. Why are you asking a question like that?"

I relayed what Jason had told me about women pursuing his father, and that one was overly possessive. "So I'm wondering if something happened that triggered a fit of jealousy that got out of hand."

"Cami, that's what the police are there for, to figure things like that out. You said Jason told you he doesn't even know the names of the women Frosty dated."

"That's true." I'd ask Mark if he'd found out any names in his investigative conversations. I glanced up at the clock: nearly a half hour until closing time, and it seemed the shopping action had slowed to a stop. "Erin, feel free to take off."

"If you're sure."

"Yeah, go ahead." I gave her a hug. "And thanks for coming in. It helped a lot."

"Hey, it helps me, too. As much as I love being with my kids at school, it's nice to have some conversations with adults, too."

"So you consider Pinky and me adults?" I teased.

"I was talking about your customers," she shot back with a smile.

Mark came into Brew Ha-Ha still in uniform as I was ringing out the cash register for the day. "Erin gone already?" he asked about his favorite person.

I nodded. "A few minutes ago. You're still working, huh?"

He adjusted his duty belt and sat down on a counter stool. "Yeah, lots of OT with this case. We're trying to talk to just about everyone who had a connection to Mayor Frost. Speaking of which, his son got to Brooks Landing this afternoon and Clint and I had a pretty lengthy conversation with him."

"Jason actually came by to see me a while ago."

"Is that right? Was that because you were the first one on the scene?"

That was a gentler way to phrase it. "Yes, poor guy. He was hoping I could tell him his dad didn't suffer." We were both quiet a moment as we contemplated that. "Did Jason tell you the mayor had women pursuing him?"

Mark leaned forward and frowned. "Not in so many words. So how did that come up?"

"He mentioned you'd asked about the diamond on the office floor and it came up in the course of our conversation."

"Between you and me, he said Mayor Frost had a woman who liked him and wanted him all to herself. But Jason didn't know who it was. We'd be interested in talking to this mystery woman if we can figure out who she is."

"Definitely. Did you ever see the mayor out on the town with anyone?"

Mark shook his head. "No. That's why I was a little surprised by the jealous woman story."

"Mayor Frost was in the public eye, and from what I witnessed when I was in Washington, it seemed like most of the single elected officials kept their relationships as hush-hush as possible. Not because there was anything to be ashamed of, but because it put the other person—and their personal relationship—out there for everyone to watch and make comments about."

"The adoring public. Huh. You're finishing up here, so I'll leave you to it."

I followed Mark to the door and locked it behind him then completed the rest of the closing up shop duties. As I was about to turn off the overhead lights in Curio Finds, Nicoline walked by and raised her hand in a small wave of acknowledgment. Did she live nearby so the shops were on her often-trod walking route? One of these days I'd find that out.

My cell phone rang and I pulled it out of my pants pocket. "Camryn speaking."

"Cami, it's Mom. I don't think I'll ever get used to Camryn. After all you were Cami most of your life." It's not that I didn't like my given name of Cami. In fact, I loved it. But I had my name legally changed when I worked in Washington to give it a more professional edge.

"Sorry, Mom, I didn't look at the dial. Not that I'm paranoid, but I keep expecting Sandy Gibbons to call and pump me for more information."

"Glory be, she probably will do that, won't she? The reason I called, and this is last minute, but your dad and I have got some lasagna in the oven and we hope you can join us for dinner."

The thought of their homemade lasagna made me salivate, literally. Like Pavlov's dog. Then my stomach responded by making noises that sounded like cats meowing inside of it. "I'd love to. Can I bring anything, like a bottle of wine?"

"No, we have that, too."

"I'll be there shortly."

My parents held me, each in own their tender way, and it brought tears to my eyes. The trauma of finding Mayor Frost really hit me when I was in their arms. Even more than when I'd been questioned by the police, even more than when I'd told my friends the details, even more than when I'd talked to his son about it. And then I thought about Jason, and the next thing I knew loud sobs were erupting from somewhere deep inside of me. My parents knew how to coax them out of me like no one else in the world. I didn't cry often, but every once in a while I wept like there was no tomorrow.

"There, there, it'll be okay," Dad said.

I nodded and sniffled. Mom handed me a tissue and they guided me into the dining room where the table was nicely set.

"How about a glass of wine to settle your nerves?" Dad said as he filled three glasses and handed one to me.

"Thanks." I took a sip of the dry red wine and smiled. "I started feeling bad for Mayor Frost's son, and that's what got me."

"It's such a sad thing. We'd heard he had a son, but not much more about it than that. Cami, why don't you go ahead and sit down? I'll bring out the lasagna and then we'll talk some more," Mom said.

"I'll help." Dad followed her to the kitchen.

I took my place in front of a big bowl of my favorite salad, a perfect complement to the main dish. Romaine lettuce tossed with sweet red peppers, grape tomatoes, carrot ribbons, cucumbers, an assortment of olives, and dry ricotta cheese. It was dressed with vinaigrette made of red wine vinegar, olive oil, honey, garlic, Italian parsley, oregano, and basil. A basket of crusty bread with pats of cold butter sat next to it.

I took another drink of wine then leaned my head back and breathed in the glorious smells wafting in from the kitchen. My parents carried in three plates and Dad set one in front of me. A generous serving of lasagna filled a fourth of the plate. They settled into their chairs and then we bowed our heads for prayer. Dad asked that the food be blessed for the nourishment of our bodies and that Mayor Frost's family find comfort and peace.

"Start the salad, Cami," Mom said when we raised our heads again.

Fresh greens tasted especially good to me in the winter, and I loaded my plate then passed it on. I helped myself to a piece of bread and then passed that, too. After we'd all munched on the tasty meal a while, my parents asked about my day.

I told them how it had started with a woman who was in Brew Ha-Ha early, waiting for me to open the shop. "She said she was interested in snow globes. But she acted more like a police officer."

Mom chuckled. "You're funny."

"Emmy called in sick, and that reminds me I need to call her when I get home to see how she's doing." I went through the list of people I'd talked to: Lila at city hall, Sandy Gibbons, Margaret at the police station, Rosalie Gorman, Harley Creighton, Marvin Easterly, and the young woman, Nicoline. I shared my concern about the bruise I saw on her face. They asked me questions about each person and offered their opinions and assessments.

Then I went over some of the things Jason and I discussed, about his father and how he had women vying for his attention. And that he'd had problems with his sister. I didn't get into details about their mother's pendant, however.

"Cami, why do you suppose Jason told you personal things about his father and his aunt?"

I shrugged. "I don't know. I guess he needed someone in Brooks Landing to talk to, besides the police that is."

10

After I got home I turned up the thermostat and was putting the leftover lasagna and salad my parents had given me in the refrigerator when my home phone rang. The caller ID read *Lewis Frost* and sent a dozen chills up my spine.

"This is Camryn."

"Camryn, hi. It's Jason Frost."

"Hi, Jason."

"My cousin Anne is here and I told her about the diamond, so we started talking about Grandmother's pendant. She said Dad kept it in a case in his safe. And she knew where he kept the code. Long story short, we looked in the safe, and it's not there."

"Your grandmother's pendant is missing?"

"All I know is it's not where Dad kept it."

"Did you call the police?"

"No, I didn't want to dial nine-one-one. I'd rather talk to either the assistant police chief or an officer named Mark. They're the two I met with earlier. I tried the numbers listed on their business cards, but both of them went to voicemail and I didn't leave a message."

I didn't think they'd care in this case, but I didn't specifically have permission to give out their personal cell phone numbers. "How about I give them a call and they can call you back?"

"You could do that, but we thought of something else that would be faster."

What, pray tell? "Oh?"

"Dad has a portrait of Grandmother hanging in his den and she's wearing her diamond pendant. You have that photo of the diamond on your phone. Anne suggested we compare it with Grandmother's diamond, see if it looks like the same one."

And I thought I had wacky ideas at times. But if it helped Jason and Anne feel better, like they were doing something to help with the investigation, it was a simple request. And something that was easy enough for me to do.

"Are you sure you wouldn't rather have the police bring you their photo?" I said.

"At this point I don't know what I'd report to the police. And I trust you. The pendant isn't in the safe, but Dad might have put it somewhere else. We're thinking that if the diamond looks like it was from Grandmother's pendant, then the chances are he had it at his office. In that case, the rest of it minus the big diamond was probably stolen."

There was some logic to that. "Okay, I can be there in a few minutes."

"Or we can come to your house," he said.

"How big is the portrait?"

"It looks like two feet by three feet."

Very large. "I don't want you to run the risk of wrecking it, so I'll come there."

"You know where my dad's house is?"

"I do."

After we hung up, I called Erin and told her where I was headed and why. When I told my friends about the diamond I'd left out the part about taking a picture of it. First Erin scolded me for keeping it a secret then she said, "I'll go with you."

"Not necessary, but thanks. The reason I'm calling is to ask you to call me at eight thirty."

"Cami, I don't like all this cloak-and-dagger stuff. What if it's a trap? You should call Mark, let him know."

"I know it's not a trap, but I'm taking extra precautions by calling you. Will you call me then?"

"Fine. Yes, I will do that. And I agree that Jason Frost seems like an up-and-up guy."

"He's a teacher, you know."

"I guess it takes one to know one."

Anne was standing in the spacious entryway ready to greet me after Jason let me in. They looked like they could be brother and sister, with the same striking blue eyes, chestnut brown hair, straight noses, lips that were on the thin side. Anne was several inches shorter, but came across as more of a powerhouse than Jason did.

"Thank you so much for coming over," she said. "This may seem a little crazy, but Jason and I are beside ourselves after what happened to our dear Lewis. And then when we found out Grandmother's pendant might have factored into that, it makes it all seem that much worse."

"Of course."

"Let me help you with your coat." Jason eased it off my shoulders and handed it to Anne, who hung it in the closet. I stepped out of my boots and patted the phone in my pants pocket.

Jason pointed. "This way to the den. The police and county deputies went through the house last night and finished up this morning, looking for possible clues. I don't know if they found anything. They didn't say one way or the other."

"When they've figured it all out, you'll get the full report. But they'd be happy to answer all the questions they can in the meantime," I said.

Jason attempted a smile, but Anne looked even sadder. We trekked around the edge of the sunken living room to the den. When we stepped inside and I looked around, my first impression was it would be a room I'd love to relax in, or work in, or take a nap in if I lived there. It had old dark paneling that went halfway up the walls, with book shelves that started where the paneling ended and followed the rest of the way to the ceiling on three of the walls. The fourth wall featured their grandmother's portrait in the center, and it was flanked by a window on either side.

I pulled out my phone, found the photo then enlarged it. I reverently walked over to the image of Jason and Anne's grandmother and studied first her lovely, serene face and then the pendant hanging on her chest. *That's quite the rock,* I thought, trying to maintain a neutral expression. I looked at the photo of the diamond, but I was not qualified to determine if it was the same one as that in the pendant. Especially given the slightly different angles of the two.

Jason reached out his hand and I gave him the phone. He looked up and down, down and up, and then passed the phone to Anne who did the same. They shrugged and shook their heads, then Anne handed me back the phone.

"Anne, how about asking your mother to take a look at it, see what she thinks?" I said.

She shook her head. "No, I'd rather not get her involved. Not yet anyway."

"Okay, well, the police can have the diamond analyzed by an expert, and compare it to the pendant. That'd be the only best way to tell with any certainty," I said.

Jason nodded. "Anne was right, we aren't thinking very clearly."

My cell phone rang and startled all three of us. Erin was right on time. "Excuse me a minute, I better take this. I turned and pushed the talk button. "This is Camryn."

"You're alive and all right?"

"Yes, thank you. Sorry, but I'm finishing up at a

meeting. Would it be all right if I called you back in fifteen minutes, or so?"

"Sure. And Mark's here, so I had to tell him why I was calling you."

"Thank you, and I'll get back to you shortly." I turned back to the cousins. "I should get going, but if there's anything else I can do, feel free to call me anytime."

It took a few minutes to say our good-byes. I sensed they wanted to pull information out of me that I didn't have. And there were questions I wished I could have asked them, but they were personal ones about their family and none of my business. We shook hands and they thanked me again.

As I stepped outside, a blast of frigid air took my breath away. The wind had picked up and felt even more bitterly cold than when I'd arrived at Frosty's house. I sat in my car a moment, letting the engine warm, and looked around at the Christmas light displays shining brightly from a number of the neighborhood houses. The warm glowing rays they cast out in every direction helped chase away some of the night's darkness. It was the inviting welcome Frosty had when he arrived home at night, and something he could appreciate when he looked out his windows.

I hadn't strung lights on my own house, and I made a mental note it was something to think about. It was my first Christmas living in a house, after all the years in apartments. Between managing Curio Finds and all the other things that had happened, it hadn't occurred to me to decorate my house. I hadn't even put up a Christmas tree. In fact, I'd never done so in all the years on my own.

Pinky phoned me when I was about to drive away. "I just talked to Emmy, and she's got a pretty bad cough and doesn't want to spread the bug to us, or to our customers, so she won't be in tomorrow."

"That's too bad, for Emmy more than for us. I meant to call her to see how she was and sort of got sidetracked by something."

"I'm afraid to ask what that was."

"I'll tell you all about it tomorrow. See you then."

"Oh, all right then. Night, Cami," she said and disconnected.

When I pulled into the back alley to access my garage, a Brooks Landing police car was idling beside it. I drove into the garage and parked. After I got out and was closing the garage door, Assistant Chief Lonsbury stepped out of his car with a sour look on his face. "I understand you've been busy, out making a house call."

Was it possible the news about the diamond photo had traveled from Erin to Mark to Clint that fast? "Come in," I said, knowing that's what he intended to do, with or without an invitation. I made a production of rattling my keys and then inserting one in the back door lock. Clint reminded me about keeping my house locked every chance he got. And I didn't need another lecture, so it was a great relief I'd remembered to lock up when I rushed over to Frost's house.

At least the house had warmed up while I was gone.

"Don't worry about your boots." I noticed he wore lace-ups and it would take too much time for him to take them off and put them back on again for what I hoped would be a short visit.

He ignored my suggestion and bent over and had them untied and off in seconds. "I learned to speed dress a long time ago."

Okay then. "Have you eaten supper?" I think the only reason that popped out of my mouth was with the hope it would ease the tension a bit and get him to stop staring so intently at me.

His eyebrows lifted out of the frown. "No, I guess I haven't."

"I ate at my parents' house and they sent the extras home with me. How about some lasagna, made by my Italian father with help from my Scandinavian mother?"

"Thanks." He managed a half smile. That's when I noticed how weary he looked.

"I'll have it ready shortly." With a full stomach, he might just go a little easier on me.

Clint moved in beside me as I got the dishes of lasagna and salad out of the refrigerator. "Camryn, what were you thinking?" Oh, oh, he was launching his attack before he ate.

I dished up a huge portion of lasagna onto a plate, popped it into the microwave, and set the timer for two minutes. Then I turned to face him. "I went over to help Jason Frost and his cousin. You had talked to Jason about the diamond on his dad's office floor. So they wondered if it was from their grandmother's pendant, but unfortunately the pendant was not in the mayor's safe where he kept it. They thought if he had it at his office, maybe someone stole it from him, minus the diamond."

"And they asked you to go over there to show them

the picture you just happened to possess to compare it the portrait of their grandmother who was wearing it."

"Yes."

"And how did you get the photo of the diamond in Mayor Frost's office?"

The time for the confession had arrived. "I took it."

Clint exhaled a long "Aaaaah." He held out his hand. "Let me see your phone." I gave it to him and with a couple of swipes of his fingers he had the diamond photo on the display. "You took unauthorized pictures of a crime scene?"

"I took one, and not of the crime scene, just of the diamond."

"The diamond was part of the crime scene. Why did you do that?"

"It looked so odd lying there, and I'd never seen a diamond that size before. I don't know."

He took another look. "It's going away." He deleted the image then handed the phone back, lifted his arms, and ran his hands through his hair. The microwave beeped and I removed the plate and carried it to the table, along with the container of salad and a bowl to put it in. The bread was in a bag on the counter. I grabbed that and some silverware to complete the setting. Clint watched in silence then walked over to the table, slipped off his jacket, hung it on the back of a chair, and sat down.

"What would you like to drink, water, milk—"

"Water's fine."

I got us each a glass and debated whether or not to join him at the table. My manners won over my desire to escape to my bedroom and lock myself in, so I sat down in the chair at his left. If he wanted to give me the evil eye I wouldn't be conveniently located across from him. He'd have to turn his head to do it.

The thing I noticed the couple of times I'd seen Clint eat was how intensely he concentrated on his food when he did. Maybe it was a cultural thing in his family. One where you talked before and after the meal, but not during. My family kept any number of conversations going during every meal. I decided to remain silent and appreciate the quiet. When Clint moaned a pleasurable, "Mmmm," I considered it a good sign.

He used his bread to absorb the last of the sauce on his plate then leaned back in his chair, put his hands on his stomach, and smiled. "I've never had better lasagna."

"On that much we agree." I tried to stifle a yawn, but couldn't.

"I can see you're wiped out. Yeah, I guess I am, too. But before I go, I'd like you to tell me more about the missing pendant and anything new you might have learned when you talked to Jason Frost and his cousin."

I highlighted the details, and assured him that I'd advised Jason and Anne to work with the police department. "I told them you'd be the ones who would find a diamond expert to make a comparison for them."

Clint nodded. "That gem is locked away in evidence. The missing pendant adds another layer, no question about that. The mayor could have moved it to a different spot, say, to a safety deposit box. If he had it in the office, and was showing it to someone, say, an appraiser, one who was less than honest . . ."

That gave a possible motive for someone outside the list of suspects I'd been considering. "And I'm sure you've gone through his calendar, his list of appointments," I said.

Clint raised his eyebrows. "One of the first things we did." But that was all he'd say on the matter. "I better shove off." He stood, gathered his dishes, and carried them to the sink. I grabbed his jacket and we met at the door. He put on his boots then I handed him his jacket. He took it with one hand and slid the other under my chin. "Let the Brooks Landing Police Department handle the investigation, Camryn." He kept his eyes trained on mine as he lowered his face closer and closer until his lips touched mine. My heart started hammering so ferociously when the kiss deepened that I thought it might burst out of my chest. "Okay?" he said as he slowly pulled away.

Okay? Far more than okay, it was the best of the best. Then it dawned on me he was not talking about the kiss. He was coaxing me into agreeing with him, and he was using unfair tactics. The quandary that posed for me was, with the way he kissed, it was entirely possible he could get me to agree to almost anything.

"Clint, I'm sorry I took that picture. I'm not trying to act like the police."

He narrowed his eyes. "Good. Don't forget to lock the door behind me."

I didn't answer, or I might have said something snippy about him not needing to treat me like a child. When I shut the door, I clicked the lock louder than was necessary. How could Clint be so sexy, so sensual one minute and then slide back to his old irritating self the next? It was enough to drive me to distraction.

I put away the rest of the food then turned off the kitchen lights and made my way to the bedroom and got into my pajamas. After washing up and getting ready to wind down for the night, I went back into the living room, turned off the last lamp in the house, and opened the blinds covering the large picture window. I stretched out on the couch then reached over and pulled the handmade patchwork quilt from the armchair. My parents had found it for me at a church bazaar sale on one of their shopping adventures. I leaned my head back on a throw pillow and pulled the quilt up to my chin, appreciating its warmth and the comfort it gave me.

My neighbors' lighted Christmas displays were visible from that vantage point. The gloom that had hovered around me since I'd found Frosty lying lifeless on his office floor began to dissipate. Not that the heartbreak of his death would ever completely go away, especially for those who dearly loved him. But the darkness that enveloped them would gradually lift, and their memories would shift, focusing more on his life than on the circumstances of his death.

I honed in on an angel wearing a long white gown standing peacefully in the snow. Lights shone out from inside her translucent form. Her long yellow hair flowed over her shoulders, and a golden crown encircled the top of her head. She was holding a long horn to her mouth like she was playing a beautiful piece of music, one that couldn't be heard.

I closed my eyes imagining what it might sound like

if there was a real angel playing an instrument out there. I'd heard orchestras play so magnificently, and choirs sing so divinely they were more like heavenly beings than earthly creatures. My mind drifted to memories of my parents—my biological parents who had been in Heaven for over thirty years—and I smiled. As much as I wished they were still here with me on earth, it was a great comfort knowing they were forever safe in Heaven. I hoped Jason would someday feel the same way about his parents.

11

I was in Clint's arms, smiling up at him. A bell was ringing in the background. As a light came on, my eyes
opened and my arms were empty. I was alone on the
couch covered from head to toe with the quilt. My cell
phone was jingling, and light was streaming in the living
room window. I sat up with a start because the sun didn't
rise until just after 7:30 a.m. I had overslept.

My phone was on the coffee table, within easy reach.
"H'lo?"

It was Pinky. "Cami, are you still sleeping?"

"I was. I must have really crashed. What time is it?"
I craned my neck for a look at the cuckoo clock hanging
on the living room wall.

Pinky said, "Seven fifty," just as I saw the time for myself.

"I'll get ready and be there soon."

"No rush, I just wondered if you'd pick up a gallon of cream on your way."

"A gallon, really?"

"Yeah, get four quarts. Please. Besides putting it in coffee and the creamy cocoa, I've been whipping more than ever to dollop on top of the hot chocolates."

"Yes, you have."

"I talked to Erin, and she said she'll help us out again after school."

"We're lucky she's been available."

"She told me about your little escapade last night. Cami, why didn't you take one of us with you, or better yet, not have gone at all? Mark and Clint and the other police officers are trained to run into burning buildings and down dark alleys. And they have guns and all those other things on their duty belts to use if something dangerous happens."

"Pinky, there was no reason to think I was in danger. But, I had my canister of Mace handy. And Clint already lectured me about it and deleted the picture from my phone."

"Clint?"

"He was waiting for me when I got home. Can you believe I lived in Washington, DC, all those years and somehow managed to stay away from danger and out of trouble? With the exception of the Peter Zimmer incident, that is."

Pinky sniggered. "It's hard to believe, all right."

As I was walked up to Brew Ha-Ha's door with a grocery bag in each hand, Nicoline came up from behind me, slipped her hand on the knob, and pulled it open. The little ding prompted both Pinky and the couple at her counter to turn and look at us. It was Jason and his cousin Anne. With their drawn faces and bloodshot eyes, neither of them looked like they'd slept a wink. My heart went out to them and I smiled sympathetically. "Morning."

Jason said, "Hi." Anne said, "Mornin'."

Nicoline hung back a bit. Perhaps she sensed the sadness surrounding them. Something was amiss in her own life, and it may have increased her sensitivity to the bad things others were experiencing. I was searching for something to say when Pinky called out, "Hallelujah! My new friends here need some cream in their coffee. They were about to settle for milk. I used the last quart with a group of shoppers that just left."

"Here you go." I handed the bags to Pinky across the counter then turned to the young woman as I slipped off my coat. "Nicoline, will you join me—us—for a cup of something?"

She nodded shyly. "If it is not too much trouble. I have money."

Pinky poured cream into a metal container and set it on the counter for Jason and Anne. Then she took a look at Nicoline. "Nicoline, you say? Nice, a very pretty name. So, as long as we're getting acquainted, I'm Alice—call me Pinky. And this is Jason and Anne. And you know Cami, right?"

They nodded at Nicoline and she nodded back as she unzipped her jacket. She kept her stocking cap in place, and I wondered what her bruise looked like now. I hung my coat on a rack Pinky kept for customers against the wall across from the stools, then joined Pinky behind the counter and asked Nicoline what she wanted to drink. "I will have a hot chocolate, please. One with mint in it, if it is not too much trouble."

"Did you learn to talk like that at a special school? Formally, I mean." Pinky said to her.

Nicoline blushed and shifted, clearly uncomfortable.

I gave Pinky a mild tap on the leg with my foot, not enough that she'd yelp, but enough so she'd get the hint. "I mean, it sounds nice, the way you talk. I've seen those shows where young people are taught how to speak properly, and what forks they should use for different courses, things like that."

Fortunately, Pinky came up with a good save then stopped talking before she stuck her other foot in her mouth.

Nicoline shook her head. "No."

"One minty chocolate coming right up," I said.

"And I'll have some cream whipped and ready in a sec," Pinky said.

When we'd assembled the drink, I set the mug on the counter in front of Nicoline.

"We're on our way to the police station to talk to the assistant chief, but we thought we'd stop here first for a cup of coffee to toast Dad," Jason said.

Pinky's hands flew to her chest and she inhaled loudly. "That is so special. And really touching."

Jason and Anne raised their mugs so Pinky did the same. They waited while I poured some of the daily special in a mug and held it up, too.

Jason looked at Anne to start. "Here's to my dear

uncle, Lewis Frost, the man I counted on for so many things that I can't even begin to name them all. Rest in peace, Uncle Lewis."

The four of us carefully clinked our mugs. Nicoline was looking down with her eyes glued to the mug she held onto with both hands. I debated whether to invite her to join us or not. But she didn't look like she cared to participate. As a newcomer in town, she'd have no idea who we were toasting.

"To our mayor who was also our friend," Pinky said. Then Jason added, "Hear, hear. So long, Dad, until we meet again," as we clinked a final time.

Nicoline stood up with a troubled look on her face. "I did not realize the time. I am sorry but I must leave."

"Here, I'll pour your chocolate in a to-go cup," I said and took care of that for her.

"Thank you." Nicoline smiled slightly as I handed her the cup, then she made her way out of the shop lickety-split.

Jason asked for their beverages to-go as well. Pinky got them ready, topping them off with more coffee. After they'd left Pinky turned to me and plunked her hands on her hips. "Who is that strange girl, Cami? She was in here the other day, too."

"Nicoline? I don't know for sure and that's what I'm trying to find out. So far I've managed to find out her name, that she lives nearby, she's not as young as she looks, she may be interested in buying a snow globe, she likes minty hot chocolate, and that she is hiding how she got a big bruise on her cheekbone."

"Get out of here."

I lifted my shoulders slightly. "I think she needs help and I'm hoping to get the full scoop, but she shuts down when I ask questions she's not ready to answer."

"Like when I asked her about the way she talks," Pinky said.

"Yes, that's why I was trying to tell you to cool it, because I'd already mentioned it to her myself."

"Oh. Well it seems like a reasonable thing to ask her about. She has a different way of talking."

"And some people don't like others telling them they're different," I said.

"You're right. Now you've got me a little worried about her, so let me know if there's any way I can help."

"Will do. But for now I think the best thing for us is to be friendly and try not to pry."

"Speaking of prying, that reminds me, what happened at Mayor Frost's house last night?"

"Not much." I told her about it then said, "To look at a portrait of a pendant with a diamond in its setting and try to compare it to a photo of a diamond lying in carpet is beyond my expertise. They'll need a specialist for that."

"I guess." She patted my shoulder. "Well, you tried anyway."

The shops were busy until late morning when we finally had a little reprieve. I sat down on the stool behind my checkout counter with a cup of hot tea sweetened with honey. Thoughts of Frosty and Jason and Anne and

Nicoline were taking turns consuming me. And then Clint and his glorious kisses would edge their way in here and there.

Mayor Lewis Frost was dead, the person responsible had not yet been identified and was still roaming free in the meantime. I wasn't ready to rule out any of the three people I considered likely suspects. Marvin Easterly had had two meetings with Frosty the day he was killed. So had Rosalie Gorman. Those were the ones I knew about. Harley Creighton hadn't given me a straight answer when I asked if he'd met with Frosty that afternoon, after he'd talked to him at Brew Ha-Ha that morning. In fact, he'd gotten defensive, and had turned my question around instead of giving me a simple yes or no. That was more than a little suspicious.

Then there was the issue of the missing diamond pendant and the giant gem lying on Frosty's floor, minus whatever piece of jewelry it had been in. The experts would be able to analyze it, take the necessary measurements, and determine whether it belonged in the pendant or not. Meanwhile, their grandmother's missing treasure was adding anxiety to what Jason and Anne were already dealing with.

And where was Anne's mother? She should be at her nephew's and daughter's side. Her absence made me wonder about the kind of person she was, no matter what kind of a falling out she'd had with her brother. Maybe it had been more serious than Jason thought or was willing to talk about.

My friend Mark came through Brew Ha-Ha's archway

as I was jotting down a couple of notes on my observations. I shook my head at him. "Thanks for ratting me out."

He stuck his thumbs in his belt. "I will do just about anything in the world for you, and my other friends, too. But when it comes to withholding information I find out about during an active investigation, well, I can't do that."

"I know, Mark."

He nodded. "So now that it's out in the open, tell me about your observations. Did it look to you like that diamond came from the grandmother's pendant?"

"Could have, yes, but the question is, did it? That's for diamond experts to figure out. And that reminds me, you were checking on when the mayor's office was last vacuumed."

"Right, and it turns out it was the night before his death, after the council meeting. The cleaning crew comes in after hours. They don't need to vacuum the offices every day, but it so happens they did on Tuesday night."

"Okay. So if the diamond belongs in the pendant and it fell out of its setting in the mayor's office, it must have happened after that."

"You raise a good point. We talked with Jason and his cousin this morning, and according to them, the pendant was kept in its original box in a home safe. When we went through the mayor's house with the county crime lab team, looking for clues for why he may have been killed, we found nothing suspicious. We didn't even know he had a safe, so it must be well-hidden. Not that the warrant allowed us to tear the place apart. Clint went back to Frost's house with his son and niece a while ago. He's going to check out the safe and will in all likelihood dust it for prints."

"If it turns out to be the diamond from the pendant, you have to wonder why Frosty took it out of his safe and had it in his office. And what happened to the rest of the pendant and the box it's stored in?"

"Exactly what we're trying to find out."

"Still no one reported it missing?"

"Nope. We're keeping details about it as quiet as possible. And haven't released that to the public."

"Any other good leads on your end to help solve Frosty's murder?" I persisted.

"Not yet. I've watched the video of the council meeting a few times now—the parts where things went to hell in a handbasket, that is—looking to see if there's someone in the crowd we still need to talk to, but we've interviewed all of them."

That got my attention. "What video are you talking about?"

"You know, the city council meetings. They tape 'em and put 'em on the city's website."

"Thanks, I didn't know about that." And it was very valuable information indeed. Watching the council in action—their interactions and reactions to each other and members of the public—would be much more telling than reading about it in the newspaper.

"Are things cool between us then?" Mark said and lifted his hand.

I slapped the palm of my hand against his in a high-five. "We're cool. Remember, I was there when you took your oath, when you got sworn in as a police officer. Of course you need to honor that. Even if it means siccing the assistant police chief on me."

Mark smiled. "You've been defending truth, justice, and the American way since we were in elementary school, and that's a long time ago now. I've always looked up to you for that. It's just that we don't want you risking your personal safety doing it."

"We" meant Mark agreed with Clint. One of my oldest friends was siding with Clint and his safety obsession. I rolled my eyes and groaned. "I know."

Mark glanced at his watch. "And speaking of defending justice and all reminds me that I need to get back to work. Pinky said you guys are working short, with Emmy still out."

"Yeah, she's got a bad cold, hopefully nothing worse. So our faithful Erin is coming in again after school."

"Good. I'll stop back later for coffee. You know, Cami, you may need to get more help for the next few weeks before Christmas."

"We'll see. Hold good thoughts for Emmy's recovery."

"Will do."

After Mark left, I moved my stool closer to the computer, signed onto the Internet, and found the City of Brooks Landing, Minnesota, website. A minute later I was viewing Tuesday night's council meeting, keeping the volume very low in case anyone, including Pinky, came into the shop. The chamber where the mayor and council members sat was arranged in a semicircle on a platform about a foot and a half higher than the rest of the room. Mayor Frost had the center seat, and the others, I noticed, were in alphabetical order, left to right: Harley Creighton, Rosalie Gorman, Wendell Lyon, and Gail Spindler. Frost sat between Gorman and Lyon.

The first part of the meeting was routine. And then the gloves came off, first over the microbrewery debate. A number of citizens took the podium to speak against it, and an equal number spoke in favor of it. Harley was very vocal, defending the opposing side. Wendell Lyon had been on the city council for some years and was the one who asked multiple questions, delving into the nuts and bolts of the owners' business plan and why they believed they would be successful. That's where Harley Creighton jumped in with, "They'll be preying on the people who have no tolerance for alcohol by encouraging them to have this new experience." To which Mayor Frost said, "Councilor Creighton, it's not the only place in town that serves alcohol, for crying out loud."

Creighton's face was strained and red when he retorted, "Those other establishments were approved before I was elected to this council. And if I had my druthers, they'd all close up shop. Meanwhile, I won't stand by and let another one open."

Rosalie Gorman physically shifted away from Creighton and moved closer to Mayor Frost when she made the motion to approve. Creighton whispered something to her then she shook her head and said something back to him. I wished their microphones had picked up what they'd said.

Wendell Lyon seconded the motion. Creighton was

the only member of the council who appeared to be against it, but when it came to a vote, Wendell Lyon voted with him. Three ayes, two nays. It passed. Harley Creighton didn't try to hide his dismay when the microbrewery was approved. There was some disruption from the public, but Mayor Frost hammered his gavel and it quieted down.

The last item on the agenda was the proposal of annexing ninety acres from Chatsworth Township into the City of Brooks Landing for the children's clothing factory. An attorney, Robert Harris, representing the owner of the company, showed a PowerPoint presentation touting all the benefits to the community. The company had looked at a number of areas around the state and decided that Brooks Landing was where they wanted to locate.

Wendell Lyon was again the chief questioner after the attorney representing Wonder Kids Clothes gave his report. When Lyon asked for the names of the owner or owners of the company, the attorney said they did not yet wish to be named in a public meeting because they were looking to incorporate, and also were working with banking institutions on the financing details. And there were other reasons he was not at liberty to disclose.

A supervisor from Chatsworth Township went to the podium and told the council that getting a letter telling the township what they were proposing to do was a heck of a way to find out about it. "I know it's part of the orderly annexation agreement between us, but it would've been nice if you'd had the courtesy of paying us a visit, or at least calling us," he said. He may not have been in favor of it, but he wasn't overly upset by it, either.

There were members of the public who thought the factory would be a great thing, providing new jobs and opportunities for local people to work right in their own backyard. Not to mention the economic growth to the community.

Marvin Easterly and two men, possibly his cronies, took turns speaking against the proposed factory. Although Easterly was not alone in his opposition, he was the most vehement in expressing his resistance. "There is no reason that factory needs to go there. There's land on the other side of town that would be better suited, if you ask me."

The attorney answered him, "Sir, I can assure you my client approached a number of land owners who had property that was considered suitable for the factory building and campus."

"That's what I'm talking about. They're not talking about a single building. It's a whole damn campus that'll cover up valuable farm land with concrete and asphalt."

That's when people on the opposite sides of the issues started shouting back and forth, and paid no attention to Mayor Frost's plea for order. When Marvin Easterly and company, as well as the supporters in favor of the factory, were asked to leave the meeting by Assistant Chief Clint and Officer Mark, they were escorted out without further incident.

After things had quieted down, Lyon leaned forward and spoke slowly and deliberately to the attorney. "Mr. Harris, the people you're representing are not here tonight. Is there any reason for this council to think that's because they're not disclosing something?"

"No, sir, there is not."

But that wasn't enough to convince Wendell Lyon. Or Harley Creighton. They voted against the project, and Mayor Frost, Rosalie Gorman, and Gail Spindler voted for it. Again, it was a 3–2 vote.

It took me a few hours to view the video because I'd put it on pause when customers were in the shop then resume it again when I was alone. I watched for anything telling in the body languages of the mayor and other council members during their verbal exchanges.

One thing I noticed that struck me as curious was that Rosalie Gorman sent Gail Spindler a dark look a number of times. And every time she did, Spindler would briefly return it with a nondescript glance of her own, and then cast her eyes downward like she was reading a document. It appeared they were upset with each other about something, but what?

The women voted the same way on the two major agenda items. Was Gorman silently putting pressure on Spindler to vote with her on the controversial issues? I'd heard that Spindler was a woman of few words, but she didn't utter even a single one during the entire meeting outside of Aye. Even Gorman hadn't contributed much of anything to the discussions. Everyone knew she liked to talk and was in no way shy about expressing her opinions. Something was going on between the two women, no question about it.

Gorman had been up in arms the next day when she'd tracked Frosty down at Brew Ha-Ha. Evidently, she was

still not in a happy place by then. Was it a carryover from
the meeting itself, or a different matter altogether? It
seemed to me the disagreements between the council
members inside their meeting chamber had spread outside of it also. Not a good thing. I'd been approached to
consider a seat on the council so I needed to find out
whether I'd be walking into a hornet's nest.

12

The UPS man surprised me when he bounced in with a delivery around two o'clock. "Sorry," he said, more hurried than ever. "I missed this one on my truck, or I would have dropped it off earlier." He carried the box past me and set it on the counter.

"Not a problem," I said as I signed for it, not even looking to see who it was from. I was swamped with shoppers. Plus Pinky had a line at her counter and neither of us was able to help the other.

Mark was right: We'd probably need to hire an additional worker for the last weeks before Christmas, especially if Emmy wasn't back soon, or was unable to put in as many hours. Nicoline came into the shop right when I was in the thick of things. After her abrupt exit that morning I wondered if I'd see her again.

She apparently felt the need to help me because she slipped off her jacket and laid it on the floor against the wall by the checkout counter. But she left her cap on. Then she set about straightening the shelves where people had set snow globes and other items in no particular order after they'd looked at them. That was another surprise. I watched her for a moment here and there as I waited on customers, admiring her naturally artistic decorating talent.

I'd thought the window display my parents and I had put together was well-done, but it was evident Nicoline could likely turn it into something more imaginative, more magical. For some reason, it triggered an old memory. I thought about the time I'd brought Almond Joy bars to a gathering. They were luscious and gooey, but didn't look nearly as special as they tasted. When I set my plate down next to the others, all the other treats looked like they had been created by a professional baker or cake decorator. I'd never seen such a variety of beautiful confections on a sweets table. They all had added touches that made their goods look more tempting and perhaps even better than they actually tasted.

That's the memory that watching Nicoline stirred up. She knew how to take a display that looked perfectly fine to me, and probably to the majority of people, and turn it into something exceptional. She had that eye, the ability to arrange the various items that both set them apart and blended them together at the same time. I didn't know we were missing that at Curio Finds. When I had the opportunity, I went over to her. She gave me a shy smile, and quietly said, "I hope you do not think I am too bold. But you were with so many people and I saw how they were setting the items in places they did not belong."

"Not at all. I appreciate what you've done, and I'm impressed with how nice you're making the shelves look. It's like seeing a masterpiece painting before and after it's been cleaned and restored." I thought she'd be a great asset to our shop, and I'd consult with Pinky about it when things slowed down. "Nicoline, if you're interested in some part-time work for the next few weeks, maybe longer, we could really use your help. We hired two women last month, but lost one after the first day. And our other helper hasn't been able to work the last couple of days."

"Oh. Well, I would be happy to help you out. I believe that will be fine, but I will need to check first with my uncle." Was he the one who had hurt her?

"Sure. The pay might not be what you're used to, but it's not bad."

"I will be happy with whatever it is."

"I'll get an application printed for you to fill out. Just basic information, nothing too extensive like some places require for employment."

"That will be fine. I have not been in your city long and have not worked here. I was a nanny in Boston for a few years."

"What brought you from Boston to Brooks Landing?"

"My uncle needed my help."

A group of shoppers came through the front door and ended our conversation. But Nicoline stayed, moving among the shelves of merchandise, looking at what we had and rearranging things as she did. When there was a little break in the action I told her I'd be back in a few minutes and went next door to let Pinky know I'd offered Nicoline a job.

Her head moved inward and outward, stretched as far as her long neck would allow. "Cami, you don't even *know* her," she said in a stage whisper that could no doubt be heard a block away.

I lowered my own voice. "I know she's got a great eye for decorating and arranging shelves and that she moved here to help her uncle, after working as a nanny. Both those things mean she cares about people. We'll get her to fill out an application, and I'll check her references." Then I mouthed the next words. "And I'm concerned about her and want to find out what's really going on in her life."

Even if I'd known how everything would eventually shake down, I would still have felt the same way.

Pinky put her hands on my shoulders, leaned over, and briefly touched the top of my head with her forehead. Then she pulled back, looked at me, and nodded. "Okay. You've even got me worried about her," she mouthed in kind.

I went back to Curio Finds and spotted Nicoline rearranging another shelf. I was about to print an application form when a middle-aged couple came in. They were looking for a gift for their granddaughter to add to her snow globe collection.

Nicoline's face brightened as she picked one up and carried it to them. "This one is special. When you turn it on it lights up, and the colors change from red to blue to white to green to pink, and all the while the snow is moving around inside of it. Sometimes the snow swirls quickly and sometimes more slowly, gently." She flipped the switch on and handed it to the woman.

"What a sweet thing you are. And what a cute touch—you wearing an earflap beanie to sell snow globes. It gets people in the mood to buy them," she said and when she smiled, a score of fine wrinkles deepened on her face.

Nicoline responded with a smile of her own. I was pleased the woman had added a positive spin on why she thought Nicoline was wearing the cap.

The man put an arm around his wife and leaned in for a closer look. "Well, sweetie, I think this snow globe is just the ticket for Jenny."

The woman nodded. "I think so, too." She handed it back to Nicoline. "Will you gift wrap this up for us, please?"

"Certainly," I said when Nicoline looked to me for the answer.

I took the snow globe over and when I carried it to the counter I nearly tripped on the box the UPS man had delivered. I pointed to it. "Nicoline, would you mind putting that in the storeroom? It's just back there. Thank you." I pointed at the door.

She nodded, picked it up and carried it to the room. When she returned she had a troubled look on her face, making me wonder if she was worried about her uncle, or about the prospect of working at Curio Finds, or just plain thought the storeroom needed organizing.

I found a gift box and had the snow globe wrapped for the couple in no time. They paid and left in high spirits knowing they'd found a unique gift for their grand-daughter, one she would love.

"Would you like to open the box I put in the store-room?" Nicoline said.

"No, I'll do that later, after I catch up a little."

"I will help you if you like." It seemed she was itching to get more merchandise out on the shelves so she could add to the displays.

"That's okay. For one thing, I want to get that job application ready for you." She waited as I went online, found the same template we'd used for Emmy, and then printed a copy. "Here you go."

Nicoline took it from me and looked it over. "I will fill this out and return it to you. Is tomorrow all right?"

"Sure thing. I know tomorrow is Saturday, but if you don't have other plans, it'd be great if you'd be able to work for a few hours."

She nodded. "I have no plans so I will be happy to do that."

"Good. Is nine o'clock an okay time? Hopefully we'll be able to get some training in before it gets too crazy."

"I will see you then. Would you like me to do anything else before I leave?"

I shook my head. "You've helped out a lot already. See you tomorrow."

As I watched her put on her coat and head out the door, I felt optimistic I'd learn a lot more about her in the coming weeks. Pinky came into my shop a minute later looking like she was all done in. "Holy moly, Cami. This is the busiest day we've had all week."

"I think so, too. And our cash registers should back that up. When Erin gets here, you should take off."

She glanced around the shop. "Nicoline gone?"

"Yes, she left a few minutes ago. I'll say this about her. She certainly is ready and willing to pitch in."

"And she certainly is strange."

"Pinky—"

"Well, she is. But you're right about her artsy eye. I thought the shelves looked good before but they look even classier now. Maybe she can help me figure out something cooler to do with my muffin and scone displays."

"I don't think you need help with that. They sell fast enough as it is."

She chuckled then stretched her arms halfway to the ceiling. "You've got that right. I've been making oodles and oodles of extras and I still can't keep up."

The bell on Brew Ha-Ha's door dinged. "Oh, Lordy," Pinky said.

I slid off my stool. "You sit, I'll go." But Pinky followed me instead, and when we saw it was Erin, she said, "Yay, saved by the bell."

"Literally," I said.

Erin grinned from ear to ear, and she wasn't the only one smiling. We all were.

"Erin, you look like you won a trip to the Bahamas," I said.

"Not quite. It's that feeling I get—and have since I was a kid—on Fridays after school lets out. TGIF."

"Golly, I can remember how that felt," I said.

"Yeah, the good old days," Pinky said.

Erin pulled a snow globe out of her bag. "Here's a sample of the big art project we made this week."

Pinky and I took turns holding and admiring it. It was a simple scene of two deer standing by a group of pine trees.

"Very nice, Erin. And the snow is grated Styrofoam?" I said.

"Yes. It worked pretty well. The kids had the best time figuring out their scenes. And with me and two volunteers operating the hot glue guns, none of them got burned."

Pinky handed the snow globe back to Erin. "I swear you could open up your own craft shop. It's really nice."

Erin put the globe back in her bag. "Maybe after I retire from teaching."

I gave Pinky's arm a pat. "You get out of here and enjoy the rest of the afternoon. Do something fun or go home and relax for once."

"Is that okay with you, Erin?" she said.

"Of course it is. And after we close up shop, how about I pick up some supper and bring it over? Tell me what you're hungry for."

Pinky's eyebrows lifted then she smiled. "Chinese. Sweet and sour chicken, maybe some beef and broccoli. Pick up a few different things we like and we'll share."

Erin nodded. "You're making me hungry. How about you, Cami, are you in?"

It'd been a while since the three of us had hung out together and shared a meal. "I am in. It sounds like fun. Back in junior high, we did that a lot. Just the three of us."

But as it turned out, it was not just the three of us. Our little gathering would end up being double that number.

The crowd in the coffee shop was smaller the rest of the afternoon so Erin managed fine without much help from me. I had spurts of customers, and when I was alone in between them, my thoughts returned to Mayor Frost, his grieving family, and the missing pendant. And then I'd wonder about the hot ticket issues discussed at the council meeting. And Frosty's emotion-filled visits from farmer Marvin Easterly and Councilors Harley Creighton and Rosalie Gorman the day after.

It was nearing 5:30 when I sat down to take another look at the Brooks Landing City Council meeting. At least the highlights—or low points—when the micro-brewery and the children's clothing factory were being hashed around. I'd watched for about ten minutes when another customer came into the shop. I remembered him from the other day, first because of his size, and second because he was interested in the snow globe the mayor had purchased. The same one Nicoline liked.

With the way it turned out for Frosty, I wished with all my heart that either this man or Nicoline had seen the snow globe and purchased it first. It may not have prevented Frosty's death, but at least he wouldn't have died because he was hit over the head with the snow globe I'd sold him at Curio Finds. I hit the pause button on the video and greeted the man, once again awed by his mammoth size. "Is there something I can help you find?"

"I'm looking, thank you." He visually browsed through the merchandise. "Perhaps you can help me. Might you have a snow globe with bears in the scene?" Like the other snow globe he'd admired.

"Not at the moment."

"So you have not gotten more in this week as you had thought?"

I tried to remember if I'd said that specifically, or not. "No, we haven't. I'm not sure when more will come. But I can check with my parents. They're the owners of the shop and do most of the ordering. They've been at it for so many years and know much more about it than I do. I can give you a call to let you know what I find out."

He shook his head. "That's not necessary. I pass through here often enough. I will stop in again."

"All right."

He turned to leave as Margaret from the police station came through the door. The man stopped abruptly then threw up his hand, probably as a wave, but it almost looked like he was covering his face. Then he turned and headed the opposite direction instead into Brew Ha-Ha, like he suddenly needed a cup of coffee.

Margaret glanced at his back and shrugged. "I'm here to find a gift for my daughter, and I can't tell you how happy you made me when you gave me the certificate. Not that you had to do that, but it was really nice."

"It was my pleasure." And then I took a chance and

ribbed her a little. "So no other crazy woman has burst into your office this week besides me?"

I was relieved when she smiled. "No. And I wanted to tell you that if I had been the one that found Mayor Frost like that, and got his blood on my hand besides, I'd have acted a little crazy, too, maybe worse than you did."

Maybe she would have. "Poor Frosty. And his family, too. I know the police have a lot of potential suspects to weed through, but I hope they can find his killer soon."

"We all do."

I took a small breath and changed the subject. "So what kinds of things does your daughter like?"

"She has good taste and likes pretty things. When she was young she had a snow globe she really loved. Her grandmother gave it to her for Christmas when she was about thirteen, but it got broken a few years after that. I got to thinking that I bet she'd appreciate another one."

"Well, you have come to the right place." I picked up a globe that was similar to the one Nicoline had sold the couple earlier on in the day. It didn't have the same variety of colored lights. Instead they were varying shades of violet tones, from pale lavender to a deeper purple. And the scene inside was of a young couple skiing down a slope.

I turned the switch on, and Margaret let out a little yelp. "Audrey will love this. It's perfect. Purple is her favorite color and she met her husband when she went on a ski trip to Colorado."

Life was full of twists and turns, much like people skiing down the hills of a mountain. Two short days before, Margaret had not cared for me one bit. And now she was standing in my shop, thanking me, and happy as a clam that I'd helped her find the perfect gift for her daughter.

I wrapped the snow globe for Margaret, and she thanked me over and over again. She was barely out the door when the official-looking woman—the one who'd been waiting in Brew Ha-Ha early yesterday morning for Curio Finds to open—came in.

"Welcome," I said.

"Hello. My friend was in here a short time ago. A large man, wearing a long coat, fur cap."

"He was, yes."

Her eyes moved from one snow globe to the next. "Did he find anything, buy anything?"

"No, he didn't."

"Thank you. I didn't think so, but I needed to verify that."

She left without another word, and I found myself shaking my head. More unusual people than ever before seemed to be coming out of the woodwork and into my shop lately. Was the wintry December weather affecting people and bringing out some strange behavior? Erin and I met in the archway between the two shops. "You look a little perplexed," she said.

"I don't know what it is, but there must be something in the air." I told her about the bear of a man and the woman interested in him and his purchases. And about Nicoline and that we were about to hire her.

"Cami, I know you're short on help around here, but

hiring someone you don't know, and are actually worried about, may not be so smart."

"Maybe not, but I'm letting my instincts be my guide with her."

She leaned in and raised her eyebrows. "As in, keep your friends close and your foes closer?"

I gave her a little push. "Erin, she's more a friend than a foe."

Mark strolled into Brew Ha-Ha and let out a long exhale. "Hi, girls. I got tied up and missed my coffee break earlier. How's it going?"

"Good." Erin pointed at the Betty Boop clock. "Five minutes 'til closing time, so we're winding down."

"'Winding down.' Good one, Erin," Mark said.

Her comment had gone over the top of my head.

Erin shrugged and grinned. "You've been putting in some long days, Mark."

"That we have, and we've interviewed more people than on any other case I can remember in my whole career. Things just aren't adding up yet, but we'll get there. So what are you two doing tonight?"

"Picking up Chinese and taking it to Pinky's," I said.

"Hey, I know three handsome eligible bachelors that would love to join you."

"Really? Where'd you meet them?" Erin managed to keep a straight face.

But it made Mark smile. "In the line of duty. Actually, Clint told us we need some R & R after the last few days of hitting it so hard. We were talking about grabbing a burger and a beer."

"Who's the third handsome eligible bachelor?" I said.

"Jake Dooley." Another Brooks Landing police officer.

"What do you think, Cami?" Erin said.

"Sure, if it's okay with Pinky."

"I'll call her." Erin spent a couple of minutes on the phone and when she hung up said, "Pinky thinks it'd be fun. She got a little power nap in and is feeling way better."

"What time?" Mark said.

"We're heading over right after work," Erin said.

"How about this? I'll talk to the guys, see what they want to eat, you tell me what you want, I'll call in the order, and we'll meet you there at . . ."—he looked at his watch—". . . six forty-five, or so?"

I left it up to Erin and Mark to figure out the food order and went back into my shop. Our little get-together had expanded into a party that included men. Not that I was trying to impress any of them, but I didn't want to offend them, either. I needed to clean up and get out of the clothes I'd worked in all day.

I took a last look at the shelves and once again admired Nicoline's handiwork, hopeful she'd give me some pointers. I rang out the cash register, very pleased with the day's total, then checked the bathroom to be sure the light with a mind of its own was off. When I went into the storeroom to get my coat, I saw the box that UPS had dropped off and I'd all but forgotten. I picked it up and looked at the return address. It was from Van Norden Distributing in Amsterdam. An hour ago I'd told the man I had nothing else to show him. I felt a little guilty and wished he'd left his phone number so I could let him know there were more snow globes after all. A box of them.

Erin stuck her head into Curio Finds. "I'm locking up. Mark is going to pick up some beverages. I'll stop at home to freshen up then pick up the food we ordered. See you at Pinky's."

13

The eaves, front windows, and bushes of Pinky's house were decorated with strings of pink lights. Naturally. She'd been ecstatic when companies added a variety of color choices and started selling her favorite one some years back. She had a white artificial Christmas tree in front of her living room window full of varying shades of pink ornaments including birds, glass balls, beads, poinsettias, even a nutcracker. Plus more strings of pink lights, and garlands, and feathers stuck here and there among the branches. It was stunning.

I was tickled she was hosting a party that included manly men surrounded by an array of pink objects and accents. Would they notice, or think anything of it? I knew Mark didn't. He'd known Pinky almost as long as

I had, and we always agreed that to know her was to love her.

Mark and Jake were in the kitchen, helping Pinky fill her refrigerator with bottled water, soft drinks, and beer when I let myself into the house. There were a few bottles of wine sitting on the counter. "Hi, Cami, welcome," Pinky said.

Mark held up a bottle of soda and pointed it toward me. "Par-ty time. You know Jake, right?"

I nodded. "Hi, Jake." I'd met him once in passing when he walked through the park on patrol. We'd said little to each other at the time, except to exchange names. Seeing him again I realized he was closer to my age than I'd originally thought.

"Camryn," he said then we shook hands.

Mark's phone rang twice and quit. He looked at the display. "That's Erin's signal that she's in the driveway with a load of food. I said I'd carry it in for her." He dashed out the door.

"Should we put the white wine in the fridge, Pink?" I said.

"Sure, go ahead. Do either of you know what wine you're supposed to drink with Chinese?"

"I'm more of a beer man," Jake said.

"That's the thing, in this group we're all more beer than wine people," I said.

"Believe it or not, Cami was raised with an Italian father who knows something about wine, and she still prefers beer."

I shrugged and raised my eyebrows. "I like a good wine, but it's true, I do prefer beer. To answer your question, Pinky, I've heard people in the know say a German Riesling is a good choice. But the ones I've tried are too sweet for my taste." I looked at the labels on the bottles. "There isn't a Riesling here, anyway. And my opinion is drink what you like. We're getting a variety of dishes that have beef, chicken, pork, or shrimp in them. Wine experts tell you to drink red with one thing, white with another. Right?" I said.

Mark and Erin, with Clint picking up the rear, came into the kitchen carrying some delicious-smelling food. The aroma drifting out of the boxes was so strong it was like being smack dab in the middle of the Chinese restaurant kitchen. "Holy moly, how many more people have you got coming here tonight? This looks like enough to feed an army," Pinky said.

Erin smiled. "Look at these guys. They're like a small army themselves." They were all big boys. Six feet tall and over. Muscular. Jake was far from fat, but was broader and heavier than either Clint or Mark.

Clint inclined his head toward the living room. "Pinky, you certainly do a fine job living up to your pink-loving reputation." I listened for sarcasm in his voice, but it wasn't there.

Jake leaned in toward Pinky. "When I was a little kid, about two, I think, my mother was taking videos and asked my brother and me what our favorite color was. Travis was four and said, 'Black,' I said, 'Pink.' That's a true story and my confession about it all rolled into one."

Pinky laughed and moved closer to Jake. A man whose favorite color had been pink, even if it was for a short time, had obviously scored high points with her.

Mark set an armload of food on the counter. "And what's your favorite color now, Jake?"

Jake grinned. "Pink . . . mixed with blue, and that makes a shade of purple."

Clint came up behind me. "Camryn. Keeping out of trouble?"

I turned to him and instead of snarling, I smiled. "For the most part. How about you?"

His brown eyes darkened as they searched mine. "For the most part."

"We've got a nice little buffet assortment here, if we can all open a container or two," Mark said. We had everything ready and arranged on the long counter in short order.

"The plates and utensils and napkins are over there," Pinky said and pointed at the opposite counter.

"Go ahead, everyone, and pop the top off the beverage of your choice. They're in the fridge," Mark said.

"If anyone wants wine, I'll open a bottle," I said.

Erin touched one. "I like this red blend. I'll have a glass of that, thanks."

Pinky's dining table easily accommodated the six of us and we settled around it with filled plates and our drinks. Erin and Pinky had wine, and the rest of us had beer. As we ate and drank and talked and joked, I was amazed how well Clint and Jake blended in with the rest of us, like they, too, had been our friends since childhood. Clint was much easier to get along with in a crowd than when we were alone. Except when he had his arms around me and wasn't talking about the things I needed to do to stay safe and out of trouble, that is.

It seemed like he'd read my mind because he caught my eye and raised his bottle like he was toasting. Then he smiled. Not so much that his teeth showed, but enough so the crow's feet by his eyes deepened a tad. I tried to keep a neutral expression on my own face, but he was so doggone easy to gawk at that I felt my cheeks warming. I didn't look away from him fast enough, and it was obvious when his face colored slightly that he'd noticed it, too.

When we finished eating we all helped put away the leftovers, then washed and dried the dishes. Then Pinky pulled out a trivia board game called Party Smarts from her closet. "My brother gave this to me last Christmas and I haven't gotten around to playing it yet. I don't want to tell him that, so are you all agreeable to try it?"

None of us had played it before, and everyone was willing. "As long as it doesn't drag on like Trivial Pursuit can," Erin said.

"We can cut it off if we need to," Mark said.

It turned out to be a fun game. We all took turns reading the questions, and each of us knew a respectable number of answers, so nobody looked bad. And the bonus was it was a quick game. After the rough week we'd all had—some of us more than others—we needed to call it a night fairly early. We finished in less than an hour, with Erin as the declared winner. Besides being as smart as a whip, she knew things like what states bordered other states, and remembered who the tenth president of the United States was. Clint came in a close second. By nine o'clock we were thanking Pinky, saying our good-byes, and climbing into cold vehicles for the short drives to our houses.

Clint walked me to my car, but didn't say anything about following me home as he so often did. I assured myself that was fine. A part of me longed to be with him more and more, but another part of me was afraid to let that happen. Too many times he'd brought out a snarky side in me I didn't even know was there. He pushed buttons in me. Again, ones I didn't know were there.

Sometimes he acted like he was attracted to me. And other times he treated me like a naïve kid with no street smarts at all. Like he was doing me a favor by guiding and directing and protecting me. And that's when a big red button inside of me pressed down on my heart, and it hurt. A lot. But instead of striving for a reasonable conversation with him about it, my cattiness came to life instead.

My house felt lonelier than usual when I unlocked the door and stepped inside. Maybe it was because I'd been with people all day. It was so quiet, the only sound I heard was the ticking clock in the living room. The wound I'd had since finding Mayor Frost's body cut deeply. I was sad for his family and for the community he served, and it filled me with an intense need to find out who had killed him. Just because I wasn't a policewoman or private detective didn't mean I couldn't snoop around and ask some questions.

I decided to watch the video of the city council meeting again. As my computer came to life, Pinky phoned me. "Cami, where has Jake been hiding all this time?"

"I don't know, Pink. I understand he started with the PD about the same time I came back to Brooks Landing, so about nine months ago, not all that long. Mark said they've worked different shifts and haven't hung out much together."

"Well, better late than never. I think he's really cute and he's so nice besides."

"And he likes pink."

"Okay, maybe that was one of the selling points. But even if he didn't I'd still think he was cute."

"He is, in a strapping, strong kind of way."

Pinky sighed. "I haven't had that much fun in a long, long time."

"I agree. When Mark first suggested having the guys join us, I was disappointed thinking they'd take away from our girl's night. But they definitely added to it. You could tell by looking around when we were eating and playing the game that it was the kind of evening each one of us needed."

"That's a good way to put it, Cami. It really was and we need to do stuff like that more often."

"Sounds good to me."

"My bed is calling me, so I'll see you in the morning."

"Sleep tight, my friend."

"You, too."

Thinking about Pinky calling Jake cute brought a smile to my face. She'd been married for a short time and was too scarred after it ended to think about diving into another relationship anytime soon. So one year passed and then another without her getting serious about anyone. If Jake turned out to be a good fit for her, we would all celebrate.

Back to business. I sat up straighter in my chair, logged onto the city's website, then found the meeting video. I moved the cursor over to the twenty-three-minute mark, when the microbrewery discussion started. I wanted to delve deeper by observing everyone's conduct and their interactions with each other. The mayor and councilors had distinct, and very different, personalities that came across during the meeting.

Mayor Frost was a natural peacekeeper. I'd witnessed that many times when a citizen questioned him about issues, sometimes when he was getting his morning coffee at Brew Ha-Ha. Or when I'd overheard him trying to settle Marvin Easterly and Harley Creighton down when they'd been so riled up. His talent for diplomacy was evident in the council chamber also.

Wendell Lyon was professional and tended to be more on the logical and thoughtful side in his approach. Gail Spindler had been silent during the discussions, making it difficult to get much of a read on her at all. However, the looks she and Rosalie Gorman exchanged spoke volumes, like poison-pen chapters of a novel. And Gorman was much quieter than normal.

And finally, there was Harley Creighton. What was the reason he was so adamantly against the microbrewery? He might have had a drinking problem or been raised to believe that alcohol was the root of all evil. And no doubt, alcohol abuse had destroyed countless peoples' lives. Something worth checking about him.

Besides the city council members, Marvin Easterly was the only other person at the meeting who raised any red flags for me. Probably because, in addition to the loud protests that got him ousted from the meeting, he'd paid two separate visits to Mayor Frost on the day he was killed. And I'd heard with my own ears how angry he was.

I went back to the part when Wendell Lyon was asking the attorney Harris if there was any reason the council should be concerned about the clothing factory deal and the attorney said there wasn't. Mayor Frost had shifted in his seat and raised his hand a little, like he was going to say something but then changed his mind.

On Wednesday morning, when Marvin Easterly was yelling at Mayor Frost, before Harley Creighton interrupted their discussion, he'd told Frosty he suspected him of something underhanded. His words came back to me: "There are people that wonder if you've got some special interest in that clothing factory, the way you've been talking it up." I moved the time indicator back to take another look at Frosty's face when the attorney said the council should have no concerns. He was uncomfortable. Had he been involved in the children's clothing factory deal, beyond visiting the Murphys on behalf of the company?

Wendell Lyon and Gail Spindler were on my list of people to talk to. I needed to get their take on a few things. But not tonight. Lyon had been around a long time and it seemed he paid close attention to what was going on and studied the issues that came before the council. He'd be a good source of information for a new council member, whoever that might be. Observing Gail Spindler's behavior during the meeting brought the expression "Still waters run deep" to mind. Were those waters always still, or was there something that was pulling her under the surface so all she was able to do throughout the meeting was tread that water?

I honed in on Rosalie Gorman again, and there was no mistaking she'd sent Spindler a number of dirty looks during the meeting. And I was willing to bet that Spindler could not wait for the council meeting to conclude so she could take her leave. I was curious if the women had words before the meeting, or if Gorman was saving them until after it was over.

Four council members, one mayor, and two issues that had led to heated discussions. Did that add up to anything underhanded? Or did one of the individual council members have another reason to want the mayor out of the picture permanently?

I shut down the computer and moved to the couch to relax before bed. I looked at the ceramic bowl on the coffee table where I'd dropped every penny from heaven that had mysteriously appeared in my path through the years. It was growing to be a sizable number, and the question was, what would I do when the bowl was full? When I found one I was getting some sort of a heads-up. So the more I pondered it, I realized there was no earthly reason to hold onto them forever. It'd be far better to cash them in at the bank, and then find a family in need or a worthy cause to donate the balance to. I smiled at the revelation. Paying it forward by gifting others was at the heart of the Christmas spirit.

I woke up Saturday reflecting on the bizarre dreams that had filled my night, wondering what in the world had sparked them. My biological parents were in most of them, but they didn't have an active role. They were there as observers more than anything else. I was in Mayor Frost's office looking at the diamond on the floor. I bent over and picked it up. My parents were next to me so I extended my arm then opened my hand for them to see it. They held each other's hands and closed their eyes.

They were in others, but I couldn't recall any specific details about them. Except the last one, the one that woke me up. My mother, father, Mayor Frost, and I were sitting at a table in the mayor's office. My father had a bowl full of gigantic diamonds sitting in front of him. He slid it over to the mayor. Frosty looked down at it. First he frowned, then he nodded, and then he was gone. Visible then invisible. In what seemed like the same moment, my mother handed me a bowl of pennies. It was my own ceramic bowl and it felt like it weighed next to nothing. I was about to set it on the table when I noticed the bowl of diamonds was sitting in front of me. The bowl of pennies was suddenly too heavy for me to hold and I dropped it on top of the diamonds causing one of them to bounce out of its bowl. Then I woke up.

I shook my head, amazed how people who had been gone for over thirty years could be sitting at a table with someone who'd recently died, and someone who was still alive, and it could seem perfectly normal in a dream. My parents were frequent visitors in mine and it was natural and comfortable having them with me. My mother handing me the bowl of pennies made sense because I believed she'd sent them to me in the first place. One by one. But my father giving Mayor Frost a bowl of diamonds was strange. What was the significance of that?

Pinky called as I was ready to walk out the door, just before eight o'clock. "Hey, Cami, guess who just had to call in sick again? Emmy's friend Lester finally talked her into going to urgent care, to check for pneumonia."

"Pneumonia? Poor Emmy. We should bring her some hearty soup."

"I offered to do that. She said she appreciated the thought, but we absolutely should not do that because she doesn't want to expose us. Emmy's worried enough that Lester will catch it."

"It's a relief knowing she has Lester looking out for her, anyway. I'm just leaving, so I'll see you in a few."

"Good. We got Emmy out and Nicoline coming on board. Do you get the feeling we're in for another crazy day?"

We hung up and I heard the little bird pop out of the living room clock and deliver eight consecutive cuckoos. "Very funny," I called out as if he could hear me. I was hoping it wasn't a sign of things to come. Or eight of them.

I drove to work with my dreams whirling around in my mind. I loved it when my parents were in them. The funny thing is, at age thirty-seven, I was ten years older than my mother, and eight years older than my father had been when they'd died. Yet in my dreams I always felt they were older, and certainly wiser, than me. And every once in a while when I looked in the mirror it struck me that while I kept getting older, my parents would always stay their same young selves.

14

My cuckoo clock had been right: Pinky's shop was so wild with customers when I arrived I could barely squeeze by their bodies to get around the counter to help her. I dropped my coat on her rack and my purse on the floor by the refrigerator when I got to the other side. And before I knew it, it was time to open Curio Finds. Nicoline was waiting patiently by the archway, telling the inquiring minds that we'd be turning on the lights shortly.

She was nicely dressed in brown slacks, a tan turtle-neck, and a button-down knitted brown sweater that had some horizontal tan lines woven in. It was the first time I'd seen her without a cap covering her dark brown, long, and wavy hair. She had it parted on the side and pulled into a loose ponytail at the base of her neck. The bruise on her cheekbone had lightened to a pale shade of green. No longer very noticeable. I smiled as I hustled by and waved her in with me. "I'll get the lights, if you'll unlock the door and turn the sign to Open," I said.

We barely had a chance to talk over the next hour as people spilled in both from Brew Ha-Ha and from the street. Nicoline was great with the customers, assisting them as best she could. My main jobs were ringing up orders and gift wrapping some of the purchases. There were no cries for help from next door, but as it neared ten o'clock, I asked Nicoline to check in with Pinky to see how busy she was.

She was back in a minute. "Pinky said your friend Erin is on her way in to help. And Mark is there now, making drinks."

"*Mark*?" I said and she nodded. "All right, I'll be right back." I walked over to the archway and sure enough, Mark was behind her counter wearing jeans, a soft plaid shirt, and a pink apron. And I'm not kidding. No doubt he had stopped in for a cup of coffee and gotten roped into making them for others instead. I snickered and got back to work. I saw Erin scoot by the archway a few minutes later.

Both shops quieted down just after eleven o'clock, so our growing crew of helpers took the opportunity to straighten up the shops, then take a short break. All five of us grabbed a coffee and scone or muffin, and sat down at a back table. Nicoline resisted at first. "I will sit in Curio Finds and watch for shoppers."

But Pinky put an arm around her and guided her along with the rest of us. "Don't be silly. Sit down and join us."

"Mark, I gotta say, you look good in pink," I said.

"I know. It brings out the best in me." He took too big of a bite and muffin crumbs dropped onto his plate.

"Erin, Mark, I would have been in such deep doo-doo if you hadn't come in," Pinky said.

"Glad to help out," Erin said.

"Ditto," Mark managed around his mouthful.

A woman in a long quilted coat came through the archway from Curio Finds. When she pulled off her wool hat I recognized her right away. Gail Spindler. I stood up and went over to greet her. "I apologize, I didn't hear you come into the shop. I should install a bell like Brew Ha-Ha has," I said as I guided her into my shop.

"And I'm sorry for interrupting your break. I came by earlier but your shop was packed." She extended her arm. "We haven't officially met, I'm Gail Spindler."

I shook her hand. "Camryn Brooks. No biggie about the break. How can I help you?"

"I've thought of calling you a number of times, but a personal visit seemed better," she said and unzipped her coat.

"Sure. Can I take that for you?"

"Thanks, but I won't be long, seeing how busy you were not long ago." She looked around, like she was considering the best place to talk.

"I've got an office, let's go back there. It's small, but it's more private."

"That sounds good."

I stuck my head into Brew Ha-Ha and waved Nicoline back into the shop. "We'll be in the office for a bit, if you'd mind the store. But call if you need help, okay?"

"I will."

I led the way to the office. It wasn't much bigger than the shop bathroom, about six feet by six feet, and held a small desk, a file cabinet, and two bentwood chairs with round seats. An office chair would have taken up too much space. I sat down in the chair behind the desk and Gail took the other one.

I guessed she was about five-four and shopped for her clothes in the petite section of stores. She wore her high-lighted brown hair in a becoming shoulder-length bob. She studied me for a moment and it felt as though her wise-looking eyes belonged on a much older person. Like a ninety-year-old, not a sixty-year-old. Her overall persona was calming. Maybe that's how she dealt with her abrasive counterparts—she was able to rise above them and their antics.

I was dying of curiosity, secretly willing her to spit out what she had to say.

"Camryn, I'm here for two reasons really. First of all, I know Lew—Mayor Frost—talked to you about the council seat after Harley Creighton said he was stepping down."

"He did. He told you about that?"

Gail smiled shyly. "He confides, I mean confided, in me about most things. And I did the same with him. We've been very close for some time. I've loved Lew for years, but I'm not in love with him, if you know what I mean. He's been a dear friend, a shoulder to cry on. Not everyone understands that, and it's caused some disruption among the council members. Some jealousy."

Was that what Rosalie's sour looks were all about? Was she the possessive unnamed woman in Frosty's life?

"Gail, I watched the video of Tuesday night's council meeting, and it was evident Rosalie was upset about something, and it seemed she was directing her unhappy looks at you."

Gail nodded. "This has been one of the worst weeks of my life. I'd like you to keep what I'm about to tell you between the two of us."

"Of course."

"Rosalie was convinced Lew and I were having an affair. I've been faithfully married for almost forty years, and I'm *in* love with my husband."

"What made her think you were having an affair?"

"I was giving Lew a comforting hug on the anniversary of his wife's death a few weeks ago when Rosalie burst into his office. She made some remark about the two of us always whispering together about something, and hasn't let it go."

Lila had made a similar comment about the way Rosalie entered Frosty's office the afternoon he died. Was she a drama queen, or was there something more disturbing going on with her?

"Did you talk to Rosalie about it?"

"I tried and she wouldn't listen. Lew said to just let it go, that she'd simmer down eventually. But if you ask me, she's just gotten worse, to the point that I think she needs professional help. She and Lew went out a couple of times and she got the wrong idea of how he felt about her. Lew was never interested in a personal relationship with Rosalie, for many reasons. One of the big ones, of course, is they served together on the city council. And the other big thing was her possessiveness."

I nodded as I considered her words. Rosalie was likely the one Frosty was talking to his son about.

"Camryn, the reason I told you all that is because I know Rosalie has paid you a visit and I was concerned she'd said things about me and Lew that weren't true."

"Yes, she did come to see me. But no, she didn't say anything about you."

Gail smiled. "I guess I could have just asked you that right off the bat. And I don't make it a practice of talking badly about my fellow council members, but I needed to clear the air on that."

"I appreciate that."

"The other reason is, Lew had spoken highly of you and your family, so when he told me he thought you'd do well on the council, I agreed wholeheartedly. It appears Harley won't be stepping down after all, but now we have "—her eyes filled with tears—"an empty seat."

"I can tell you this much—I'm thinking about it."

"That's good to hear."

"Gail, did Mayor Frost talk about his mother's pendant, or ever show it to you?"

Her eyebrows rose, showing her surprise. "Why, no, he didn't. The police asked me about that, too."

"I thought they would have. Back to council issues for a minute, if I could. Some people think Mayor Frost was cutting a deal under the table with the clothing factory he wanted to bring to town, like giving the company tax incentives to build it."

"To tell you the truth, I wondered about it myself. But he wouldn't talk about it at all, even to me."

"If there was one person you had to name that you think killed the mayor, who would it be?"

She looked down at her hands then back at me. "I don't know. I left the office about three o'clock that day. His door was open and so I stuck my head in to say good-bye. He was doing some paperwork and told me to have a good night. The last thing he said to me was, 'I'll see you tomorrow.'" She dabbed at her wet eyes with the back of her hand.

Nicoline appeared in the doorway. "I am sorry to interrupt, but we have a number of customers."

Gail and I stood up. "I appreciate you coming to see me. I planned to talk to you, but hadn't made it yet," I said.

She nodded. "Maybe we'll talk again."

A new wave of shoppers kept us busy until noon. "Why don't you take a lunch break, Nicoline?"

"I am fine. I noticed when I hung my coat in the back room that the box I put back there for you is still unopened. Would you like me to unpack it now?"

The box I kept forgetting about. "Sure, that'd be great." I reached in a drawer behind the counter, found the box cutter, and gave it to her. "Here you go, to cut through the packing tape."

She took it and headed to the storeroom.

I'd started gathering together the credit card receipts we had thrown into a drawer when Nicoline returned with the open box. She set it on the checkout counter and

I peeked into it. The smaller boxes inside were arranged like the last order they'd sent. Nicoline withdrew one, opened it, and pulled out a snow globe. "Very pretty," she said.

I took it from her and gave it a shake. It featured a baby polar bear lying beside an adult bear in a wood. "This company sure seems to like bear scenes," I said.

"I like it."

"So do I. This one anyway."

Nicoline's mouth formed an O.

We each took a turn removing a box and opening it up. But the next one I picked up was weightless. "That's odd." I opened it and confirmed there was nothing inside. I held it so Nicoline could see for herself. "How in the world did they not notice that?"

Nicoline shook her head and looked away. It seemed she had shut herself off for a second, as she sometimes did.

"We'll have to let them know," I said and set the empty Three Bears by River box on a shelf under the counter. I found the wholesale prices on the invoice and marked the snow globes accordingly. Then Nicoline found tasteful ways to show them off on the shelves. I looked at the invoice. A funny feeling ran through me as I read the name Three Bears by River again. The last three bears snow globe we'd gotten had been used in a crime. I was not an overly superstitious person, but I started thinking maybe something bad would have happened to the person who purchased it. Like it had to the mayor.

There were people who believed objects could be cursed. I'd seen a special on the Hope Diamond. It was over 45 carats and had been cut from the 68 carat French Blue Diamond to disguise it after it was stolen from the French Crown Jewels. The French Blue had been cut from the Tavernier Blue Diamond, a gigantic gem of nearly 120 carats. One legend was that a man named John-Baptiste Tavernier had stolen it from a Hindu goddess statue in India, and then brought it back to France. The diamond had been one of her eyes, and when the priests discovered it was missing they put a curse on whoever had stolen it.

The program didn't say what, if anything, happened to the other eye or if any of the other diamonds cut from the Tavernier were involved in unfortunate events, but the Hope Diamond had supposedly claimed at least ten victims. Truth or fabrication, I had no idea. The jury was still out on that one as far as I was concerned.

I lifted the invoice from the counter and saw a penny lying underneath it. *Heads up, Cami.* I shook my head and slid the penny next to a jar of pens we kept by the cash register. Nicoline finished her shelf arrangements. "I would like a short break to go on a walk, if that is okay."

"That's fine, and take time to eat, if you'd like. It seems like everyone in town shopped this morning with the way it's quieted down."

Nicoline grabbed her coat and backpack from the storeroom and headed out the door. I jogged over to the door then braved the cold and stepped outside to watch where she was headed. I couldn't quite get a handle on her. She wore a protective shell around herself, and whatever secrets she was keeping about her life were locked inside. Nicoline went north to the end of the block, crossed the street then walked to the end of the next block and turned right so I lost sight of her.

I stepped back into Curio Finds and vigorously rubbed my arms to warm them up. I went into Brew Ha-Ha and found Erin behind the serving counter and Pinky sitting on a stool drinking a glass of water. "Hey, girls, can I swap cars with one of you for a while tonight?" I said and sat down next to Pinky.

She turned and looked at me like I'd asked her to fly me to the moon. Erin threw a dish towel at me and crossed her arms on her waist. "Cami, I know you must have a good reason for this rather strange request," Erin said.

"I do."

"What is it?" Pinky said like she really didn't want to hear the answer.

"I want to find out where Nicoline lives, and she's seen my Subaru so she knows what I drive."

"You've got her job application, look at her address."

"It's a PO Box."

"How about asking her?" Pinky said.

"I did that a couple of days ago, and she evaded the question."

"And you still thought it was a good idea to hire her. Why?" Erin said.

"For one thing, she's creative and does a great job arranging the merchandise. She's a hard and willing worker. And I think she's got an undesirable home situation."

"I'm with Cami on finding a way to help Nicoline get out of a bad relationship, if that's what it is," Pinky said.

Erin nodded. "As a teacher I agree with you, you need to at least try. So you can swap cars with me, Cami. I'll stay until closing."

E rin was my partner in crime. A little before five o'clock she went to the lot behind our shops, got her car, and parked on the street out front, one space back, so it wasn't directly in front of Brew Ha-Ha. I'd carried my coat and hung it on the rack in the coffee shop earlier without Nicoline noticing.

"Nicoline," I said pointing at the clock, "It's time to call it a day."

She nodded. "It has been a good day. Thank you."

"Thank *you*. We appreciate you helping us out like this. You have no idea."

We'd agreed on a tentative schedule earlier. Pinky and I took turns opening Brew Ha-Ha on Sundays, and most of the year it was doable for one person to manage both shops. But it had been extra busy, so for the meantime, we'd set Pinky's shop to open at 8:00—an hour later than the other six days—and my shop opened at noon. Both shops closed at 4:00 on Sundays.

Nicoline got her things. "So I will be in at noon tomorrow."

I nodded and smiled. "See you then, and have a good evening, Nicoline."

"And you as well." Nicoline waved as she left the shop.

I made a mad dash, as fast as my body would carry me, grabbed my coat off the rack, and pulled it on with what seemed like lightning speed. "Good luck," Erin called as I scurried out the door. I took a quick glance down the sidewalk to be sure Nicoline hadn't stopped, and when I saw her walking away, I jumped into Erin's warming vehicle. When Nicoline was halfway down the next block, I shifted into drive and followed her.

She made her turn, and I didn't want to lose her, so I braved the turn myself. She headed into the historic Huber Hotel. I pulled over to the curb and stopped. It was a four-story building that dated back to the early 1900s, about the same era as our shops. A large gathering area lobby, front desk, and owner's apartment comprised the first floor. The next two floors had sleeping rooms, rented by the day, week, or the month. There were a few studio and one bedroom apartments on the fourth floor.

I was able to see Nicoline through the large front window of the building. She headed directly to the staircase located on the far side of the carved wooden desk, and was no longer visible after the third step. I sat there wondering if she was staying there, or if that was where her uncle lived and she'd stopped by to visit him. I stayed in the car for some minutes then decided to have a chat with the young male clerk sitting behind the front desk.

He looked up at me from his iPad when I walked in. "Greetings, are you looking for a room?"

"No, actually, I'm looking for my friend." I held up my gloves. "I need to give these to her, but I don't have her room number. Nicoline Ahlens."

He held out his hand. "I can take care of that for you."

"Thanks, but I'll just run them up."

"You might want to take the elevator, since they're on the fourth floor, room four-oh-four."

I nodded but ignored his suggestion, maybe to show him I was not as out of shape as I may have looked. Three flights of stairs up and back down again would be like a short workout at the health club. And if I'd gotten more aerobic exercise lately, it wouldn't have been as tough as it proved to be. Of course the heavy coat didn't help. My heart was pumping and must've doubled its beats in the minutes it took me to reach the fourth floor. Add to that the apprehension I felt wondering what I'd say if I ran into Nicoline.

The room at the top of the stairs was 401. The hallway was open both directions, and I took a right. I was glad she wasn't in 402 because she would have had a view of the street where I'd parked from her windows. As I was about to round the corner from 403 to 404, I heard its door open with a slight creak. I threw my back against the wall knowing there was no place to hide, no place to run without being seen.

I heard Nicoline's voice say, "All right." Then the door closed with another creak, followed by heavy footfalls. The aging wood floor let out sounds of protest under the weight. The person headed the opposite direction, and I uttered a silent thank-you. I knew it wasn't Nicoline because she was "a little slip of a thing." The person walking down the hallway was much heftier, and I assumed it was her uncle. When he stopped I held my breath until I heard the elevator doors open and close again after he'd stepped inside.

I crept closer to room 404, staying near the wall where the floor was tighter and not as squeaky. The apartment door didn't have a peephole so I wouldn't be seen unless

CHRISTINE HUSOM

someone opened it. I stopped and stared for a moment. The old hotel seemed like an odd housing choice for a young woman. But then again, she was old-fashioned in many ways. I stuffed my gloves in my pocket then moved past her door to the stairway and down the steps. I was actually sweating by the time I reached the lobby. The clerk glanced at me then nodded when I said, "Mission accomplished." My hope was he wouldn't mention my visit to Nicoline.

I started Erin's car, drove a block then turned around so I had eyes on the hotel to watch any comings and goings for a while. The clerk had recognized Nicoline's name as a guest or resident, confirming she lived there, and had allowed me to go up to her apartment. I'd heard about some questionable people that had overstayed their welcome at the hotel in the past and were asked to leave. It was a good indication there wasn't a bunch of unsavory characters bothering Nicoline anyway. Outside of her uncle, that is. After there had been no activity for ten minutes, it was time to call it quits.

"Well?" was the first word out of Erin's mouth when I got back to Brew Ha-Ha. She frowned when I told her where Nicoline lived. "I wonder if that means she's not planning on being in town long."

I dropped my coat on a counter stool and sat down on another. "Not if she signed a lease. I don't know if they have to there, or if people can rent apartments by the month." I thought about my past impressions of the hotel.

· 206 ·

"Erin, remember when we were young, it seemed like more of an old folks' home."

"It did. You'd walk by and see older people sitting in the lobby reading or playing checkers."

"That's right. I don't know what the rooms are like, but it's pretty nice inside with the old wood-paneled walls. Plus, it's clean."

Erin smiled. "If you say it is, then it must be so, Ms. Clean. And you're right, I have no idea how long people stay there."

"You weren't swamped when I was gone?"

"Hardly. Only one couple stopped by for coffees to go."

"I doubt we'll have much more business in the next half hour 'til closing. I've got paperwork to keep me busy, so go ahead and take off."

"You sure?"

"Yep." When she came around from behind the counter I gave her a hug. "Thanks again."

"Ah, sorry, I almost forgot, Emmy called and she's got bronchitis, so the doctor put her on antibiotics and gave her strict orders to rest as much as possible until she gets better."

"Bronchitis. Yeah, she needs to take it easy, all right. But now that we've got Nicoline to fill in for her, Emmy won't have to feel pressured to rush back."

15

I sat at my checkout counter contemplating all that had happened since the day Frosty had died. The police were putting in overly long days interviewing lists of people I wasn't privy to. Gail Spindler had given me her take on Rosalie Gorman, but when she said she didn't like to talk negatively about her fellow council members, I decided not to press her about Harley Creighton, too. Wendell Lyon was the last councilor still on my list.

The overhead lights in the shop went off for no good reason, but the ones in Brew Ha-Ha kept me from being in total darkness. I said, "Not funny, Molly," and the lights came on again. If I was really talking to a ghost, at least she was listening and responding. "You are not crazy, Cami. Just keep telling yourself that." I picked up the penny I'd found on the counter earlier and stuck it in my pocket.

It took me a minute to get my train of thought back on track. Wendell Lyon. No time like the present. His home phone was listed on the city website, so I tried the number and he answered right away. "Wendell speaking."

"Hello, Mr. Lyon, it's Camryn Brooks."

"Yes, Camryn, I've been meaning to contact you, but I wasn't sure when you'd be ready to talk about, um, things."

I wasn't clear on what he meant. "Talk about things?"

"Specifically, Mayor Frost's death."

"It's okay, I can talk about it. But I'd rather do that in person."

"I agree. Would you like to meet somewhere?"

"I'm at Curio Finds now, or I could swing by your house a little later."

"I'll tell you what. I need to go the drugstore anyway, so how about I meet you at your shop first. Does that work for you?"

"That'd be fine."

Waiting for Wendell gave me a little time so I picked up Nicoline's job application. Her phone number had a Boston, Massachusetts, area code, as did her two references. Perhaps I had jumped the gun, hiring her on the spot without checking her job references first. Then again, we hadn't dug into either Emmy's or Molly's backgrounds before we'd hired them, either. But I knew enough about them to believe they'd be trustworthy employees.

With Nicoline, it was different. I couldn't give her my full measure of trust for a couple of reasons. Mainly because she didn't completely trust me, not enough to tell me what was happening to her at home. She'd lied about how she'd been injured, and to me that meant she was protecting someone she shouldn't be, one who should be held accountable instead.

The other reason was—and it was another aspect of the trust issue—there were times I'd noticed her with a peculiar expression on her face. It was as though she was contemplating something that caused her to feel both pained and guilty, like when we'd discovered the snow globe was missing. Nicoline was a conflicted young woman, if nothing else.

I'd been so lost in thought it caught me by surprise when the shop door opened and Wendell Lyon walked in and up to the counter. We shook hands. He was in his mid-sixties and sported a neatly trimmed gray beard. There was a twinkle in his eyes that hadn't come across on the video. Maybe it wasn't there during the heated meeting. "Thanks for meeting with me, Mr. Lyon."

He smiled. "Glad it worked out. And call me Wendell."

I pointed at the coffee shop. "Let's go sit down. Can I get you something to drink?"

"No, thanks. We had an early supper and I'm stuffed." We headed to the back area of Brew Ha-Ha and took our seats. Wendell slipped his arms out of his jacket but kept it around him. "There's something you wanted to talk to me about?" he said.

"Yes, a couple of things. The police are investigating

Mayor Frost's death, of course. But since I'm the one who found him, it makes me want to help out as much as I can."

"I can understand that."

"Wendell, you're the council member that's known for doing his homework and asking pertinent questions."

"That's the attorney in me, what I was trained to do."

"I thought you had a tax business."

"I do now. I opened it after I stopped practicing."

"Got it. I watched Tuesday night's meeting video, and things got pretty intense."

"Tell me about it. I can sympathize with Harley and the problem he has with establishments that sell alcohol. That's why I voted with him on that issue, more as a support for him than anything else. I'm not opposed to a microbrewery, and I figured it would pass without my vote, judging by the positive response it's gotten from so many of our residents."

"Why is Harley against places that serve alcohol?"

"It's not a secret that he and his wife both had serious drinking problems when they were young. Harley sobered up, and this is many years ago, but his wife didn't. She'd been overserved in a bar one afternoon then picked up their daughter from daycare, and crashed her car. They were both killed."

I sucked in a breath. "That's awful. Didn't the daycare people notice she was drunk?"

"Apparently not. But seasoned drinkers don't always exhibit obvious signs of impairment."

"True. I heard Harley yelling at Mayor Frost about the

microbrewery, right here, in fact, and then he said he was quitting the council because of it."

Wendell shook his head. "The mayor told me all about their tiff, and he also said he thought you'd be a good replacement if Harley decided to leave."

I nodded then shrugged. "Then Harley changed his mind after the mayor died. It makes you wonder." When Wendell didn't respond I had the feeling he felt the same. "And the other issue, the proposed factory. Mayor Frost got a funny look on his face and acted like he wanted to say something when you asked the attorney if there were any reasons the council should be concerned about the proposal."

"Really? I didn't see that. I guess I'll have to take a look at the video myself."

"When you asked your question, was it because you had a particular concern?"

"I did, frankly. Frosty was acting sheepish about the whole thing, and I think it made all of us question why that was."

"Wendell, did you know about the mayor's diamond pendant, the one his mother left him?"

He shook his head. "The police asked me about that. Frosty didn't talk to me about it and I'd never noticed a pendant of any kind in his office."

"You've known the mayor a number of years. Is there anyone he was having any real trouble with?"

His bushy eyebrows drew together. "You mean enough to kill him?"

"Yes."

"No, at least not on purpose."

"So there's someone you suspect who could have done it accidentally, then?"

"I didn't mean to imply that, Camryn. People get into arguments, tempers fly. Did something like that happen? I don't know, but we need to find the son-of-a-gun who did it and put him away for life. Frosty wasn't only my colleague, he was one of my closest friends."

I thought about everything Wendell Lyon had said as I went about my closing up duties. After double checking the machines in Brew Ha-Ha to be sure everything was off, I locked the door, turned down the heat, and shut off the lights. As I walked into Curio Finds, Clint startled me when he came through the entry door. He was in uniform, still on duty. "It's well past closing time, so when I saw your lights on I thought I'd better check to be sure everything was okay," he said.

"Everything's fine. Wendell Lyon stopped in for a visit, and he just left."

"Any special reason?"

"We're all trying to figure out what happened to Mayor Frost."

"Ah, and in my mind that translates to you were pumping Lyon for information."

"Not exactly."

He moved to an arm's length away from me. "Camryn, it seems like we've had a discussion about that once or twice before. Probably more than that."

Then all the shop lights went out, again. But this time,

there was no light spilling over from Brew Ha-Ha. Clint slid a hand around my waist, resting his arm on my back, bringing us side by side like we were preparing for a quick getaway. "What in tarnation? It doesn't look like the power went out, because the security night lights are on in the building across the street."

"Pinky would tell you the place is haunted. *Molly.*" When I said her name, the lights came back on, almost making a believer out of me.

Clint shifted so we were face-to-face. "How did you do that?"

I lifted my hands. "I promise you I have nothing up my sleeves."

He touched my fingers then slid his hands up my arms and rested them on my shoulders, all the while studying my face. "I believe you."

The mystified look on his face made me smile. "Sure, now that you've frisked me."

He smiled back. "That wasn't much of a pat down. In any event, you should get the wires checked in this place."

"The electrician did a thorough check last month. He even replaced some wires, but more as a precaution than anything else."

"Well I think you should get it looked at again. Try a different guy."

"I'll talk to Dad about it. But right now, I need to close up shop for the night."

Clint's police radio clicked on. "Buffalo County to a Brooks Landing officer."

"Three-oh-one, go ahead."

"Report of a suspicious person going up the fire escape steps of the Huber Hotel."

"Ten-four. You'll be all right, Camryn?"

"Ten-four," I said.

He ran out the door so fast, he'd probably get to the hotel before the guy got to the top of the fire escape steps.

It took me a few minutes to get out of the shop then another five to let the engine in my car warm up. I shivered and lifted the front of my coat so I could breathe into it and not fog up the windows as much. I wanted to get to the hotel to see if Clint had caught the suspicious character. As I drove the few blocks I realized I'd never noticed the hotel even had fire escape steps. They weren't on the front, and as I approached the hotel, I slowed down to a crawl and glanced at the west side. No steps.

I kept going past the hotel front to the east side. Nope. I took a right at the next street and continued until I had a view of the backside. That's where they were located. On the same side as Nicoline's apartment. In fact, unless there was an inside landing area that separated the apartment from the exit, it seemed the emergency egress was directly outside her apartment. Had she felt threatened by someone on the steps and called 911 to report it?

I didn't see either a suspicious character or our assistant police chief in pursuit of him, so I drove home.

Clint called my cell phone as I was heating the last of the leftover lasagna. "Did you make it home?" he said.

"I did, and all in one piece besides."

"I didn't like leaving you like that, with your shop lights acting up and you blaming it on a ghost, so I needed to be sure you're feeling okay. You're not coming down with whatever Emmy's got, are you?"

"I'm not ill. You know, Clint, there isn't always a simple, physical explanation for things that go bump in the night."

"I don't like the thought of you being alone in your shop with those unexplained bump-in-the-night things going on."

"Don't worry about it. Really. I admit that it's a little disconcerting at times, but I feel perfectly safe."

"Well—"

I cut him off, "Did you catch the fire escape climber?"

"No, he was gone before I got there. Those steps lead to an apartment on the fourth floor, so I went up there to see if the people that lived there had used them, but no one answered. My guess is, if it wasn't a Peeping Tom, it was probably some kid showing off for his friends who didn't mind freezing half to death in the process."

I remembered doing some goofy things with my friends when we were kids. I considered telling Clint I'd been snooping around that same apartment, but why open up another debate? "Why are you working again tonight? It seems like you've been putting in sixteen hour days this whole week."

"I'm not counting. We're short one officer, until we can get another one hired. And one called in sick, so it was either me or one of my other guys who have been putting in about as many hours as I have."

It was moments like that when I liked Clint a lot. "How's the investigation going?"

"You could say we're making progress with the number of people we've interviewed, but we keeping hitting one brick wall after the next. Nothing seems to be adding up."

As long as he seemed receptive to sharing information, I tried for one more answer. "Did you find out if the diamond came from the mayor's pendant?"

"Not yet, that might take a while. But a positive thing for the family: the medical examiner's office released the mayor's body this afternoon, so they'll be able to make the funeral arrangements."

"I guess that gives them some closure, in a sad way of course. Did the medical examiner say what caused his death?"

"Yes, Mayor Frost took an initial blow to the head by a round object, but it was striking his head on the desk that caused the fatal injury."

In a small way it gave me some comfort knowing the snow globe had likely knocked him out, but hadn't killed him. "So the blood on the desk was from Mayor Frost?"

"Yes, the tests confirmed that it was."

"This might sound like a strange thing for me to say, but I'm glad it was the mayor's and not the killer's. I didn't want the killer's blood on my hand."

He let out a loud breath. "I don't blame you, I wouldn't either. Well, I better get back to work. Good night, Camryn."

"Night."

I hit the end button on the phone and shook my head. Clint had actually been decent to talk to after we'd established I was safely at home. And not suffering from an illness. My meal had cooled so I zapped it another minute then carried the plate and glass of milk into the living room. Leaning back on the couch with my feet up, using my lap as a table was more appealing than sitting at one tonight. The lasagna tasted even yummier than it had on Thursday. Lasagna had been one of my forever comfort foods and I felt a little better with each bite.

I had talked with a number of people about Frosty since he'd died. The police had the names of far more people to investigate than I had, yet Clint indicated they hadn't gotten the information they needed to solve the murder. Of the people I knew, farmer Marvin Easterly and councilors Rosalie Gorman and Harley Creighton were still my obvious suspects, and I wanted to talk to them again. But what about the people I didn't know? Mayor Frost had contacts galore.

When my plate was empty, I carried it to the kitchen, rinsed it out in the sink, and then picked up my notepad and pen from the table and went back to my spot in the living room. Both Gail Spindler and Wendell Lyon confirmed that Frosty had not disclosed any secret deals with bringing the children's clothing factory to town, but my observation about Frosty's reaction to the attorney's comment about it had given Wendell pause.

Another Saturday night. What were Easterly, Gorman, and Creighton all up to? Was one of them toting around a burden of guilt, waiting for some damning evidence against him or her to be brought to light?

Nicoline. The person who'd left her apartment when I was creeping around in the hallway had to be her uncle. He either lived there or was paying her a visit. Nicoline had come to Brooks Landing to help him. I puzzled over what kind of assistance he needed. He wasn't bedridden, and he was able to be alone all day while she was at work. I picked up my phone and called the number she had put on her application. It rang four times before she answered, "Hello." I heard men's voices in the background, likely coming from a television or radio program.

"Hello, Nicoline, it's Camryn."

"Hello," she repeated. The voices got quieter and more muffled.

"I thought I'd check in to see if you're starting to feel comfortable working in the shops."

"I am, thank you."

"You said you're in town because your uncle needed your help, and I got to thinking that I hope you'll be here for a while."

"Oh. Well, I have no plans to leave."

"Good. I finally got a chance to go over your application and I noticed you listed a post office box instead of your address."

"Yes, that is my address."

"It's your mailing address. The reason we need your physical address is in case we can't get a hold of you by phone."

"It is not so you will be visiting me?"

Her question confirmed that she was not ready to let me in on what was going on in her personal life.

"No, not at all. We're talking about an emergency situation."

"Oh. Well, I will give you my address. It is Two-hundred, Second Avenue Northeast."

"All right, I'll jot that down on your application. And I'll see you tomorrow."

"Yes. Tomorrow."

If Nicoline ever showed up with another injury, I'd make sure Clint or Mark arrested her uncle so fast it would make his head spin. Maybe then she'd be able to get free of the hold he seemed to have over her.

I was staring at nothing, trying to find even one piece of a puzzle to match with another when I got a call. "Hi, Camryn, it's Jason Frost."

"Hi, Jason, how are you?"

"I go between feeling numb and then very sad. Sorrowful. The police called to tell me they took Dad to the funeral home earlier. We'll be meeting with the directors tomorrow."

"Are your cousin and aunt going with you?"

"Just Anne. My aunt is acting strange about it, and said we should take care of the arrangements. I found out there was another layer to their dispute that I had no clue about. Anne confided in me about it."

"I'm sorry to hear that, Jason. You found out there was something other than your father being willed the pendant?"

"Yes, that was personal. This is business. But back to the pendant, I've been going through some of Dad's papers and things, trying to figure out what he might have done with it, and I came across his bank safety box key. That's where I would have kept it if I were him, so we'll soon find out. I also found the insurance information on the pendant. If I'd known it was valued at over two million dollars I would have talked to Dad about it, made sure I knew what his wishes were. And that he kept it in a very secure place. I had no idea it was that valuable."

I almost dropped the phone. "Oh my gosh. It looked huge, but wow."

"Ten carats is a big one all right. I know my grandfather couldn't have paid that much for it when he bought it all those years ago."

"Still, a very generous gift to your grandmother."

"For sure. The police told me they got two sets of fingerprints from his home safe, and I found that curious. Dad's had the same cleaning lady for years, so the police are going to talk to her, see if she even knew about the safe. With the way it's hidden, it's hard to say. I'll go to the bank on Monday to look in the safety deposit box."

"You got so much on your plate, Jason. I'm sorry."

"I didn't mean to unload it on you, Camryn."

"Not to worry. Feel free to talk to me anytime."

"Thanks. I called to let you know about Dad."

"I appreciate that."

After we hung up, I contemplated what kind of business disagreement would cause a rift so deep that Frosty's sister wasn't willing to put it aside and help her nephew through such a difficult time. A true crying shame.

The missing pendant had even greater potential significance than I'd thought. How long would it take a diamond expert to determine if the diamond I'd seen belonged in the pendant? But if it didn't, that opened up a whole new can of worms. It was rumored Frosty had a fair amount of wealth, but if he could afford another large diamond that meant he was extremely rich.

I got my laptop, settled back down on the couch, and

logged onto an Internet search engine to read up on diamonds, and what would make one worth over $2 million. A half hour later, I'd read more technical information than I would remember. The main factors that determined the value of a diamond were its shape, its anatomy, and what was referred to as the four Cs: its color, clarity, carat weight, and cut. Frosty's diamond must have been a fine one.

16

After a night of crazy dreams, I was out the door bright and early on Sunday morning to open Brew Ha-Ha and get it warmed up before Pinky arrived with her dozens of muffins and scones. "Have you ever thought of upgrading the commercial kitchen here instead of baking at home?" I said when she came in with a box full.

"No, then I'd really be tied down here, or we'd need to hire a full-timer for sure because I'd be back there baking." She looked worn out, a little out of sorts.

"I guess you're right." I took the box from her and carried it behind her counter.

"We'll use up the ones I have in the freezer first," she said and headed for her storeroom to get them. She came back with a few bags and gave them to me.

CHRISTINE HUSOM

I visually assessed her. "Are you okay, Pinky? You're not getting sick are you?"

She sat down on a counter stool and dropped her chin into the palms of her hands. "Holy moly, Cami. I think I am. Lovesick, that is."

That was the first time I'd heard her say that in close to twenty years. "You fell that hard for Jake that fast?"

She nodded. "I can't get him out of my mind. I didn't sleep much at all last night. It's like being a teenager again with all those crazy hormones flying around."

I gave her shoulders a squeeze. "Oh, Pinky, I hope it works out with Jake."

She smiled. "Thanks. He did ask me out for a bite to eat later this afternoon."

"That's promising."

Pinky sighed. "Jake told Mark he thought I was captivating."

"Captivating, huh? Well it's nice to know he has good taste. And he seems like a really decent guy." I gave her my best smile.

After we'd decided on the coffee special of the day, Pinky went home, hopefully to get a long winter's nap.

It was a relief when Nicoline walked through Brew Ha-Ha's door, all in one piece. That's when I realized I'd become a helicopter employer. I was as concerned about her personal safety as Clint was about mine. Maybe more so. She smiled like she was happy to be there.

"Hello, and how are you doing today?" I said.

"I am well, thank you. And you?"

"I'm doing fine except I had the strangest dreams about diamonds all night."

By the look she gave me you'd have thought I poked her in the stomach. Her eyebrows lifted and her mouth dropped open like she was gasping for air.

"What's wrong?"

She shook her head. "Nothing at all. Only a little cramp that is going away already. I'll hang up my coat and bag and then you can tell me your dreams, if you would like." She was gone for a minute and returned ready to listen. I knew she was probably just being polite.

I couldn't share the details of the missing pendant so I said, "I was talking to a friend last night about a diamond pendant that's been in his family, and it got me curious about diamonds and what makes some more valuable than others, things like that. So I did some online research and that must've triggered the dreams. You were even in one of them."

"*Me*?"

"Yes, we were watching a diamond cutter work, cutting this huge diamond that he'd graded as an FL."

She frowned at my answer.

"That means the clarity is completely flawless under magnification."

"I see. Well that does not seem like a strange dream if you were reading about them before you went to sleep."

"No, I guess not. The thing that was peculiar, bordering on creepy, was that Mayor Frost was hovering near me most of the time, and pointed his finger at the diamond. He never said a word, he just pointed."

Nicoline waved her hand toward Curio Finds. "What shall I do to help?"

I glanced up at the clock. "I guess it is about that time.

We'll get the shop open, then I'd like you to take a look at the front window decorations. See if you can spruce the display up somehow. You're so good at making them look better."

Nicoline's smile lit up her face. "Thank you. I will be happy to. There are no customers at the moment, so I will get started. But I will be here to watch for them."

"Sounds good." I unlocked the front door, turned the window sign to Open, and flipped on the overhead lights. We left the tree lights on in the window display around the clock during the holiday season. "The coffee shop was busy earlier. I've got mugs to wash and muffins to replenish, so I'll be next door. Holler if you need me."

I was filling the muffin and scone display case when I heard a man's voice in Curio Finds. I finished my task and then headed back to the shop to help. As I walked through the archway, I got a partial view of a tall man going out the door. "Was he looking for something special?" I said.

Nicoline was rearranging a tree and didn't turn around. "No, he was curious about what was in the shop is all."

A while later Nicoline found me to say she had finished the window display, if I'd like to take a look. I joined her in the front of Curio Finds. We stood for a time, admiring the results of her labor. She had moved the three Christmas trees closer together, so they were no longer spread out in a row. Now they appeared as a unit, like trees in a dense forest with the smallest tree in the forefront. She'd removed the white garland from the trees and had woven it around the gift boxes under the trees, like they were sitting on fluffy snow. And she changed up the snow globes, adding three that lit up with changing colors and swirling snow.

"I love what you've done. Our mayor appreciated the way it was, but you've made it so much better."

She looked away then back at me.

I stepped outside to see what it looked like from there. I was very pleased. The display had taken on a warmer, more inviting character. "You'll have window shoppers stopping just to watch the snowing snow globes," I said when I was back inside.

"Then it is all right to leave them turned on?" Nicoline asked.

"Why not? During business hours that is. I have no idea how long the batteries last, but we have a supply in the storeroom, and we can always get more." I gave Nicoline an impulsive embrace. When she flinched, I realized my mistake. "I'm sorry."

"No, no. Thank you for the hug. It is just that I was not expecting it."

"My friends and I tend to do it without thinking sometimes."

Nicoline nodded. "That is very nice. To have friends you are so comfortable with."

"How about you, did you leave all your friends behind in Boston?"

She frowned slightly and it took her a minute to answer. "I had friends there, yes."

"Well, until you get to know more people here, I hope you'll consider me your friend."

"I do, already."

Progress. "I'm glad."

Both shops were fairly steady with customers the rest of the afternoon, and Curio Finds was the busier one. I dearly wished Nicoline would let down her guard and spill out her secrets, but she was not to be rushed. Even some of my simple comments seemed to draw out a negative reaction in her. Removing her barriers, one at a time, might be a slow, slow process.

Jason Frost phoned to let me know they'd set his father's funeral for the following Saturday afternoon.

"I decided to fly home tonight. I'll feel better being with my family and my students. My kids didn't know their grandfather very well, but they're sad, just the same. The police will keep me informed as they learn more through their investigation. And checking Dad's safety deposit box for the pendant can wait a few days." I would have been too curious to let that go, but it was not for me to decide.

"I'm sure it'll be good for you to get back to your family. Thanks for letting me know. Travel safe and we'll see you Saturday," I said.

As the day went on I reflected more and more about Mayor Frost and his grieving family. I felt an increasingly strong need to have another conversation with Marvin Easterly, Rosalie Gorman, and Harley Creighton. I didn't think Easterly would have knowledge about Frosty's pendant, but the other two might. And I had another question for all of them, one that, by their reactions, could tell me what I needed to know.

Nicoline seemed reluctant to leave at the end of the day. "Your mayor? He was a well-loved man, was he not?" she said as I turned the sign on the front window to Closed.

I nodded. "By most people, anyway. His family and friends in particular. Certainly a well-respected man in the community. He was good at solving problems, and at promoting the business community here, too."

"I am sorry for his family and for Brooks Landing."

"Me, too."

"I will see you tomorrow at nine o'clock."

"Thanks, Nicoline, I'm so glad you came to us right when we needed you."

I'd hoped my words would be encouraging, complimentary. Instead, she looked sad when she nodded.

After Nicoline had left, I phoned Rosalie Gorman. "It's Camryn Brooks."

"Yes, Camryn."

"I was wondering if I could talk to you about a couple of things."

"Like the council seat?" She was all business. "What do you want to know?"

"I'd rather talk in person and can meet you at your convenience."

"That'd be fine. I'm the Realtor on duty today and was just about to leave the office."

"I'm at my shop if you'd like to swing by here."

"I'll be there shortly."

I hadn't contacted Van Norden Distributing about the missing snow globe, so I sat down at the computer to send them an e-mail. I was typing away when the shop lights went off. "Molly, I've got a visitor coming in a few minutes, and it might freak her out if you're playing with the lights." Coincidence or not, the lights came back on. "Thank you." I sent the e-mail then saw Rosalie Gorman standing at the door, a second before she knocked on it. I let her in, and then locked up again.

"Thanks for coming over. Would you like a cup of coffee or something else to drink?" I said.

"I'm fine, thanks."

"Let's go sit in Brew Ha-Ha."

"All right." Rosalie spoke quietly, not her usual brusque self. "Have you heard Lewis's funeral is Saturday?"

"I did, yes."

"I can't believe he's gone," she said.

I waited until she sat down so I could sit across from her. "You're right, it doesn't seem real." Including the part when I found him on his office floor, lifeless, and pointing at the broken snow globe. "Rosalie, I was wondering about a couple of things you may know something about."

She focused her weary eyes on mine. "What?"

"Did Mayor Frost show you his mother's pendant?"

"No. I didn't even know about it until the police asked me about it."

"So he wasn't intending to give it to you?"

That took her by surprise. "Why, no, I wouldn't think so. You might as well know about Lewis and me: I already told the police." She took a moment. "I was in love with him. I hoped he was starting to feel the same way, but he wasn't ready to admit it yet. And then he, well, you know."

I nodded. "The afternoon he passed away, you went in his office and slammed the door. What were you so angry about?"

"I went through all this with the police."

"I know, but I feel . . . I guess I'd like to hear it, too. If you're willing to tell me."

She lifted her eyebrows then nodded. "Okay. I wasn't exactly angry. I was upset because he'd been spending more time with Gail Spindler behind closed doors. And she's a married woman. I wanted to tell him it didn't look right."

"I can see why you'd been concerned. What did he say about Gail?"

The thought of Gail and Frosty together obviously agitated Rosalie. Her voice got louder. "He said she was just a good friend. Ha! I've seen the way they look at each other. And then I asked if he'd take me out for dinner that night, but he said he couldn't. Because we served on the council together, we needed to keep our relationship professional. Can you believe it? It hadn't stopped him from cozying up to Gail."

Rosalie's whole body tensed up. She was on edge, and perhaps would benefit from some professional help, as Gail had suggested.

"Did the mayor show you the new snow globe he'd bought?"

Another surprised expression. "No, he didn't. Do you think it was a gift for me?"

"Gosh, I don't know who he bought it for."

I was starting to feel sorry for her, but needed her opinion on one last thing. "Rosalie, you were close to the mayor. Who do you think hurt him?"

Tears popped out of her eyes. "I can't think of a single person who'd want to."

I leaned in and laid my hand on hers. "Rosalie, it's obvious how much you're hurting. Do you have a minister or a counselor you can talk to about it?"

"Is that your way of saying I need a shrink?"

"No, all I'm saying is it'd be good to talk to someone you trust. We all need to do that at times."

My conversation with Rosalie Gorman had given me another way of thinking about her nickname. Stormin' Gorman was in an emotional whirlwind, with a storm a brewin'. I sat down at my checkout counter and added her to my list of councilors who had no knowledge of the pendant. Nor had she seen his new snow globe. With one last council member to go, I phoned Harley Creighton. It went to voicemail, and I decided not to leave a message.

At four thirty I climbed into my cold car and gave the dashboard a pat when it started right up. When the engine had warmed, I drove west of town to the farm property under debate. The city council had given the Wonder Kids Clothes people the go-ahead to move forward with their feasibility study. As a prospective future council member, I had an excuse to ask a few questions. Right?

I knew who the Murphys were, and had heard the scuttlebutt about the deal they'd been offered, but didn't know much more than that. I pulled into their driveway and their outside motion-detection lights came on, illuminating the whole side yard. It sat on the outside edge of Brooks Landing, not two miles from downtown, but I felt like it was miles out, in the middle of the country. It was an old farmstead. And one that Marvin Easterly wanted to remain that way.

I left my car running and went to the side door, similar to the setup at the Easterly farm. I knocked on the door, grateful the late afternoon air had stilled. It took a minute then Rusty Murphy opened the door. "Hi, I'm Camryn Brooks. I think you know me from the curio and coffee shops."

"Sure, come in." Rusty pointed at the kitchen table. "To what do I owe the pleasure?" His red hair and beard explained how he'd earned his nickname.

I hung by the door instead. "I'll only be a minute. This isn't common knowledge, but I'm thinking of trying for the open seat on the city council."

He clicked his tongue on the roof of his mouth. "Isn't that just a heck of deal about the mayor?"

"Awful." We chatted about that a minute then I launched into my questions. "Rusty, your land was a big topic of debate for the council. I understand Mayor Frost himself paid you a visit on behalf of the company to make you an offer on your land."

Rusty nodded. "What he said was he'd been approached by someone who was looking for a piece of property on the outskirts of town, and that they had so much to spend. Let me just say it's more than either the appraised or the assessed value."

"That would be tempting all right."

"It is. Mina and I have mixed feelings about selling, but if we take what the company is offering, we can buy another farm and move into a for-profit operation. We're talking about raising organic beef and some other things. Since this property is in the orderly annexation plan, it's just a matter of time, whether that clothing factory deal pans out or not. We'll have to see."

"Marvin Easterly is certainly opposed to it."

"That's who we feel sorry for in all this. We've never seen him upset like this before. He rents our fields and has always been the ideal land tenant. He's kind to our kids. But this has caused some hard feelings between us, no doubt about that."

"You don't consider him a violent guy?"

Rusty's face wrinkled up, like he'd never heard anything so silly. "Violent? No. His bark is way worse than his bite from what I've seen. He can be gruff at times, that's a fact, but he's a gentle guy. You should see the way he treats animals and kids."

But what about the adults he's angry at? I extended my arm and we shook hands. "Thanks for your time, Rusty."

"Sure, and good luck with your decision about the council seat."

As I headed for home, my cell phone rang. I pulled over and fished it out of my coat pocket. "Camryn speaking."

"Hi, it's Harley Creighton. I see I missed a call from you."

"Yes, thanks for calling me back. I was wondering if we could meet in the next day or so."

"What did you have in mind?"

After the "I think you're kinda cute" look he'd given the last time we spoke, and the way he'd just asked that question, meeting in a public place was decidedly in order. And grabbing a beer somewhere was off the table, thank goodness. "If you're going to be at city hall tomorrow, I could meet you there."

"How about I stop by your shop, say around ten?"

"That works. Thank you, Harley."

It felt like it had been the longest week of my life, and I was torn between stopping in at Erin's house to chill out with her or go straight home and crash. I opted for some friend time. When she opened the door I must have looked worse for the wear because she gave me a hug. "Look what the cat dragged in." But she said it in a kind way.

"Are you busy?" I took a quick look around her living room.

"Not too. I was going over my lessons for the week. Come on in."

I followed her to the kitchen. Her planner and papers were spread out on one end of the table. We sat down at the other. I slipped my coat onto the back of the chair behind me. "Erin, things just aren't adding up with the usual suspects in Frosty's death."

"I know. Mark said they've been getting more and more frustrated as they go along."

I told her about my conversations with the councilors, Lila at city hall, Jason Frost, Marvin Easterly, and Rusty Murphy. "I need to talk to Harley Creighton one more time, and maybe I can weasel something revealing out of him."

"Cami, I know you were good at researching and investigating issues in Washington, but solving murders is a whole different ballgame. Police have all kinds of cool tools in their kit, making them able to do things like collect fingerprints, run criminal histories, and interrogate people in intimidating little rooms."

"Yes, they do. But sometimes people tell other people things they don't want to tell the police."

"Like what?" She leaned closer.

"Well, take Nicoline for example. I think she's wary of the police for a reason, one that I hope to get out of her someday soon."

"People in abusive relationships are usually threatened with more harm if they tell anybody, especially the police."

"I know. But, hey, she told me where she lives so I'm making progress."

Erin smiled. "So you don't have to sneak around anymore."

"I still don't want to push my luck by showing up at her doorstep for no good reason." I tapped my fingers on the table. "Hey, changing the subject here, so Pinky's got a date, huh?"

"You'd think she was sixteen again, the way she's acting."

"She told me that's the way she feels, too."

Erin took a peek at her kitchen clock. "Jake should be picking her up any time now, and I have a feeling we'll be hearing all about it."

We smiled and crossed our fingers, wishing our friend the best of luck.

17

Pinky had stars in her eyes and kept messing up orders. "I asked for a cranberry scone," a woman at her service counter said and pushed the plate holding a muffin back at Pinky.

"Oh. Sorry. Here you go." Pinky gave her a new plate with the scone and the woman joined her friends at a table.

"Maybe you should go for a walk, burn off some of your nervous energy, maybe get some fresh air," I said.

She snapped her dish towel. "Ten degree air is a little too fresh for what I wore to work. I left my boots and parka at home."

I would have offered her mine but we weren't the same size. "We've got some time before Curio Finds opens, if you want to run home for them."

"Nah, I'll go do some laps in your shop." She shook her hands and released some of her nervous energy. "How can this feel so good and so painful at the same time?"

When her hands quieted, I took them in mine. "One of those sweet mysteries of life. Your text message said you had a great evening."

"Jake is sooo fun to be with. Not to mention that he's an absolute hunk. I love how he makes me feel."

"Then so do I." I released her hands and she went on her inside walk.

She popped her head through the archway a few minutes later. "I forgot to tell you Emmy called earlier and is feeling way better, but she's still got a little cough. She's thinks she'll be back tomorrow or the next day."

"That's good news."

Pinky went back to doing laps around the shelving units in my shop, and I thought again, for the one hundredth time at least, how lucky for us that Nicoline had shown up right when we needed her. How was I to know it was more than happenstance she'd come into our lives when she had?

Nicoline was even quieter than usual when she reported for work. "Is everything okay?" I said.

"Yes. Thank you. I had a little trouble sleeping last night, but I will be fine."

"Why don't you go make yourself some hot chocolate, that'll help perk you up."

Her lips lifted in a smile but her eyes looked sad. "In a little while, I will do that."

We had customers in our shop right off the bat, but we'd gone into a little lull by the time Harley Creighton arrived promptly at ten o'clock. I was able to break away without putting too much stress on Nicoline. There were a number of people at the tables in Brew Ha-Ha, so I steered him toward the office, wishing it were a larger room. I went in first so I wouldn't have to squeeze by him.

When we sat down the first thing he said to me was, "Did anyone ever tell you that you look like Marilyn Monroe?"

Oh my goodness. I didn't care to get into the fact that dressing up like Marilyn Monroe was my costume party choice. When I styled my hair like hers and covered my sprinkling of freckles and put in blue contact lenses, I had to admit I looked a lot like her. But in my normal life, when I looked in the mirror I saw Camryn, not Marilyn. I mumbled, "I have heard that before. To let you know, Harley, as far as the city council is concerned, I haven't made a decision about that. But there were a couple of other things I'm wondering about."

He leaned so far forward, I was glad there was a desk between us. "Shoot."

"I know you didn't get along very well with Mayor Frost—"

He didn't let me finish. "Now, now, I think that needs to be clarified. I got along fine with Frosty, personally. But there's no sense denying we had our differences on a number of city issues."

"Okay, well then maybe you did know about a pendant he had inherited from his mother."

"No, no, that I didn't, and I told the police that, too."

"So he didn't say he was planning to give it to anyone? You didn't see it in his office?"

Harley shook his head. "No."

"How about the new snow globe he'd just bought? Was that for anyone special?"

"A snow globe?" He shrugged. "He didn't mention that, either."

"Oh, I thought maybe he showed it to you in his office Wednesday afternoon."

"The day he died? No, he was pretty busy with visitors, from what I saw."

I looked for a hint of dishonesty, but it wasn't there. He was open in his responses. It disappointed me a little that I believed him. Not because I wanted him to be guilty, but like Mark and Clint had said, no good suspects had yet risen to the surface. And somebody had killed Frosty.

I stood up. "I need to get back to work, but thanks for stopping by, Harley."

He got up and nodded. "No problem. And be sure to give the council some serious thought."

"I will." I lifted my hand. "After you."

I got an e-mail back from Van Norden Distributing stating that although they didn't know what had happened with the three bears snow globe, they would assume responsibility for it and subtract it from the invoice. They also wrote that another order was en route, leaving me to wonder again why Van Norden was shipping them in several small orders, instead of one bigger one. Unless their suppliers were having difficulty keeping up with demand and shipped them to retail outlets as soon as they got some in. My parents had told me it wasn't all that unusual during the Christmas season for companies to do that. The faster they were on retailers' shelves the faster they could be sold.

Nicoline went between the two shops, helping Pinky with drink orders and washing dishes and me with customers. I'd received another special order request and got it packaged up, ready to send. I asked Nicoline if she'd take it to the post office. She looked a bit frazzled by the request. "How shall I pay for it?"

"I'll give you a check and you can fill in the amount."

"All right."

She was barely out the door when the UPS truck pulled up to the curb, and out hopped the driver. He certainly didn't need to go to the health club in December. He got two boxes out of the truck and jogged into the shop. "Mornin'." He set the boxes on the checkout counter.

"Good morning. How's it going?" I signed for the orders.

"It's going. Have a good one."

He was halfway out the door when I said, "You, too."

No one was in the shop, so I looked at the boxes. One was from a company in Germany that specialized in antique and valuable snow globes. The other was from Van Norden. I opened that one first. Four boxes, like the last order. I took them out and picked up the one marked Three Bears by River. The same name as the one missing from the previous order. I took out the snow globe and stared at a scene similar to the one Frosty had purchased. The bears looked the same, but this time they were closing in on a man from behind, one who was holding a fishing pole with its line dangling in the river. I held it for a moment, knowing I either had to send it back, or throw it away. There was something about it that seemed vile.

Pinky walked over and stood beside me. "What are you doing?"

"This is just as bad as the one Frosty bought, the one he got hit with."

"Eew. The hairs on the back of my neck just went up. It's kind of a frightening scene, don't you think?" She shook her head.

"Yes. And it's not going on our shelves, I know that much. I thought about throwing it away, but we'd have to eat the cost, so I'll return it instead." I put it in its box, slid open the door on the back of the checkout counter, set it on a shelf, and pushed it to the back.

The overhead lights turned off and on. Pinky looked around with her eyes opened wide. "What was that all about?"

"It's been happening more again lately. Clint said I need to get the electrician back to have another look."

"Not that I want it to happen in your shop, but I'm sure glad it's not happening in mine." She reached over and picked up a penny I hadn't seen lying between the two boxes. "Here, it must be from your cash register."

Or maybe not. "Thanks." I took it and stuck it in my pocket.

The bell on Brew Ha-Ha's door dinged and Pinky dashed back to her shop. Nicoline returned from the post office with a smile. "Here is your receipt. There was quite a long line there."

I nodded. "It's that time of year, so thanks for doing that. We've got some more items to mark, if you want to help."

"Yes, I would like that." She hung up her coat then joined me at the counter.

"I got this one opened, so we'll do these first." I pulled the three remaining boxes out and put them in front of Nicoline, then set the larger box on the floor.

She helped take them out. "Only three in this order?"

"Actually there was four, but I'm sending one back."

"Why is that?"

"I have a bad feeling about it." It was like the one Nicoline had wanted to buy so I didn't go into details.

"All right. Well I can take it to the post office for you."

"Thanks, we'll take care of it later." I handed her the box cutter. "If you'll open the other box, I'll get these three priced so you can find them a nice temporary home on our shelves."

The rest of the day was busier than I'd anticipated for a Monday. Pinky ended up staying until nearly five o'clock herself before I finally convinced her to go. "When Mark was helping out Saturday he said we should hire more staff about forty times. It'll be a relief when Emmy's back."

I chuckled at the thought of Mark working in Brew Ha-Ha wearing a pink apron. "He was a real trouper helping out on Saturday. And if you ever need Jake to work here, it's good to know pink was his favorite color when he was little."

Pinky smiled and sighed. Loud and long. "He really is something, isn't he?"

"Speaking of our police officers, I haven't seen Mark or Clint all day. Yesterday either, come to think of it."

"You're right. About today anyway. Jake said they've been putting in a ton of hours trying to solve Frosty's murder and the most progress they've made is clearing a long list of people as suspects."

"Well, that's progress, I guess, but not as much as they need."

"Right. I'm outta here, and I'll see you tomorrow."

I went back into Curio Finds and when I didn't see Nicoline I thought she'd gone into the bathroom. But a minute later she came out of the storeroom. "Doing some organizing back there?" I said.

"Oh. A little," she said. "Camryn, I can drop that package you are sending off at the post office on my way home."

It took me a second to remember I'd told her about returning the snow globe. "That's okay, the post office is closed now. And there's no real hurry. We'll get it taken care of in a day or two."

"All right. Would you like me to stay until closing?"

She probably needed the money. "If you'd like to, sure. Go make yourself a cup of something to drink. And check to see if anything needs wiping down in the coffee shop. I'll wrap up things in here."

"I will do that."

We finished our jobs and were ready to leave by 6:00 p.m. Nicoline turned and looked at me like there was something on the tip of her tongue. "Is there anything you wanted to talk to me about?"

"Oh. No. Good night, Camryn."

"Night, Nicoline. See you tomorrow."

"Yes."

We walked together for the short distance to the walkway between our building and the one north of it, then I took that turn and she continued on. I sensed she was getting closer to telling me about her life and her uncle, or whoever it was, but she hadn't quite worked up the courage. *Maybe tomorrow*, I thought. I had no way of predicting all the things that would spill out of her mouth once the flood gates were opened.

As my car warmed, I thought about Frosty and decided to swing by his house, for no good reason. If Jason had still been there, I would've asked permission to take another look at his grandmother's portrait. My dreams kept sending me back to the diamond I'd spotted on the mayor's office floor. If I'd seen either Mark or Clint, I would have asked if they'd gotten an answer yet from the gem expert.

I drove past Emmy's house on my way to Frosty's, and it prompted me to send up healing thoughts for her. As I approached his house, I got quite the surprise. There was a dark sedan sitting in the driveway and the overhead garage door was open. I pulled in across the street, parked, turned off my engine, and watched. A shorter woman in a fur coat was pressing numbers on the keypad on the outside of the garage. A few seconds later the door began its descent and the woman—who appeared to be in her late sixties—walked to her car and got in. Was she an old girlfriend of Frosty's, one who had his access code? Even if she was collecting something that was hers, it wasn't right for her to go into his house without permission from the family.

She sat for a minute before backing out of the driveway. I debated whether to call Jason or not. And what would I say? I didn't have a pen and paper handy so I called my home phone and left her license plate number on my voicemail. And then I phoned Mark.

"There is a lady who just left Mayor Frost's house. It looks like she got in through his garage. She knew the code, and I'm following her."

"Cami, if she has the code, she probably has permission. What's her license number?"

I hadn't memorized it and speeded up so I was close enough to read it. "It's S-one-W-A-four-nine."

"Okay, I'll run it, and you don't need to keep following her."

"But we need to tell Jason, see if she had his permission to be there."

"I'll take care of that." He paused and I heard him hitting keys on the laptop computer in his police car. "Cami, do you know anyone by the name of Loretta Proctor?"

"No, I don't. Where does she live?"

"I can't answer that. Are you still behind the car?"

"Yes."

"Turn around, Cami. The plate comes back to someone from out of town. We'll check it out, and if we need to file a report, I'll get your statement."

"Okay, Mark."

I didn't turn around until the car was outside city limits and figured the woman was probably headed home, wherever that was. What in the heck had she been up to at Mayor Frost's house? Loretta Proctor was the owner of the car and probably the driver.

Jason Frost phoned me some minutes later. "Camryn, Officer Mark Weston just called and told me you saw my aunt leaving Dad's house when you drove by a while ago."

His aunt? The one who had not been at her brother's house when Jason needed her, but had shown up now, after he'd left? "Golly, Jason, I didn't know who it was and I didn't actually see her leave the house. I saw her punching in the code to shut the garage door. Technically, she was in the driveway. And so was her car."

"Lea and I have been sitting here trying to decide what to do."

"Your aunt didn't talk to you about it, didn't ask your permission to be there?"

"No, before Officer Weston called, I didn't even know she had the code. Like we told you, Dad and Loretta have been on the outs for some time." He was silent a moment. "You know, come to think of it, Dad's had the same code for years. He probably gave it to her way back when, and never thought she'd go in without his knowledge."

"Are you leaving it up to the police to talk to her?"

"I asked them to hold off until we figure out the best way to handle this. I'll talk to my cousin Anne first, get her input. Oh, and Officer Mark suggested changing the code, and even offered to do that for us."

"That's a very good idea."

"I don't think it was just a coincidence you happened by Dad's house when you did."

What was he getting at? "You're right, I was thinking about him and took a little detour on my way home."

"What I meant was, I think you were supposed to do that."

Ah. "Maybe I was, Jason."

I parked in my garage and hurried into my house. When I got inside, I was glad I'd forgotten to turn the heat down that morning. I tossed my keys on the counter and stared at my refrigerator for a second trying to remember if there was anything inside worth eating for supper. Maybe it was a chips and salsa night. After I got into my pajamas.

I was leaving the bedroom, decked out in flannel pajamas, a flannel robe, and my pink bunny slippers. I had the penny Pinky had found and given to me in my hand when my doorbell rang. I groaned and threw the penny in the ceramic bowl, debating whether I should answer it or not. Then there was a knock and a voice calling out from the other side of the door. "Camryn, it's Clint."

The fact that I didn't hesitate to let him in, even at the risk of being ribbed for appearing like I was ready for bed at such an early hour, was a fair indication of how much I wanted to see him. I let him in then closed the door behind him. He eyed me from my own face down to the bunnies' faces on my feet, and then brought his eyes back to mine. "It looks like you're about to call it a night."

"Not for a while yet. It just feels good to get out of the clothes I was in for the last twelve hours. And at this time of the year, if I don't have somewhere else to go, pajamas seem like the best option."

"I can't say I blame you. Thirteen hours for me." He reached up and tugged at the inside of his collar.

That would be a long time with a bulletproof vest and all the heavy equipment he carried on his belt. "Did you stop over for a particular reason?"

"Mark called me about the woman you reported."

I lifted my hand. "Before you say any more I should tell you that Jason Frost called me after Mark talked to him and told me who she is."

Clint nodded. "You don't say."

"And also that Jason asked Mark to change the code so she wouldn't be able to get in again."

"We cruise by Mayor Frost's house regularly, but . . . in any case, thanks for being there when we weren't."

"Sure. So are you about done working for the day?"

"Yeah, on my way home."

"I was about to have some tortilla chips and salsa, if you want to join me."

He patted his stomach. "I'm good. We had a pizza delivered to the office when we were going over the case."

"Still no suspects?"

"I wouldn't say that. It's an active investigation and we're waiting on some answers so we know what avenues to pursue next. Oh, and Camryn? I know Mark's been your friend for a long time, but don't be afraid to call me if you need to."

"You mean because I called Mark instead of you about Frosty's sister?"

"Yeah, that and other things like that."

But Mark wasn't as intense as Clint was, and was less likely to lecture me. However, I was not about to argue, because he'd issued an invitation of sorts. "Okay."

"Good night."

"Good night." We both reached for the door knob, and as he bent over the side of his face touched the side of mine, and I innately responded by moving my hand to his arm and turning so we were face-to-face. "What is it about you?" he whispered against my lips before he covered them with his own.

He pulled me in tightly, and as our kiss intensified, my body responded with the most wonderful sensations possible. When he finally eased himself away from me, I wasn't sure if my legs would support me, so I leaned against the wall. "Sweet dreams," he said as he opened the door then left my house, and me all by my lonesome. I pulled back the blinds a crack and watched him walk to his car. *Clint, that kiss was the stuff sweet dreams were made of.*

18

'd lost my appetite. For food, that is, and settled in on the couch with the warm quilt covering me from the waist down. My notebook and pen were lying on the coffee table. I picked them up and as I thought about all the people I'd talked to about Frosty, and my impressions of them, I stabbed the pen into the pad over and over, trying to gather those thoughts together enough to write something down.

My cell phone rang, reminding me I'd left it on my dresser. It rang three times then it quit. It hadn't gone to voicemail that fast. I found my phone and saw it was Nicoline who had called. I selected her number and tried her back, but she didn't answer. She may have dialed me in error and hung up when she realized it. Still, an uneasy feeling settled over me. I dropped the phone into my robe pocket and then grabbed my laptop computer from the spare bedroom/office on the way back to the couch.

I sat it on the coffee table, and when the Internet was up and running, I typed Loretta Proctor's name into a search engine. A second later I had access to over 5,000 records plus some photos of her. She was listed as the Chief Executive Officer of Proctor Fabrications, a well-known manufacturer of quality clothing. Little bells started ringing in my head. Frosty had been the Chief Financial Officer of a manufacturing company. Was it at Proctor's? Had something happened between his sister and him at work, something that was at the heart of their disagreement and had led to their separation? Jason had implied as much. Add to that the personal insult of having a valuable pendant willed to her brother instead of her, as Loretta had expected.

It was a touchy subject, and not one I could talk to Jason Frost about until things had calmed down in his life. But it made me all the more curious about why Loretta Proctor had gone into her brother's house. What was she was looking for, and had she found it?

Loretta had offered Jason a place to stay at her house. Maybe so she could, as Erin had said the other day, keep her friends close and her foes closer? Anne hadn't said boo about her mother, probably not unusual knowing how close she was to her uncle. Stuck in the middle of a family battle was never a good place to be.

I didn't want to get caught up reading more about Loretta Proctor's business life, so I closed out of the Internet and shut off the computer. I picked up the pen and notebook again and wrote, "Loretta Proctor, CEO of Proctor Fabrications, likely the same company Frosty had been the CFO of. A clothing manufacturing company." What a coincidence—or not—that the mayor was working on bringing a children's clothing factory to a ninety acre parcel just outside of the Brooks Landing city limits. If the township property was first annexed into the city, that is.

Frosty had been involved with that deal. He'd represented the company when he visited the Murphys and told them what the company was willing to pay for their land. He should have disclosed that publicly, and recused himself from voting on the issue. What would the company's attorney have to say about the whole deal if he was put on the witness stand and had to tell all he knew?

Was it possible Loretta was involved in the deal and she and her brother secretly got along better than their families believed they did? I jotted that down then crossed it out because it didn't make sense. There would be no reason to hide that from those obviously hurt by their discord. Especially after Frosty's death.

I set the notebook aside then reached over into the penny bowl and picked up a small handful. I held them a moment then spread my fingers and let them fall through them, back into the bowl. "When Frosty's killer is locked up for what he did, I'll figure out a worthy organization to give all of you to." I shook my head. *It's not bad enough that I'm talking to the lights in Curio Finds and calling them Molly, but now I'm talking to pennies besides.*

I made sure the doors were locked and headed to bed for a good night's rest. And aside from dreams of my ceramic penny bowl sitting on Curio Finds checkout counter filled with diamonds instead of pennies and Loretta Proctor walking around my shop like a robot, wearing her mother's diamond pendant, and carrying the scary snow globe her brother had purchased, I had an otherwise restful night.

It was a good thing, too, because with all that got packed into the next day I'd need every bit of energy possible.

Emmy was behind Brew Ha-Ha's counter when I got to work, and I realized how much I'd missed her. She was a little tired looking, but when she smiled, her face lit up. "Welcome back," I said then went behind the counter and gave her a warm hug.

"I can't tell you how good it is to be back." She filled a mug with coffee.

I heard the coffee bean grinder going in the back room. Pinky was hard at work.

"When Pinky called me earlier she said you're planning to put in four hours or so today?" I said.

"Yes, I'll see how it goes. I know I'm not as young as I used to be, but it's taking longer than I would've thought to get my strength back."

"We hired another woman to help out, too, so don't feel pressured to push yourself."

"Pinky told me a little about her. Nicoline?"

"That's right. She'll be in at nine. She's on the quiet side and a good worker. You saw her last week, the one you said was a 'little slip of a thing.'"

"Oh, sure, I remember."

"Come and I'll show you how she's dressed up the merchandise displays."

Emmy followed me into Curio Finds and started winding her way around the shelves while I hung up my coat.

"What do you think of the window display?" I said.

"It looks very nice."

The bell on Pinky's shop door dinged so Emmy and I headed back in there and waited on the small group of women that had come in.

Nicoline had been prompt the last few days so by nine twenty when she hadn't shown up for work or called to say she couldn't make it, I wondered why. She had my cell number, and in fact had called it the night before. I phoned her, but it rang and rang without going to voicemail. What reason would she have for turning off that feature? A prepaid plan, perhaps, where voicemail would count against her minutes?

I tried her phone again late morning and hung up after eight rings. I decided it was about time I checked Nicoline's references. I called the man she'd worked for in Boston and he said she had been a very good employee, and his children loved her. He didn't mention having any reliability issues with her.

Emmy worked until noon. Her friend Lester had given her a ride to work and picked her up when she was ready to go home. "I feel bad leaving, especially since Nicoline isn't here."

"We'll be fine. Erin is coming in after school, and my parents are willing to help whenever we need them." I'd sent Erin a text message and she replied she was available. I put my parents on an imaginary "emergency only" list, like if things got crazy busy closer to Christmas and we were too overwhelmed to deliver good customer service, we'd bring them in.

Pinky joined me in Curio Finds about two o'clock when there was a break in the action. I was dusting off a shelf. "Cami, you look so stressed."

"I'm wondering if I should go check on Nicoline, see if she's okay."

"Erin will be here about three thirty."

I nodded. "Nicoline was acting out of sorts yesterday. She might have been coming down with something and is sick in bed. But you'd think she'd have called."

"You'd think."

Jason Frost's cousin Anne came into the shop while we were talking. Her face was drawn, and it was obvious she'd been crying. "Camryn, I feel just awful."

Pinky apparently took that as her cue to leave and excused herself, no doubt hoping I'd tell her all about it later.

I pulled the extra stool closer to the one behind my checkout counter and we sat down. "Did Jason talk to you about last night?" I said.

Anne nodded, then fresh tears rolled down her cheeks. She pulled a tissue out of her coat pocket and wiped them away. "I can't figure out what my mother was doing in my uncle's house. But that's not what's got me so upset." She wiped away more tears. "I was talking to my attorney yesterday, and he gave me more details about the city council meeting last week."

It took me a split second to figure out who that was. Robert Harris. The attorney that had gone before the Brooks Landing mayor and council members with the Wonder Kids Clothes proposal. He'd told them the owners weren't ready to be publicly named for a number of reasons. It all made sense now. "Your attorney is Robert Harris?"

Anne lifted her eyebrows. "Yes. After what happened to Uncle Lewis he waited to tell me. We talked for a while and then he advised me to watch the video of the meeting so I could get the full flavor of the discussion." She sucked in a breath. "People were so angry."

"Why was Mayor Frost keeping his relationship with you—as owner of the company—a secret? Isn't that a conflict of interest?"

"Technically, yes it is. When I first started looking for a good location, I didn't even discuss it with Uncle Lewis, knowing he'd feel like he was caught in the middle and I didn't want any special favors from him. Everything went through my attorney. Then after I told Uncle Lewis about it, he thought the Murphy property was ideal, and went to talk to them.

"He was planning to disclose his part if it looked like we were going to be able to pull the deal together. The reason he hadn't said anything before that was to keep my mother out of it. If she'd gotten wind that I was starting my own company, she'd have figured out a way to move in and bump me out of the deal, then take over herself."

"Why?"

Anne shook her head. "Loretta is not a nice person. When my grandfather died and left Lewis and Loretta the company, it was doing quite well. My mother's the older one. First she incorporated and changed the name from Wonder Kids to Proctor Fabrication. Then she appointed herself as the CEO. She did whatever she had to to build a huge business. Loretta does not like competition from other companies. Or from her brother, either. Or from me. And I think it's because I've been so close to Uncle Lewis."

"I don't quite understand."

"She's always been envious of Lewis." Another jealous woman in his life. "I guess she's been difficult since birth and, sadly for her, my grandparents favored Lewis. I don't think they did it on purpose, but knowing Loretta, I can see how it happened."

I thought of how calmly Frosty had dealt with Stormin' Gorman and realized that he'd likely learned good diversion skills at a very young age. Anne's choice of Wonder Kids as her company's name must have given him some measure of satisfaction, like the business his father had built was being resurrected. "It sounds like your family has gone through a lot."

Anne shrugged. "I guess." She turned to me with a pained expression, her eyebrows drawn together. "If my uncle's death was in any way connected to the children's clothing factory, I'll never forgive myself."

"Anne, so far the police haven't found anything that would support that it was." Unless Loretta had gotten wind of it and fought with her brother over it. "When was the last time your mother and uncle talked? Any idea?"

"It's been a while. Uncle Lewis got fed up with her and left the company about seven years ago. Grand-mother passed away six years ago. She was living with Lewis, and my mother would visit her fairly often. I think Lewis usually arranged to be gone if he knew she was coming." She stopped for a minute. "That's probably when he gave her his garage door code. I haven't always respected my mother, but going into his house without talking to Jason about it first is a new low for her as far as I'm concerned."

We were about to find out just how low Loretta would go.

"Why do you think she invited Jason to stay with her after your uncle died?"

"She's had a soft spot for Jason since he was born. He's so much like Lewis. My mother couldn't get past her jealousy of her brother. I think she loved his son instead."

Complicated family dynamics. "Anne, the city council meets the first and third Tuesday of the month, so that'll be a week from tonight. Are you and your attorney plan-ning to go before the council and come clean about everything?"

"Yes, I already told him we need to do that. If my mother tries anything, we'll have to deal with that. You know what they say—about how money talks. Well, Loretta has as much as it would take."

I nodded. "I'm one of those optimists that even after all I've seen in my life and career, I'm still hopeful that the good guys win out in the end."

Anne smiled. "Thanks. I'd like to think that, too."

When Erin got to the shops, I told her and Pinky I needed to check on Nicoline. I'd tried her phone again, and she still wasn't answering. The worst scenarios kept coming to mind, including her lying unconscious in a snow bank somewhere, unable to answer.

"Do you want one of us to go with you?" Erin said.

"That's okay, I think Pinky needs you more than I do. It's been busy in here."

Pinky nodded her head a bunch of times. "It was so good to have Emmy back for the morning, at least."

"For sure, I'll see you in a bit," I said.

I walked to the hotel and greeted the young man behind the desk, the same one who'd been there last time. "Hi, just stopping by to see my friend." *And I am taking the elevator this time.*

I wasn't sure he recognized me, but he gave a slight nod of acknowledgement.

My heart started beating faster as the elevator climbed to the fourth floor. Would Nicoline be there, and was she okay? The doors opened on four, and I walked to her door and gave it a good rapping. I thought I heard someone move inside, but it was possible the sound had come from one of the other apartments.

I knocked again. "Nicoline, it's Camryn. I know

you're in there, and I want to be sure you're all right. You haven't answered my phone calls."

The sound of someone walking was definitely coming from apartment 404. Then it was Nicoline's voice on the other side of the door. "I am okay. Thank you for checking. Now you should go." Thank God she was there, and not out in the cold somewhere. But she may have had a new injury she was trying to hide.

"Nicoline, please open up. When I see you with my own eyes, I'll go."

I prayed she trusted me enough to let me in. The door slowly opened and she peered around it at me, her eyes even larger, more haunted than usual. "See."

"Please let me in, for just a minute."

"I am expecting my uncle soon."

"Only a minute." I gave the door a gentle push and Nicoline stepped back and pulled it open. When I stepped inside, she closed the door and turned the deadbolt lock. It seemed unnecessary, but what did I know about her fears? The apartment was simply furnished and there were no real homey touches, except a handmade knitted afghan lying on an overstuffed chair.

"I am sorry I did not come to work today," she said.

"Are you ill?"

"I cannot tell you why, but please know that I had a good reason. A very good reason. But, really, you must leave. If my uncle comes home and sees you he will know I lied to him about something."

"Nicoline, I don't understand. Please tell me what's going on."

"I cannot."

The bell on the elevator gave a single ding, and Nicoline's entire body went rigid. "You must leave. He must not see you," she whispered. "Hurry, out this way." She pulled me to the emergency exit door. The moment she opened the door, two things happened: a key turned the lock in the apartment door and I got a quick glance at a snow globe sitting on the kitchen counter about two feet away. It was the three bears approaching the man fishing in the river, namely Three Bears by River. *What in the heck?*

The apartment door opened as far as the deadbolt allowed. "Nicoline, open the door." I'd heard that low, deep voice somewhere before.

"One moment," she said.

I was so caught up in Nicoline's panic that I didn't have time to worry about my own fear of heights as I stepped onto the outside metal grate landing. My heart was jumping around in my chest as I crouched over then grabbed the railing. I held on for dear life as I sank down onto the first step. There was no way I could walk down the steep flight of circular steps so I used the method toddlers did and scooted down on my butt.

That saved me from looking down. I hoped no one was watching me, although suffering embarrassment was the least of my worries at the moment. I actually counted each step, trying to distract myself and when I got to the ground I said, "Forty-eight," out loud. Then I got to my feet with some effort. They were shaky from the adrenaline pumping through my body. I hurried around the hotel to the front sidewalk and ran. Not what an athlete would call running, but faster than I was usually able to move. Especially wearing a puffy coat and lined winter boots.

All the while what kept going through my mind was, *Nicoline must have stolen the three bears snow globe from under the counter in the shop.* But how, and why? She had wanted the first three bears scene, but Frosty had bought it before she'd had the chance. Then when she could have had first dibs on the second one, the company had forgotten to include it in the order. After I'd made the decision to send the third one back to the company, she must have found the snow globe under the counter. Is that why she was so adamant about taking it to the post office? Because she was planning to keep it for herself?

19

I was out of breath when I got back to Curio Finds. Erin was waiting on a customer and sent me a quick, inquisitive look. As I passed by the archway, I noticed Pinky was serving drinks at her counter. What would my friends make of it all? They'd been more suspicious of Nicoline than I had, and it seemed with good reason. I assured Pinky and Erin that Nicoline was all right, but it was too busy to get into a discussion about it. I'd give them all the unbelievable details later.

As soon as I'd hung up my coat and kicked off my boots, I slid open the door behind the checkout counter and squatted down, looking for the Three Bears by River box. It was still there. I took it out, looked inside, and confirmed it was the same scene as the snow globe on Nicoline's counter. Oh my goodness. There were two possibilities to consider. Either Nicoline had gotten the Three Bears by River snow globe somewhere else, or she was slicker than I would have imagined—she'd lifted it from the second order and left its box inside with the others so we'd make the missing snow globe discovery together.

Business was steady and there wasn't a good opportunity to talk to Pinky and Erin. Jason Frost called me just before five o'clock with two revelations. "Assistant Chief Lonsbury phoned a couple of hours ago to tell me they heard back from the two independent jewelers who were comparing the diamond found in Dad's office with the one in my grandmother's pendant."

I tensed in anticipation. "What'd they say?"

"It is not the same one. They did the measurements, checked the clarity, et cetera, and they arrived at the same conclusion. The one from the office was definitely not the one from the pendant in the painting."

"So the pendant is still missing?"

"Yes. And that brings me to the second phone call I got from Lonsbury a few minutes ago. The lab called him with the results of the fingerprint search, the ones they lifted from Dad's safe. One set belonged to Dad. The others belonged to Aunt Loretta."

"Oh, Jason, I'm sorry. But that doesn't necessarily mean she took the pendant." *But who else would have?*

"Yeah. The police are on their way to question her, so I wanted to thank you again for calling them when you saw her at Dad's place. My wife and I weren't sure how we wanted to handle it and had basically decided we'd look through Dad's house with Anne this weekend to see if we noticed anything was missing. But now it's a police matter, as far as we're concerned."

"You're right. I appreciate you telling me all this."

"You didn't hesitate helping us when we asked. And I get the feeling you want answers as much as we do."

There were only a few people sipping on drinks at a table in Brew Ha-Ha, and after the last two customers left Curio Finds, I waved Pinky and Erin over to a spot on my side of the archway where we wouldn't easily be heard. "I don't know what to think, girls. I don't have proof of this, but I think Nicoline stole a snow globe from an order we got last week."

"What a lame thing for her to do," Pinky said.

"Have you noticed anything else missing? Merchandise, money?" Erin said.

"No, the cash in the till has balanced every time she's worked. And nothing else is missing, as far as I can tell."

"She didn't show up for work today, and didn't even call in sick. And you're pretty sure she stole something. We can't keep Nicoline on, Cami," Pinky said.

"I know. I just wish we could help her." I took a deep breath, filled them in on Nicoline's uncle coming home and Nicoline making me leave via the fire escape.

"How did you do that being so afraid of heights?" Erin said.

"I was more afraid for Nicoline, I guess."

"Wow" Pinky said.

I pondered whether or not to tell them what Jason Frost had relayed to me. "And here's another thing. Last night I drove by Frosty's house and I saw a woman in his driveway closing his garage door."

Pinky grabbed my hands. "Cami, you waited all day to tell us this?"

I spread my fingers and she let go. "We've had a few things going on, Pink."

"I guess. Do you know who it was?"

I nodded. "I called Mark and gave him her plate number. He called Jason Frost, who later called me, and it turns out it was his aunt, Loretta."

"The sister Frosty didn't like?" Pinky said.

I shrugged. "Something happened between them is all I know."

"What was she doing there?" Erin said.

"The police are going to talk to her about it."

"She waits until Jason leaves and then she sneaks in the house. That's even lamer than what Nicoline did," Erin said.

I thought so, too. "Anyway, Jason told me a couple of other things, but I can't repeat them yet or Clint will have my hide."

Pinky's eyes opened wider than wide. "Cami, you know how much I hate it when you do that."

"Sorry, but I got into enough trouble taking the photo of the diamond in Frosty's office."

"Cami's right. We can wait, Pinky," Erin said.

"Speak for yourself, Erin." But then she smiled.

After Pinky left, Erin took care of most of the clean-up tasks while the customers finished their drinks and conversations. We were the only two left in our shops by 5:36, so Erin went home, too. Once in a while, when I was alone in the shops after a busy day, I was struck by how eerily quiet it was. I pulled the Three Bears by River snow globe out from the under-counter shelf and studied it like it was a laboratory specimen. I was on edge. I wanted to talk to Clint and Mark and get their take on Nicoline, but after what Jason had told me, I figured they were likely questioning Loretta Proctor by now. It wasn't as though my questions about Nicoline were time sensitive.

Or so I thought.

On top of everything else, Jason Frost had to face the fact that his aunt was the prime suspect in the missing diamond pendant that had been willed to his father. A treasure insured for over two million dollars. Holy moly, as Pinky would say.

I checked the business e-mail account, and reread the response from Van Norden Distributing to my message regarding the missing snow globe in their order. They'd thought it was included, but weren't going to argue about it. So Nicoline must have taken it. The question I kept asking myself over and over was why.

Then the revelation hit me. Maybe, that's where the diamond on Frosty's floor had come from, from the broken snow globe. It had been about diamonds all along, hiding in plain sight.

Things that had bothered me started to fall into place and make sense. Van Norden Distributing had sent three snow globes with similar three scary bear scenes, and each time one arrived in an order, there was a big hoopla about it. Unlike the other snow globes in the orders.

There was no one clamoring for the more pleasant, normal scenes. Was it possible they were using Curio Finds, a small shop in a small town in Central Minnesota, to smuggle diamonds into the country? And meek little Nicoline was part of the ring? Is that why she was here, helping her "uncle"? Had she killed Frosty, and that was the real reason she'd withdrawn when we'd talked about him?

I picked up the snow globe and stared at the area where the bears were standing. Were there some diamonds under the snow-covered grounds? I tapped the base against the counter then shook it to see if anything came loose. No. They'd be hidden in the base. I tapped it again, a little harder hoping the base would separate from the glass globe. I moved the globe to my chest for some traction and held the base with one hand and the globe with the other. I used all my strength and twisted, but it didn't budge. I gave it another hard tap and a good twist. When it dislodged, I thought at first I was imaging things, but it was coming unscrewed. I set it back on the counter and lifted the globe from the base.

There was a thin metal plate over the top of the base. I used my fingernail to lift it off. Inside were cotton balls and *diamonds*. Damn. My heart was beating so fast it took my breath away. I wished we had a safe in the shop to store them until they were securely in the hands of the authorities. Was Nicoline planning to break in and search for it during the night? She wouldn't know whether or not I'd mailed it back today. Thank the good Lord I hadn't. I put the snow globe back together, placed it in the box, and then back on the shelf under the counter. I phoned Clint, then Mark, but both calls went to voice-mail. If they didn't call me back before I left, I'd have to take it home with me.

I was anxious to get going and it was close enough to six that I shut off the machines and lights and turned down the heat in Brew Ha-Ha. I put my coat on and was standing behind my checkout counter, ringing out the till when the shop door opened. The last thing I needed at the moment was a late customer. It was the huge man that had stopped in a few times on his way through town.

When I remembered he was one of the seekers of the three bears snow globe, my skin prickled. When he said, "Where is that snow globe?" I recognized his voice was that of Nicoline's uncle—the one she was afraid would see me when I visited her earlier. My insides started to tremble. He turned the sign in the window to Closed, and I felt the room spin around for a second.

"Which snow globe are you talking about?" I was surprised my voice was steady and sounded matter-of-fact. I felt like someone else was talking for me.

His voice was like a growling bear's. "I am not here to play games."

No, that was obvious. He was involved in some very serious business. "Have a look at the shelves, see if there are any you like."

When he started coming toward me with the darkest look imaginable, I pulled the canister of Mace out of my pocket, used my thumb to locate where the nozzle was, then aimed it at his face and blasted him with a full dose. I caught enough to make my eyes and nostrils burn.

"Ahhh!" He grabbed at his eyes then started coughing.

But it didn't stop him from coming toward me. I picked the Marilyn Monroe snow globe off the counter and threw it at him. It miraculously hit him right between the eyes, bounced off his nose and onto his chest, then rolled down his body. I snatched up the shop phone and was on my way to the bathroom to lock myself in and call 911, but he managed to grab a handful of my hair. He pulled me back with such force that I stumbled, causing him to lose his grip on me.

Then the shop lights turned off. I sensed the movement of the man's hands groping for me. But I had the advantage of knowing the layout of the store. He was blocking my exit so I headed toward the back office to barricade myself in. I hadn't gotten far when the shop door opened and bright streams of lights moved across the ceiling and walls. "FBI Special Agents Reese and Omann! Hands up where we can see them!"

The lights came back on with the sound of the agent's voice. The visual assault made me blink until my eyes adjusted to the light. Whether I was in trouble or not, I raised my arms to be on the safe side. The mammoth man's eyes and nose were watering from the Mace, and blood was dripping out of his nose from my snow globe attack. He used his arm sleeves to wipe his face as he lifted his hands. Two agents, a male and a female, had their guns drawn and aimed at him.

"Camryn," the female agent called to me and my first thought was, *how does she know me?* That's when I noticed it was the strange-acting woman who'd been in the shop several times the past week. She had inquired about a snow globe, one we'd gotten from Van Norden. She'd also said the man was a friend of hers and asked if he'd bought anything. Now her visits made sense. She nodded at me, and I understood that meant I could lower my arms. The FBI had no doubt investigated me and my background. I was never happier to be on the right side of the law. And to be rescued by them.

"Unbutton your coat with your right hand, keeping your left arm up," the male agent instructed the man. When he'd finished that, the agent said, "Now put your right arm up and slowly turn in a complete circle." The man did that, too. "Do you have a firearm or other weapon on your person?"

"No, I do not." His voice had lost its growl.

"Then slip out of your coat, but keep your hands where we can see them at all times. If you attempt to reach in a pocket, we will assume you are going for a weapon. Is that clear?"

"Yes."

Once the man's coat was off, the male agent moved in and cuffed his hands behind his back. The agents told him to step out of his boots, and helped him do that. They spent a couple of minutes checking them. Then he was cleared to put them back on, not an easy thing to do with handcuffs on. But he managed with one agent on either side of him. The male agent frisked the man, emptying his pockets in the process while the female agent kept her gun pointed at him.

I remained where I was, leaning against the wall through it all. My heart pounded away in my chest, and my pulse was beating frantically. As they led the man to the door, the female agent looked over her shoulder at me. "Stay put. I'll be back."

I didn't budge from that very spot until she returned. She walked over to me and shook my hand. "I'm Special Agent Omann."

"I don't know what to say except thank you. I didn't know what was going to happen to me."

"You can thank your friend."

My friend, which one? "What do you mean?"

"Nicoline. I can't go into details now, but we've been working with the CIA and U.S. Customs for some time to take down a diamond smuggling ring. They've been very clever and have managed to elude us in other locations, but we got timely intel from one of our informants, and that's why we're here. They were using your shop as a front for their operations."

"Believe it or not, I started to suspect something suspicious was going on with the snow globes. But I didn't know what it was until just a couple hours ago. You knew about the mayor's death, and the diamond found on his office floor, lying near the broken snow globe?"

"We knew about the mayor, but only found out about the diamond today. The local authorities hadn't released the details to the public. We knew he'd been struck on the head by an object, prior to hitting his desk, and that it was being investigated as a homicide. We've kept a low profile the days we've been here, and didn't reach out to local law enforcement until this afternoon.

"Long story short, we talked to Nicoline Ahlens, and she told us about Omar Brams's plans to retrieve the snow globe from your shop today. We were poised to catch him in the act and wanted to apprise city law enforcement of what we were doing here. Assistant Chief Lonsbury told us—and he said you knew this—they've been investigating the diamond's origin, and were able to eliminate one possibility today."

"That's what I was referring to. I had a phone call from Mayor Frost's son telling me they'd learned the diamond wasn't from the pendant his father owned. That's when I started piecing together peoples' strange behaviors over the scary bears snow globes. Mayor Frost bought the snow globe before either Nicoline or Omar were able to. And they had to get it back." I was heartsick thinking Nicoline was involved with the mayor's murder.

I pointed at my checkout counter. "The snow globe that man—Omar—was looking for is under the counter. It has diamonds hidden in the base that be must be worth millions and millions of dollars."

"Let me call in another agent to witness me receiving the evidence." Omann used her cell phone and a second male wearing a black jacket with an FBI arm patch and a black stocking cap joined us.

With the two agents beside me, I removed the snow globe box from the shelf and set it on the counter. Then the male agent moved me aside, opened the box, lifted out the snow globe, gave the base a twist to the left then back to the right. He replaced it in the box. "Did you count the number of diamonds in there?" he asked me.

"No, I didn't."

"All right."

Over the next hour, they put the snow globe in an

evidence bag, and the empty box from the second snow globe in another. They examined the other snow globes we'd received from Van Norden Distributing to confirm their information had been correct and it was only the snow globes with the three bears scenes that held smuggled goods. Those scenes were designed so they wouldn't appeal to 99.9 percent of shoppers in the unlikely event Omar was detained and unable to be in the shop the minute they went on the shelf. Unfortunately for Mayor Frost, that's exactly what had happened and it had cost him his life.

I answered their questions and wrote out a narrative statement of every detail I could think of regarding the three bears snow globes, Nicoline, and the man named Omar. And that Van Norden Distributing had contacted Curio Finds in November informing us they were a supplier of snow globes. I'd passed the information on to my parents and they'd placed an order. An order that was delivered in three separate shipments. I signed a release form for the items they were taking.

Before they left I needed to ask them a question "What will happen to Nicoline?"

Special Agent Omann studied me like she was weighing her words. "I can tell you this much. She has cooperated fully with the FBI, and that will play out very favorably for her." I desperately wanted her to assure me Nicoline was not being implicated in Frosty's murder, but knew she couldn't tell me that.

When they left, I reclaimed the Marilyn Monroe snow globe from the shelf the agent had set it on. When he'd picked it up off the floor, I was amazed to see it was still in one piece. I placed it in its special spot on the checkout counter. Then I sank down on the stool behind it in stunned silence, not knowing what to think or how to feel. Three FBI agents had arrested a diamond smuggler who'd used my parents' shop as a front. And spent over an hour in Curio Finds getting my oral and written story. What was our little world coming to?

Surprisingly no one had seemed to notice the activity when the FBI had stormed in with weapons drawn, or when they led Omar Brams outside and put him in one of their vehicles after his arrest. True, the streets were pretty quiet by then and the two dark SUVs the special agents drove wouldn't have alerted anyone. SUVs were common in Brooks Landing. Certainly no one would suspect they belonged to the FBI. But still.

Where had they taken Nicoline, and what were the charges against her? Would I ever see her again?

I thought of Clint and Mark, and other officers who may have been there when the FBI paid them a visit and filled them in on the smuggling operation with a Brooks Landing connection. I wished I could have seen their reactions, the looks on their faces. "Where is everybody, and who should I call first?" I said out loud.

The lights flickered, but didn't go out completely. Maybe the lights, or whoever was controlling them, liked hearing my voice. Ha. So I kept talking. "Okay, I need to tell my parents first off, and Pinky and Erin will kill me if I wait any longer to tell them. It's anyone's guess what Clint and Mark are up to, and why they haven't called me."

I picked up the shop phone and called my parents to

be sure they were home, and then I phoned Pinky and Erin and asked them to meet me at the Vanellis' house as soon as they could get there. And when I wouldn't answer any of their probing questions, they didn't even argue.

"Cami, tell us again. Everything," Dad said.
Mom, Dad, Erin, Pinky, and I were huddled in my parents' living room. My parents were shaken by the small role they had played in the international crimes. We all shared in the disbelief that the whole thing had really happened. And maybe if I repeated the story enough times, it would sink into our brains.

"Cami, I'm impressed you had the presence of mind to Mace that guy," Erin said.

"We're going to have to get that electrician back in to see what's going on with the lights," Dad said.

"I think Molly turned off the lights at just the right time to help you," Pinky said.

Mom and Dad and Erin all gave her skeptical looks.

When my cell phone rang, I looked at the display. "It's Clint," I said, then answered.

"Camryn, where are you?"

"My parents' house."

"Good. I wanted to make sure you were all right. And I need to fill you in on some things."

"Why don't you stop over? Pinky and Erin are here, too."

"Mark's with me."

"Of course he's welcome. too."

I'd made it through the retelling of getting the snow globe's base open when Clint and Mark arrived.

Mark looked around, smiled, and nodded. "Feels like old times, hanging out at the Vanellis' house."

My dad shook their hands. "You know our assistant police chief," I said. I hadn't told my parents about my relationship with Clint because I didn't exactly know how to describe it.

"Why. sure. Come in, Mark, Clint. We're all trying to digest what's been going on right under our own noses."

Clint shook his head. "Not something you'd ever expect in small town USA. Camryn, we got delayed locating the party we were looking for. Otherwise we would have been standing by when the FBI arrested Omar Brams. Sorry."

"I understand. So you found her okay?"

"We did, and it seems Loretta Proctor was in her brother's house, not to take anything, but to return the pendant she claimed to have borrowed," Clint said.

"What?" I said.

Mark lifted his hands. "Her story is she wanted to have a picture taken of herself with it on, and didn't think her brother would let her borrow it. She'd kept it for a while, and after her brother died she figured she'd better get it back before Jason discovered it was missing. Whether we believe her or not, Jason decided not to press charges."

"Since Mayor Frost had given his sister the code to his house, technically she had inherent permission to access it," Clint said.

Clint and Mark asked me about Omar Brams's arrest,

and when I got to the part about using the Mace, Mark raised his hand for a high five and as I slapped my palm against his, he said, "That's my girl."

"Your temperamental lights worked in your favor at least," Clint said.

Considering the looks she'd gotten the last time, Pinky kept her mouth shut about Molly.

"Beth, I think we could all use a drink," Dad said.

20

The next few days were far less eventful. And then Friday afternoon Nicoline paid me a surprise visit. She was free, at least for the time being. I took her in my arms and held her for a while.

"I am here to ask your forgiveness," she said.

"Let's go sit in the coffee shop. I'll ask Emmy to listen for customers." Pinky was out running errands.

Emmy had seen Nicoline in Curio Finds once, but they hadn't been formally introduced. After I took care of that detail I said, "We'll be talking in Pinky's if you need me, Emmy."

"That's fine, dearie," Emmy said.

"Would you like a hot chocolate?" I asked Nicoline.

"No, thank you."

We sat down and Nicoline studied her hands for a

moment then launched into her story. "I am from the Netherlands. I have been in the United States on a work visa. My uncle—"

"Omar Brams?"

"Yes. He has been on the wrong side of the law for a long time. I did not know all that he was involved with, but he insisted I come here, to Brooks Landing, Minnesota, to help him. I was afraid I would be doing something illegal, but I was more afraid of not helping him."

It would take three Nicolines to equal Omar's size. I'd be afraid of him, too. "Did he threaten you if you didn't?"

She nodded. "He said my mother would be in danger."

"That must have been terrifying for you."

"It was. My uncle did not tell me all of the details, but it was my job to purchase the snow globes. The first one was with the three bears and the man by the cabin. I feel responsible for your mayor's death because I told my uncle he had bought it first. I had no idea he would hurt him." I was as unwittingly responsible as she was.

"Nicoline, it is not your fault."

She shrugged slightly.

"Do you know what happened that day, to Mayor Frost?"

Nicoline shook her head. "Just that Omar went to the mayor's office and was taking the snow globe when the mayor walked in. There was a struggle and the mayor fell and hit his head on his desk. My uncle somehow escaped without being seen."

"Did he tell you there were diamonds in the base?"

"Yes. After that tragedy, I knew I should go to the

authorities, but I was afraid, and I did what my uncle had commanded. I stole the second snow globe so there would be no risk of anyone seeing it."

"And then when I put the third snow globe away, you were in a pickle."

She frowned at my choice of words then nodded. "I did not want to continue helping my uncle. You were so kind to me, and I was deceiving you. I told my uncle I was too sick to go to work at Curio Finds that day and could not look for the snow globe. He was angry, but let it go, and told me he would take care of it. He did not tell me how he planned to do that. I feared for you and was ready to go to the police.

"Then, as an answer to my prayers, Special Agent Omann paid me a visit. It was after you had been there, and after my uncle had gone out again. The agents were watching him, and watching your shop. I told her everything. She asked if my uncle had a gun, and I said no. She said that was good and they would keep you safe. I only hope you can find it in your heart to forgive me."

I reached over and took her hand. "I already have. I don't blame you one bit. And it's a great relief to me your uncle is in federal custody, mostly because that means he can no longer hurt you." We sat quietly for a moment. "So what's next for you?"

"I am not certain. My work visa expires in a few months, and I must testify if my uncle goes on trial. I understand he gave the FBI the name of the man who is his boss. The one he was getting the diamonds for. So they are looking for him. In the meantime, I am staying in what they call a 'safe house.'" She stood up. "And now

I must go, because my driver is waiting for me. They were kind enough to let me visit you." Nicoline gave me a tight hug. "I hope to see you again."

"I hope so, too. You are welcome here anytime."

She smiled in her shy way and left for parts unknown. I sent up a prayer that she would be kept from further harm.

Pinky and I had wrestled with how we'd both be able to attend Mayor Frost's funeral on Saturday afternoon. My parents planned to go, too, so we couldn't ask them to man the shops. Erin saved us once again by offering to work with Emmy so we could keep the doors open.

The funeral was the largest I'd ever been at. The church was crowded, and the service was a fine tribute to the man, Lewis Frost, and to Frosty, the mayor. It was upbeat, focusing on his life and accomplishments, instead of his tragic end.

There was a lunch served in the church basement after the funeral, and Pinky and I joined my parents at their table for a ham sandwich and some scalloped potatoes. Clint and Mark were sitting with other city employees. I watched the interactions between Jason, his wife and children, cousin and aunt. If there were hard feelings or differences, it wasn't publicly evident. I think Frosty would have appreciated that, being the natural peacekeeper that he was.

I nudged Pinky. "We didn't get the chance to meet the rest of Jason's family. I'd like to do that before we leave."

We excused ourselves, then Pinky and I went over and Jason introduced us to his wife and children. And to his aunt, Loretta Proctor. We gave them our sympathies and talked for a few minutes before Anne pulled me aside. "Camryn, I wanted you to know that after all that's happened, I've decided to withdraw my proposal to build Wonder Kids Clothes in Brooks Landing. It wouldn't feel right."

"I respect your decision. I'd probably feel the same way."

"There are other venues out there and we'll find a good spot."

Jason joined us and gave me a hug. "We really appreciate you coming today, and for your help with . . . everything." He bent his head in his aunt's direction.

Anne nodded. "Some lessons in life come late. But as they say, 'better late than never.'"

I'd understandably felt deep sadness at times since discovering Frosty's body. And learning about all Nicoline had gone through added to it. I needed to believe she'd move on to a happier life out from under her uncle's control. My friends encouraged me to focus on something positive and offered to help deck out my house for the holidays.

On my way home from the shop that afternoon, I stopped at the lot where a Boy Scout Troop was selling Christmas trees and more. I bought a Frasier fir tree, two wreaths, and many feet of pine bough garlands. One of the dads tied the tree to the top of my Subaru, and another put the wreaths and garlands in large plastic bags and loaded them in the back of the car.

When I pulled up in back of my house to unload my cache, Pinky and Erin came out to assist me. It was a mild evening with no wind and neither had bothered to put their coats on. Pinky went to work untying the tree, and Erin carried in one bag of greens. I carried in the other then went back to help Pinky with the tree. We brought it into the house and propped it up in the corner of the kitchen. My parents had dropped off an extra tree stand, a box of lights, and a container of decorations they'd been storing.

"Where do you want to set up the tree?" Erin said.

"How about in the front window?" I said.

"Good choice," Pinky agreed.

We set to work, making sure the tree was straight when we screwed it into the stand. The lights went on next, and it was great having Pinky there so I didn't have to stand on a step stool to reach to the top. "Holy moly, your folks must have a lot of decorations, if these are the leftovers," she said.

"They used to put up two trees, and they went all out with their decorating."

Erin nodded. "I remember that."

We kept busy until Clint, Mark, and Jake got there to string lights on the roofline of the house and the bushes on either side of the front steps. Mark had a pole and lifted the string of lights to the nails that served as hangers. They'd been pounded in by the McClarity family sometime in the last forty years. I hung one wreath on the front door and the other on the back door.

When everything was ready, Mark plugged the outside lights into the electrical box on the house. And Jake plugged in the ones on the tree. We were oohing over it when Erin pointed out the window and said, "Look."

Clint had set an angel figurine in the yard and was plugging it into the extension cord. I smiled at the added touch and went out on the front steps to admire it. "I thought you might like this," he said.

I shook my head. "No, I love it. Thank you."

When I got back in the house, Erin and Mark were in the kitchen pouring champagne into glasses. They waited until Clint joined us then handed each of us a glass. "What's this for?" I said.

Everyone raised a glass and Pinky said, "We are celebrating tonight because you helped break up a smuggling ring and didn't die in the process."

"Thank you. But I didn't do much of anything. The FBI did that."

"How many guardian angels do you suppose you have, Cami?" Erin said.

I raised my eyebrows, took in a breath, and shrugged. "That reminds me, we still need to add the angel to the top of the tree."

Pinky chimed in, "I didn't see an angel."

It was lying in a box on the counter. I took it out and held it up for everyone to see. "I've had it since I moved away after high school. Mom and Dad sent it with me. It belonged to my birth parents, and the last time it was on a tree was when I was five years old."

The angel had a sweet cherub face and gold wings. She was sitting in a cloud made of white spun glass and was surrounded by five gold stars. Pinky and Erin had tears in their eyes as they moved in for a closer look.

I handed the angel to Clint. "Will you do the honors?"

He set down his glass and when he took the angel he cradled it in both of his hands. The five of us followed him into the living room. Mark picked up Clint's glass and brought it with him. I found myself holding my breath in anticipation of what it would be like seeing the angel on a treetop for the first time in over thirty years. Clint set her on the top branch then straightened her into place. Mark handed Clint his champagne and we all clapped as best we could with a glass in hand.

The angel looked more magical to me than ever. I raised my glass. "Thank you, my friends for all your help. Here's to you." We clinked glasses then Clint and I locked eyes as we each took a sip of our champagne. I lifted my glass to the angel on the tree and smiled. Clint nodded. It warmed my heart and lifted my spirits having a house full of friends and an angel watching over us.

SNOW GLOBES WITH STYROFOAM SNOW

....

SUPPLIES

- A clean jar with a lid, any size or shape

- Waterproof glue

- A dense foam block

- Distilled water

- Small figures or laminated photos

Directions: Choose a jar. Create a scene to your liking then attach the pieces to the inside of a dry jar lid, using waterproof glue. Hot glue works well, too. Take care to keep the scene pieces inside the seal. Fill the jar with distilled water to the neck. Using a cheese grater, run the Styrofoam back and forth to create flakes of "snow." Drop them in the water. Attach the lid to the jar. Add, or pour off water, as needed, then reattach lid. If your jar doesn't have a tight seal, put a bead of glue around the edge of the lid before sealing. Screw on the lid, give the jar a shake, and watch the little flakes settle over your scene.

Connect with Berkley Publishing Online!

For sneak peeks into the newest releases, news on all your favorite authors, book giveaways, and a central place to connect with fellow fans—

"Like" and follow Berkley Publishing!

facebook.com/BerkleyPub
twitter.com/BerkleyPub
instagram.com/BerkleyPub

Penguin
Random
House